PRAISE FOR REMBRANDT'S SHADOW

"...a powerful, haunting story about love, sacrifice, and the rhapsodic draw of beauty...A moving rendering of a true story about an art dealer, both thrilling and historically fascinating."

—*Kirkus*

"The story of a Holocaust survivor trying to find peace by vanquishing her ghosts and embracing her rebellious son. Based on true events, *Rembrandt's Shadow* is both poignant and riveting."

—Elena Gorokhova, international bestselling author of
A Mountain of Crumbs

"...with vivid descriptions and characters with indomitable spirit...Berg weaves a story of hope, redemption, family values, forgiveness and love...it doesn't get any better than this."

—Fern Michaels, #1 *New York Times* bestselling author

"Filled with tragedy and mystery...A compelling tale of loss, family secrets, and finally redemption. Through this speckled darkness Berg bathes us in the light of what really matters—love."

—Heather Dune MacAdam, author of
Rena's Promise: A Story of Sisters in Auschwitz

"A striking riposte to the notion that the past should be forgiven and forgotten. Berg's story beautifully captures the generations through one family's amazing story."

—Christopher Santora, Trial Attorney,
United Nations War Crimes Court for Sierra Leone

"A lovely, intimate gem of a story, about a young girl becoming a woman as her world crumbles around her, and the sacrifice of a father that will haunt her for the rest of her life...."

— Anne-Marie O'Connor, author

D0181359

WITHDRAWN

REMBRANDT'S SHADOW

A POST HILL PRESS BOOK
ISBN: 978-1-68261-143-2
ISBN (eBook): 978-1-68261-144-9

Rembrandt's Shadow
© 2016 by Janet Lee Berg
All Rights Reserved

Cover design by Dmitrije Leonidov
Cover photograph by Mike Gomez and Janelle Berg-Gomez
Book design by Mayfly Design and typeset in Whitman

No part of this book may be reproduced, stored in a retrieval system, or transmitted by any means without the written permission of the author and publisher.

Post Hill Press
posthillpress.com

Published in the United States of America

1 2 3 4 5 6 7 8 9 10

REMBRANDT'S SHADOW

BY
JANET LEE BERG

Dedicated to Mother

~

This book evolved under the instruction of Jules Feiffer, Ursula Hegi, Kaylie Jones, Heather Dune Macadam, Robert Reeves, Roger Rosenblatt, Lou Ann Walker, John Westermann, and the late, great Frank McCourt.

Fiction is history that didn't happen and history is fiction that did.

—GEORGE ORWELL

AUTHOR'S NOTE

When I met my husband Bruce Berg, he told me about his family history. I filled in the blanks with research and imagination.

HOW REMBRANDT
SAVED MY FAMILY'S LIFE

AN INTRODUCTION BY BRUCE BERG

(Husband of Janet Lee Berg, Author of *Rembrandt's Shadow*)

I t is October 20, 1942, and my Opa, Benjamin Katz, and his frightened family stood at the train station in occupied Holland, unsure if the train doors would open and take them to freedom or a death camp. My sister Alma, who was six years old, would later recall the madness, as they were surrounded by armed soldiers on the platform barking orders as they wondered if a desperate last-minute escape had worked. They were accompanied by a German officer who, when he, received the order to allow the escape commented, "I would have much rather been given the order to kill all of you."

Opa's brother, Nathan and business partner, both well-established art dealers, had been working on a big trade—a Rembrandt "Portrait of Dirck Jansz. Pesser" in exchange for 25 Jewish lives.

My telling this story gives away the ending of their harrowing escape along the tracks through Paris and on to the Spanish border where they would depart on a boat, the Marque de Comillas, which took them further away from Auschwitz, and closer to the island of Jamaica where they would wait out the war in a British internment camp.

But many other members of my family were not so fortunate. Benjamin also tried to arrange for his in-laws escape, but was not able to do so and they perished in the camps.

Even though I was born in America after the war, I was long aware that my grandfather and his brother, Nathan, were art dealers of considerable reputation, but I had no idea as to the extent of their prominence in the art world. They were considered the foremost experts in the field of Dutch painting, especially Old Masters. They possessed the works of such esteemed artists as Vermeer, Jan Steen, and Nicholas Maes and at one time, acquired more Rembrandts than anyone in Europe. It was that collection that had long made them a prime target of Adolf Hitler and his Nazi henchmen.

My mother would only tell us stories haltingly, and with little detail, except she repetitively told me about seeing people holding bars of soap at the train depot.

But only in the last few years, as I have worked to trace what became of that Rembrandt and so many other works of art my family once treasured, have I learned the terrifying details of what happened after the Nazis invaded the Netherlands in May of 1940 and appeared on the doorstep of their comfortable home in the village of Dieren.

Nathan's son David, who is still alive, recalls those days, and describes a house once filled with much joy. "The residents of Dieren, who knew my grandfather, still speak with so much affection of my grandfather 's family and how their home was a magnet for Friday night Shabbat dinners." According to David, conversations turned tense with "the growing anti-Semitic movement and what to do with the children."

After the invasion in May of 1940, my grandfather testified that they were forced to sell almost their entire inventory of 500 paintings. He stated that they "would never have parted with so many paintings at one time."

PORTRAIT OF RAMAN

Portrait of Dirck Jansz. Pesser
REMBRANDT HARMENSZ. VAN RIJN - HOLLAND, CIRCA 1634

The abstract questions turned deadly real when Nazi agents, who had long targeted the art in the Katz gallery, came to pay a visit in August 1940.

"Eventually, Hermann Goering, the head of the Luftwaffe and Hitler's chief art collector, arrived. Surrounded by armed goons, he stood in our family's living room and conducted "business" with Nathan. All the children were ushered into another room and ordered to stay there. They were not even allowed to use the toilet. The visit left everyone shaken, including my mother, who soon fell ill."

(STORY CONTINUED IN AFTERWORD)

ONE

QUEENS, NEW YORK
1971

Sylvie Rosenberg Beckman resealed the letter and placed it on top of the pile. She carefully retied the lavender bow that held the stack of mail, so nothing would be detected, and she tilted her head at the sight of Michael's wavering script. "Angela" was written on the outside of each envelope; the capital "A" cradled between sketched wings. She clapped her hand over her quivering lips. Sylvie never recalled her son as being artistic.

She thought about when she was a young girl, drawing train tracks in her journal the day the German soldiers had lined them up at the depot. She was trying to teach herself *perspective* in drawing, the illusion of the train tracks getting further away in the distance. After so many years, Sylvie's life was anything but a straight path. Her memories vacillated between euphoric and tragic without order, without making sense.

Then Sylvie snatched up the receiver and dialed Angela's number.

Angela was grateful for her Friday morning slumber without the interruption of college classes, until the shrill ring of the

1

telephone woke her. She realized her parents were both out, and stretched her slight torso in her four-poster bed.

"Hello?" She yawned.

"Angela? Is this Angela Martino?"

"Yes. That's me," she said in a fog.

"This is Michael's mother. Sylvie Beckman."

Angela was quiet. *Mrs. Beckman?* Her eyes opened as she recognized the woman's thick glottal accent and felt a powerful jolt in her half-sleep. She hadn't heard the woman's voice for over two years now. Not since that dreadful summer night they met.

"Angela, find a pen. I will wait."

"A pen?" Angela sprang up to a sitting position and fumbled for a pen on the nightstand. The curly white phone cord twisted around her long dark hair as she tried to make sense of what was happening. "But, Mrs. Beck—"

"Quickly. The pen. Before I change my mind."

"Yes," she said, ripping her hair loose. "I have a pen."

"Now, write down these directions."

Angela felt a clamp tighten across her skull with an instant headache.

"I've moved," Sylvie said.

"Yes. I know ... I tried to—"

"Do you have something to write on?"

Angela looked for a clear spot on the back of her homework assignment. "Yes. But, Mrs. Beckman, how is—"

"Shhh! You must come see me in person."

Angela remained silent as she wrote down the directions. *Talking to this dragon woman is impossible!* "Mrs. Beckman, please. Please tell me, how is—"

"We'll talk when you get here. It is important—an emergency. I can no longer keep this to myself—this secret...."

"Secret? What secret? Hello? Mrs. Beckman, are you still there?"

Angela blinked. She moaned. As if to mock her, the dial tone moaned back. She stared at the starkness of the ceiling and exhaled. Then she drew a deep breath and wildly thrashed her feet to free them from the tangled bed sheets. The image of a mermaid freeing her tail from a cluster of seaweed came to mind as she dove off her bed and landed on top of her crumbled Levis on the floor. She left her white nightshirt on and jammed her legs into her jeans, hopped on one leg, and tucked the scribbled directions into her back pocket.

She ran her fingers through her hair and rubbed her front teeth clean with one finger, while searching the room for her moccasins. *What is wrong with her? Who does she think she is, giving me commands like that? The same old arrogant, overbearing, self-centered—Oooh—that's who she is!*

Her mind raced as Angela scooped up one of her moccasins with her big toe, and squeezed her foot inside the fleece lining while she scanned the room for its mate. Dropping to her knees, she pulled back the dust ruffle and felt for the softness of the suede under her stretched fingers. *Where's my shoe? Where's my shooo? Where's my—?* She sat back with her legs tucked under her rear end, as tears came to her eyes, and all the emotions came rushing back to her—first the heartbreak, then the anger, and then finally being honest with herself. She covered her mouth with a shaking hand. *Where's my Michael?*

DIEREN, HOLLAND
1930s

B ecause she was the daughter of Josef Rosenberg, a noted
Dutch art dealer, sometimes Sylvie believed her father
loved art more than he loved her. That is, until the day
he traded a Rembrandt to the Nazis in exchange for her life.

As a baby, unaware of her own worth, Mother had propped
her up in a high chair and fed her with a silver spoon too big
for her mouth. She often clamped her mouth shut on it or spit
out its contents. Sylvie Rosenberg had the birthright to do so.

The nanny from England, the one with the alabaster eyebrows, somehow single-handedly managed to get pabulum
down Sylvie's obstinate little throat. On the nanny's day off,
Mother had to deal with the unpleasant task by herself and
she could only get Sylvie to eat if she doused the food in honey.
Not wanting to soil her own clothing if her child should spit
up, mother donned an apron to cover her fine dress. Because
the child tried her patience, her mother noticed one of the
copper-bottom pots hanging on the rack overhead wasn't
properly buffed, confiding in Sylvie that she'd have to repri-
mand the help.

The other two siblings weren't as stubborn by nature, and
hardly caused a fuss, so Mother could attend luncheons, the
garden club, and shopping. The more Father got engrossed in
his business, the more items Mother came home with from her
sprees.

How exhilarated she seemed after a day out, hours upon end, caressing the finer fabrics—crepe de Chine, silk moiré, and taffeta in the best shops on the avenue. The week the nanny was called away to visit her ailing relative in London, Sylvie developed a fever which her mother had ignored too long. The child, half conscious, was carried into the back seat of the Bentley by one of the servants, the one who always carried a dust cloth saturated in lemon oil. Raleigh, their English driver, rushed her to the physician where she was diagnosed with yet another ear infection. Mother blamed the nanny's absence for the child's suffering, and her partial loss of hearing in one ear. She told her not to bother coming back. She immediately hired a new nanny from England, the one whose breath smelled like cooking vanilla.

There was word of anti-Semitic demonstrations going on, especially outside of synagogues, but it had little bearing on the Rosenberg's lifestyle as they were secular Jews who didn't attend temple.

Sylvie's sister, Gretta, a straight-laced type who wore her hair tied back severely from her face, distanced herself from her younger siblings. "No, Sylvie, I can't possibly fit in that tiny chair," she told her five-year-old little sister. "I'm ten, which is practically a teenager."

Sylvie had waited all day with her rubber dolls seated around the small wooden table for Gretta to return from private school, imploring her to join the tea party she had painstakingly set up with miniature china cups and saucers so delicately placed on doilies.

In the center of the table stood a dainty three-tiered server she had promised Mother she'd be extra careful with that held plump crème puffs drizzled with caramel sauce.

"Besides," Gretta said, "You have your doll friends. Look, Marta finished her tea, and she's asking you to refill her cup."

Sylvie protested. "You're making that up! Marta doesn't talk. She's a doll!"

"I've got more important things to do, do you understand? Maybe Mother can find a friend for you, call a neighbor, or—or *hire* someone."

Seven-year-old Wilhelm, always making boy noises and shooting pretend-guns, came soaring through the playroom with his arms extended out at his sides like a fighter jet in a flash, ready to bring down the entire tea party and Sylvie's make-believe world. The doll's face smeared with crème, made Wilhelm laugh and laugh, and Sylvie wail so loud, Father could hear her from his office at the other end of the house.

"What on earth is all that ruckus?" Papa called. He had been studying a painting in his office, behind closed doors with Dr. Visser; the two of them calculating the value of art for hours on end.

Wilhelm glided out of the playroom with his radar searching for a good landing spot, while Gretta slipped out to the courtyard for her cello lesson.

A servant came to pick up the mess, and to sooth Sylvie, who had developed hiccups from crying so hard. "Let's have a sip, shall we?" the maid said and patted Sylvie's shoulder. With her arms crossed over her chest, Sylvie elbowed the woman's hand away.

"No, I hate tea parties!" Sylvie cried, throwing the place settings back onto the Persian carpet. "Now, you clean them up!"

Sylvie turned eight and had long abandoned her tea set and dolls. She would not get a baby sister of her own to play with for years to come and had to become accustomed to playing alone at home. Without any of the servants noticing, she slipped out the back door one weekend to wander about.

Sylvie wanted friends and to be like everyone else. She skipped along the sidewalk that ran next to the cast-iron fence of the unfamiliar playground. Some of the children spotted her, and to her delight, they motioned her toward the entrance.

"What's that on your necklace?" the smallest of the girls asked, studying her through the steel openings that separated them. "A star?"

Sylvie nodded, hopeful she found a new friend.

The girl unlocked the latch, and let her in, and whispered something to someone else. The gate closed behind her. Suddenly, Sylvie felt *different*, as if she didn't belong there. The sky shifted. So did her smile. Light raindrops ricocheted off her head. She simply stayed put. Her feet, pointed in contradiction.

The other children started drawing something in the wet dirt with a stick—a giant symbol. Someone with a small voice said, "I think the mark means 'good luck.'"

One of the girls, much bigger in girth and older than the others, called everyone over to where she was standing and eyed Sylvie the hardest. "We're going to play a game now. It's called Catch the Jew."

Sylvie's neck tensed up. The girl looked familiar. *Ingrid?* She remembered seeing her in school one day. Wasn't she the one who made nasty comments? She was pretty sure of it. All the students were instructed to hide in the school basement during one of their practice drills. *Yes, that's her* . . . the one who complained the loudest that day about doing the emergency rehearsal, the one who had said "It's all the Jews' fault."

Sylvie wondered if her older sister ever had such confrontations when going to private school. It seemed, overnight, that sending all three of the Rosenberg children to the 'fancy' schools was suddenly prohibitive for her parents.

The other children at the park shouted and snickered as they chased Sylvie in circles. Ingrid was the first to throw the mud, and the others soon followed. Then they caught her. Sylvie was forced to stand in the center of the ancient-looking letter they engraved in the dirt; she didn't learn the significance of the *swastika* until later. Whatever it meant, to her it stood for humiliation.

As her fine shoes sank into the sludge, minutes seemed forever. She refused to make a spectacle, refused to make eye-contact with those she thought were her peers. *So these are Christians.*

She tried to focus on something else. Anything. In a tree, she spotted a thick clump of twigs in the branches. Had a mother bird tried to build a home there? Would the young chicks be happy so high above the other birds? She wondered.

Maybe she should tell all the gentile children that her family wasn't a *religious* one, but that probably wouldn't change her from being a Jew. The other kids stepped off to the side; she thought of the parting of the Red Sea, as the titan made her way up to Sylvie's frozen face.

"Hmmm...what did we *catch* today? Something unlike the rest of us, I believe. Do you think you are *better* than us? Deserve special treatment?"

Sylvie said nothing. She wasn't sure how to stop the tears from coming. Should she blink a lot or continue to stare?

The troublemaker picked up a long, thin branch off the ground and pointed with it at the dirt on Sylvie's shiny shoes. "You think you have *better* looking shoes than us, don't you? *Used* to have better looking shoes, I should say!" Sylvie heard giggles from the others.

Then, the leader of the pack tickled Sylvie with the twig, dragged the stick down each arm, and left a track of dirt everywhere it touched. "Such a fancy blouse with fancy ruffles. I'm afraid you are nothing but a *dirty* Jew now."

Sylvie's eight-year-old mind raced. The stick lightly poked at the bridge of Sylvie's nose, and she inhaled deeply. *I smell dog poop on your breath, you big kak!* Sylvie wanted to scream. Instead, she recited the alphabet in her head, backwards.

"Even your eyes are dirt-brown," Ingrid added.

Sylvie refused to let one tear drop from her dirt-brown eyes onto her milky-white skin. Ingrid continued the taunting, glancing the stick slowly down Sylvie's spine, walking behind Sylvie, then in front of her, brushing the twig on her cheek and down her neck. Sylvie thought of her science lesson in school; how the moon rotates around the earth.

Then the beastly girl stared closer at Sylvie's necklace. "Looks like *real* gold to me, no?"

Sylvie's father had given her the necklace. She concentrated on Papa's soft voice—when he used his "forever words." Her favorite lesson—the day he taught her how to draw the hexagram—two triangles laid over each other. His gentle words were slipping away, replaced by the hateful words of this wretched girl. Sylvie had learned a new lesson now.

Somehow, she would turn things around, get even. She'd come up with her own strategy that would serve her for the rest of her life, so she'd never again have to stand on that horrific insignia. With her mud-streaked face and shoulders erect, Sylvie looked the captain of the bullies straight in the eye and smiled a potent smile that said she was *different, all right*—different because she *was* better, nicer looking, smarter, and more powerful, especially more powerful! She told the big bully all this without saying a word.

She *had* to come up with a good plan. Her eyes went to the tree again, darting from branch to branch like a squirrel. Finally, Sylvie opened her mouth. "You like my jewelry? There's more where *that* came from. I bet *you* would like some for yourself."

A torrential downpour ended the staring game between the two and their unlikely conversation, confirming a time. "Three o'clock, it is then."

"Yes," Sylvie answered. "Do you know where I live?"

"Everyone knows where you live," Ingrid said.

The children ran in circles again, slinging the mud at one another, as if nothing had happened. They were all dirty now, all the same, and the children's game ended.

Sylvie was about to bury her muddy clothes in a pile of rags in the basement, promising herself she would never wear them again or set foot in that park again, ever. But wouldn't that be letting that horrible girl win? No, she'd let one of the servants wash and press everything. She'd wear those clothes again and in front of that same bully. Ingrid was poor, and not very smart. Sylvie had *things* she wanted. She could win her over, and the power that would come with it.

Sylvie tossed in bed the entire night, because of having second thoughts about the invitation she had extended to the big brute. She dreamt the bully sat on her until she suffocated. She awoke gasping for breath, ripping at her bedcovers in a panic.

At three o'clock the next afternoon, Sylvie, dressed in her freshly pressed and starched blouse, kneeled on her window seat, and watched the street from her third floor bedroom window, as she waited for her plan to unfold.

There she is. That's her! But who's that girl with her? Oh, I remember. She had also been at the park—the pint-sized one, the spineless one who had stood back and watched like everyone else; the one who said the symbol stood for "good luck."

"Hmm, maybe she's right, after all."

The two girls, Ingrid and Maxine, walked past the lamppost boxes filled with flowers and turned up the slate walkway through the perfectly pruned shrubbery.

"This isn't a house. It's a mansion!" Ingrid said coming to a halt.

"A mansion?" the smaller girl repeated the word.

The girls looked up at the gabled roof with open mouths. "See. I told you. Papi was right. She *is* a rich Jew."

"Should we use the knocker?" Maxine asked in a wee voice.

One of the servants opened the door. "May I help you?"

"Umm. Is Sylvie at home?" Maxine peeked through the hinges of the massive door.

"Please go around to our guest entrance." The servant pointed to the sunroom to their left of the front entrance. "The door is unlocked. You may go in and wait there."

They entered the sunroom and closed the door behind them. In the corner, there was a faded sage toile settee and six petite wood chairs in a line, where visitors would wait until they were announced. The two girls looked at one another, then looked around the room. The walls were made up of many partitions, tiled in blue and white delft with sprigs of green. The girls sat on the stiff chairs without speaking. Then Ingrid got up and went to the divan, and extended her legs out long.

"I feel like a mo-o-ovie star," she enunciated. "Why don't you come on up and *see* me sometime...."

Maxine didn't comprehend her bawdiness. She stretched her neck and looked to see where the housekeeper had gone when she had disappeared past the foyer through the tall French doors that led to a world beyond her imagination. On a far wall, she spotted delicate figurines on a very high shelf.

"My Papi also said her father's a big shot art dealer. Owns more of Rembrandt's paintings than anyone in Europe," Ingrid said.

"Who's Remember-ant?" Maxine scratched her chin with a dirty fingernail.

"Nevermind!"

Minutes later, the woman returned to the waiting area and said, "Miss Sylvie will see you now."

The girls followed her down the long hall and paused in the main foyer at the over-sized cherry secretary that Ingrid told Maxine probably had once belonged to the queen herself. They passed dark, heavy-framed oil paintings and ascended the central staircase on tiptoes, as they held onto the banister. The stairwell was squared-off as it went up to the private third floor; it would have been fun to slide down had it been spiral, Ingrid indicated.

As the girls stepped on each riser, they tried to peer at the rooms below through the railings—Maxine's imagination saw the all-white porcelain kitchen with copper pots hanging above the counters; the flowery powder room; the busy laundry area with orderly shelves stacked high with linens and folded towels.

"I bet the master suite is where they keep a giant safe with a giant lock," Ingrid whispered while touching a tall vase at the landing.

The maid snapped at her. "Ah-Ah-Ah—fingerprints."

Ingrid leaned closer into the girl's ear. "She's a real sourpuss, isn't she?"

Sylvie opened the door and Ingrid entered first, walked in slow circles around the room, and glared at Sylvie, reevaluating her.

Sylvie looked at Ingrid, and then at the other girl.

"Oh, that's just Maxi. Maxine," she informed Sylvie, pointing with her chin at the diminutive one.

Maxine chattered incessantly. "You have your very own

servant? Is *she* the one who folded all those towels? Does she pour your drinks, too?"

"I pour my own. To the top of the glass. Why do you ask? Are you thirsty?" Sylvie queried.

"Where's your mother?" Maxine questioned.

"She's out. So is my father. He works a lot. And mother is very, um, social. Only the servants are home. But they stay on the first floor." Sylvie got busy, ignored Maxine snooping around at her things, and showed Ingrid her doll collection and all her splendid games and toys.

"Doesn't *she* pour?"

"Who?" Sylvie asked Maxine, annoyed.

"Your mother."

"I told you. She's *out* somewhere. In fact, my whole family is out today." Sylvie continued rooting through her jewelry box until she found the glittery necklace she had been looking for, and then picked it up and dangled it in front of Ingrid's face. The contrast of the shiny necklace in front of Ingrid's face made her look even uglier. Sylvie pretended to beam as she offered to put it around the girl's thick neck.

"You can keep it." Sylvie felt her throat constrict at her own words.

"Really?"

The slight girl tapped Sylvie on the shoulder. "I live in a small house, and my mother is *always* home."

"Good for you!" Sylvie barked.

"When does she come home, your mother?"

"You ask a lot of questions, don't you, Mousy Girl?" Sylvie said.

"That's not my name!" Maxine protested.

"Yes it is. That's what I'll call you if I want to—Mousy Girl. Mousy Girl."

"Stop! Stop calling me that!"

"Ooh, look, there's a mouse in the house." Sylvie teased.

Ingrid looked delighted as they squabbled. Sylvie made believe she was enjoying this, and said, "I have an idea. Let's play Seek and Find. I'll hide these bags of chocolate-covered jellies somewhere on the third floor. Let me tell you, it is the *best* Dutch chocolate in all of Holland."

Maxine wore a worried expression. "What if *she* finds both bags?"

Ingrid licked her lips as Sylvie left the room for a few minutes. When Sylvie returned she shouted, "Ready? Go!"

Maxine scooted off toward the west wing, but before Ingrid headed for the east wing, Sylvie grabbed her chubby arm and pulled her back into the room. Then she opened both her hands which she had kept behind her back and exposed the bags of candy.

"You never hid them?" Ingrid's eyes widened.

"No. Come with me," Sylvie said. "I know how much you love playing *Catch*. How would you like to play Catch a Mouse?"

They could hear the teeny girl rummaging through a closet in one of the spare bedrooms.

"Shh!" Sylvie whispered, putting one finger to her mouth while twisting the key in the lock. "Good. Now, we get to have the candy to ourselves," she said, knowing the piggish girl would love that idea. Maxine banged on the door, nonstop, while Sylvie undid the wrappers, and talked to her through the crack. "Oh, you poor mouse," she said. "It's unfortunate you found your way into *this* closet—the one with the broken lock. It gets stuck sometimes, you know. Hold on, while I try to get you out."

Ingrid laughed so hard her shoulders shook, and the delicious dark brown saliva bubbled between her teeth. Sylvie wished she could cover her eyes and ears. The piggish girl leaned her back against the door and slid down until she hit her rear end with a thud. Then she looked at Sylvie. "You have *so* much at your house! Can I come visit tomorrow, too?"

Tears formed in Sylvie's eyes. She was benumbed, unable to respond.

She knew all along exactly where to find another whole bag of chocolate-covered jellies to stop the girl from her pathetic crying—in the second kitchen cabinet from the right. Her mother always made sure there was extra everything in whatever she desired... *almost* everything.

It seemed a very long time, and Sylvie did nothing to help Maxine in the closet, just as the girl did nothing to help Sylvie the day before at the park.

That night, Sylvie lay awake in her giant-sized bed, sick to her stomach, thinking about everything—the games—the silly children's games. *I had to play! I didn't mean anything by it!* She had hoped if there was a God, maybe he understood. How she wished her mother would come home and give her her *forgiving* kiss when she'd tuck her in, and rub her belly in circles with her smooth, cool hand. The only thing that came to her was the deep sound of the clock bonging from the downstairs foyer. She counted. *Eleven times.* She wondered where Mother was this time.

TWO

THAILAND, SOUTHEAST ASIA
1970–1971

The blackness Michael Beckman dug himself into was dark and destructive like a holocaust, darker and deeper than the genocide his mother had escaped. Three decades later, the ghosts of two generations intertwined....

Naked under the stark white hospital sheets, Michael no longer wore the six-pointed star that had always hung from his neck. He had given it away. To a girl, a gentile girl. He wanted to give her something to remember him by.

Now all he wanted, as he was drowning in uncertainty, was his daily doses of morphine and to sleep, to disappear...his throat was dry, his voice was snatched away by some demon. He saw strange faces in his haze, heard strange voices:

"Where shall we put him, Dr. Hope?"

"Wheel him this way," Dr. Hope instructed the attendant. "That's good, right there's fine." The preoccupied doctor adjusted the overhead light while the rest of the medical team stood behind him, waiting for his commands.

"Dr. Fear's still scrubbing up?" he asked, not looking at any others on staff.

"I'm here now," Dr. Fear answered in a foghorn voice, as a nurse tied his face mask from behind, and he joined the rest of the group hovering over the patient.

Michael stirred. He tried to lift his head. *Dr. Hope? Dr. Fear? What is this, a joke? What's that in my mouth? It feels like a rag. Why is there a rag in my mouth? What the hell's going on here?*

"Hmm..." Dr. Fear shook his head and directed his comment to Dr. Hope. "Look at the location, lodged right there at the spine—a short circuit to the nervous system."

What? What's lodged up against the spine? Are you talking about me? I can hear you! Where am I? The straps at Michael's wrists tightened up as he tried to break free.

One of the nurses covered his eyes and whispered to another. "Poor guy. Someone turned off his electricity."

I heard that! Don't talk about me like I'm a god damn lamp! Shit! At least if my eyes weren't taped shut I could blink and let you know that I can hear you. I beg you to take the tape off my eyes. Please, oh please....

Michael heard the doctors snapping their surgical gloves on their hands. He heard the chiming of the medical instruments. He felt a teardrop trying to escape from underneath his taped eyes. He imagined Dr. Fear's face, the face of a cockroach. And Dr. Hope was a Praying Mantis...he thought of the bugs he used to play with in his backyard. He gave them names, let them have bug races on dirt tracks.

What are they doing? They're going to operate?

"Too bad it's Dr. Numb's golf day. I'm sure the kid would appreciate an anesthesiologist right about now." Dr. Fear laughed a long laugh.

Please, oh Jesus, don't let them. They're going to cut *me?*

Dr. Fear said, "Soon, we'll determine if a piece of bone has been splintered or partially crushed. I do believe there's permanent damage here—paralysis."

Dr. Hope cleared his throat. "I beg to differ. I predict when we go *in*, we'll find severe inflammation around the nerve."

Yes, that's it, just some swelling, temporary swelling. You'll find

that out when you go in. GO IN? What am I saying? You can't go in!
I have to give them a signal. If there's a God, help me. Let me give
them a signal, let them know I can hear them, feel them touching
me . . . someone—anyone? Help me.

"Relax. I'm right here, Michael. We haven't met yet. I'm Nora,
the new nurse on duty. You probably don't even remember the
last shift," she said, wiping Michael's forehead with a wet cold
cloth. "Are you okay? I think you need some more sleep."

Michael stared at her, relieved. He no longer had tape over
his eyes or a rag in his mouth. Her pale blonde hair made her
look translucent and saintly. If he had the strength to lift his
hand, he thought it would go right through her. Tears mixed
with sweat.

"Huh?" he uttered softly, pretty sure she could hear him.

"I said you need to rest now."

Thank God, she hears me.

She felt his pulse and patted his hand. "I think you were
having really bad dreams. At least your temperature is finally
going down. That was some nasty infection," she said, closing
the light switch.

He thought about how easy it is to turn electricity on and
off—light, then dark. Michael used to like sitting in the dark,
especially on clear summer nights when he had a quiet mind.
He was uneasy about being left alone in the dark hospital room.
He tried to replace the drip of the IV bag with the gurgling
brook that had once eased him to sleep under a sickle-shaped
moon. It was where he had planted his tent in the middle of
the woods on his road trip.

He fought off sleep, because of the nightmares. The only
solace was thinking of her . . . with her eyes half-closed, Angela
had once asked Michael, "Do you ever imagine jumping from

star to star? I like to squint when I look at the stars," she said, tilting her head from side to side. "Then you can see beams of light span across the universe like beacons. And do you know why I close my eyes *al-l-l* the way?"

He looked at her again, at her long upper eyelashes meeting her lower lashes. He leaned in gently for the kiss. Light-years ago, the darkness was magical.

"The button is right by your hand," Nora said to Michael, who had closed his eyes again. "If you need anything at all, just ring."

How simple, he thought, all I have to do is ring a bell and an angel will come. *I must be dead.*

* * *

Angela always kept the story in her mind, what had happened the day she was born in 1950. She was inside her mother's womb, witnessing the world in the dark, afraid, but she was anxious to be a part of the excitement. There were loud sirens. The police officer had escorted them into the hospital. The father-to-be was called immediately.

"Well, let's just see how far along you are, shall we?" The senior nurse handed the starchy white hospital gown to the woman in labor who had, moments before, stormed through the double-faced doors of "Maternity." Two orderlies pried her tight grip from her husband's side when they had to be separated. The expectant mother looked dazed. She had stopped crying, and cradled her distended abdomen, stroking it with outstretched hands. "But, but I'm a few weeks early."

The younger nurse smiled, and she pointed at the bathroom door where she would help her get undressed. "What's your first name?" she asked.

"Jean. It's Jean."

"Opening to the back, Jean," she said.

The pregnant woman's spindly legs trembled beneath her belly. Her weight, so out of proportion, forced her to hold onto the doorknob to balance herself. In the pitted mirror she glimpsed at the unfamiliarity of her own face which had aged over the past few hours.

Through the crack in the door she could hear other nurses speaking softly. A tear rolled from her reddened eyes down her pink cheeks. She licked the saltiness from the corner of her mouth. *Sea water.*

She leaned in closer to hear them. Were they whispering about her—they probably already heard the news about the tragedy. *Only hours ago. Why does bad news travel so fast?* She was the distraught woman on the beach, the poor woman in her eighth month of pregnancy—the woman who may lose the *next* child, too, from the trauma—the one who will go mad with the memory.

Part of her wanted to prove she could get through this ordeal, and another part was consumed by the same wave that ripped her first child out of her life. That part wanted to just go away with the gas they were about to administer, and never awaken.

When the doctor examined her, he confirmed, "Well, my lady, it looks like this is it. Nurse, let's get her prepped."

"Last name's Martino" the older nurse said and slapped the wrist band on the woman in labor. The next thing she knew, she was on the hard delivery table. She strained her neck, staring in disbelief at the oddness of her swollen belly under the florescent light; the belly she wished to disassociate from over the past two hours.

The labor grew more intense each minute. "Please, I need some water." Her tongue twisted in her mouth from the dryness. Her neatly-styled hair came loose from the criss-crossing of the bobby pins.

"Sorry. You're not allowed to have any water," the nurses said in unison.

"Please, an ice cube. Wet my lips, anything..."

She became delirious with the pain, which was somehow still there in the gas-induced sleep. Her mind played cruel tricks on her. She was under water, flailing her arms, screaming for help, but no one was there to save her... not a lifeguard around.

Dear God, this is a mistake! Please, somebody's got to help me! Save my baby! The screams that escaped her mouth sounded far away and foreign to her own ears and she wished her hands were free to cover them.

She imagined herself floating, free from the straps that bound her. *Free as a bird*, she thought; she gasped at the air like a baby sparrow that had been pushed out of its nest by a sudden gust of wind that had taken a wrong turn.

Overcome with exhaustion, her hair was lacquered onto her forehead like wet black paint. She thrashed about, jerked her cold, bare feet stuffed into the metal stirrups and yelped like a trapped animal, like the ones she had saved down at the wildlife shelter when she was a kid. For some reason she had always found creatures with broken wings or limbs, or they had found her. She wished she could save them all, nurture them.

"Ten centimeters, doctor," the senior nurse said.

"Time to push now," the nurse in training said. "Next contraction... come on, you can do it. You can do it," she coaxed.

The older nurse gave her co-worker a look, and then spoke in a stoic voice. "Just breathe deep, my dear."

The nurse in training squelched her cheering. The silence in between became louder than the screams that had pervaded the room five minutes earlier. Voices came in and out like bad reception on the radio.

"Ahhh God!" *Please let this baby be okay.*

"Give a really hard push on the next one."

"There's the head," the doctor announced.

She panicked, her face flush. *Is there something wrong? Death and birth, birth and death,* raced through her mind. Half conscious, she envisioned the baby with the head of a bird, its wings emerging first. There weren't any toes and fingers to count.

When she came to, she was given the same instructions: "Okay, push again, one more push," the doctor's gruff voice commanded. "Push," he said in a forceful tone that she was sure she deserved. Suddenly, he had the face of a hunter in the woods, wearing a camouflage suit with a gun in his hand, shooting ducks out of the sky for the fun of it... *such pretty mallards.*

"Yes," he sighed, surely for medical affirmation, "Here we go, the baby's coming. Here it comes. Push, push, pu-u-ush."

She was scared silly, the mother-child, with no one there to hold her hand, no one there to see her or hear her. She was invisible. No one was aware she was dying. She wasn't worthy of being saved, she told herself. Then something more dreadful occurred to her—the baby—it was the baby who was dying.

Is it breathing? Is the baby breathing? The idea of air simply passing through lungs, simply breathing air, simply living, engulfed her. The obstetrician hovered above with calculated authority.

She heard a choking sound. She panicked—*suffocation? Asphyxiation?* In a fleeting moment, she wished she could put the baby's hand in her own palm and keep it safe and warm, but she wasn't worthy of another child. *Someone else will have to raise it, care for it. I'm not capable.* She had no strength to form the words and lost her concentration.

The way the doctor held the new life in his large hands looked like holding a slippery red football. He spared the time to turn around and show the mother.

"The baby's okay?" she asked.

"Well, of course, the baby's okay. And, congratulations, you have a darling baby girl."

She watched him from behind, as he checked the infant's vital signs, cleaned her up. His movements seemed abrupt. He turned back in full view, and ordered the nurses, "Okay, let's wash the mother up now and get her into recovery."

He must have had a long day. Maybe he's anxious to go home to a full course dinner waiting for him that must be cold by now; it'll have to be reheated to his liking. Maybe, meatloaf and mashed potatoes with gravy and green beans.

She had heard a muted cry, the snip of the umbilical cord. Everything went by so quickly—one child's death, another's life—in a flash—a shooting star, too quickly to know.

Once again a mother, she peeled the fuzzy warm blanket back and looked at the stranger before her. Her pink face was as tiny as a fist. "Oh, my precious," she whispered. The mother relieved of her duty, trembled uncontrollably, as she was being wheeled down the corridor with the six-pound baby close behind. She wanted any excuse to give up all feelings, bad and good. She wanted to stop feeling all together—afraid of the past sorrow, afraid of the new joy that could be taken away like the one she'd held in her arms for *seven* years.

She closed her eyes and wanted sleep, wanted to stop thinking. Before sleep came, she thought, *the nurses will find my husband in the waiting room and tell him the good news. 'She's a cherub,' they'll say, 'that fell from the sky.'*

She raised her head to look over at the *replacement* child

in the pink bassinet. She wasn't making a sound. In the silence, no answers came from life past. And no answers came from what lay ahead.

How can I be sure no harm will ever come to her? That she'll always be loved and protected? I can't be sure. I can no longer be sure of anything. I don't know how to give her that. How do I give her the perfect life? Her sister Anna's was cut so short.

She dropped her head back onto her pillow and examined the infant's face again. *She's sweet as an angel. I will name her that—Angela. Her name is Angela!*

THREE

SOUTHAMPTON, NEW YORK
1969

Acumulus cloud wandered overhead as Angela floated on her back in the ocean. She was numb to the water temperature as she watched the cloud slowly moving by, studying its heavenly form—its snowy-white wings and flowing robe. Angela often thought about her sister while she was at the beach. Anna had been gone almost twenty years already—Angela's very own beach angel that drifted over the many shades of blue.

She tried to ignore the shadows in the water, long tendrils of hair flowing among seaweed, her pregnant mother letting go of the child's hand...one endless wail by the shore, watching Anna's red pail moving back and forth with the waves.

Angela had been the eight-month heavy weight...it was *her* fault her mother was unable to dig her heels into the sand that day and dive into the murky sea. From within the womb, she heard her mother's cry for help and came into the world that very day curious about life and death.

She wanted to *know* the sea because it was what heard Anna's last prayers and whispers, the last to caress her innocent body, her last breath, before taking her, grabbing her by the knees and pulling her away forever.

Angela floated farther out into the water and breathed

heavy with anticipation, reminding herself she shouldn't be swimming alone—mother's strictest rule, you know, because of the *accident*. That's how her mom referred to her sister Anna's drowning whenever it was talked about, which was rarely. But it was obvious she blamed herself every minute of every waking hour.

This wasn't the first time Angela had disobeyed. It was as if the beach beckoned her; it was *her* church, where she knew there was God. She squeezed her lids tight as oyster shells and the hazel in her eyes became sightless pearls within. If dark images came before her as she dipped below the water's surface, she'd think of how the ocean was *filled* with life, from ameba to whale.

Moving with each cresting wave, Angela looked at Sea Horse tied to the same petrified piece of driftwood she always used when she went horseback riding. Her sandals, cutoffs, and T-shirt were left in a heap at the stallion's hooves. She'd have to dry off before she returned to the barns where she worked. She'd put her wet two-piece daisy print bathing suit in the horse's pouch and let the wind dry her hair on the jaunt back.

She concentrated very hard, not to lose track of her counting. She had to break her record. The beach was almost empty now, an unseasonably warm afternoon in the month of May. There was no one nearby to witness her while she tested her gutsy skill, her unflagging game of courage, swimming out past the breakers. When she tired, she allowed her body to move up and down with the upward heave of each swell, becoming part of the rhythm.

Since she was little, she had obsessed about being *under* the water, always trying to hold herself down as long as possible and then allowing the water to bring her up at its will. To her, the sea was alive with deceiving beauty and pleasure; it was to be respected and understood. The chilly water forced her to tread, to swim, to dive its surge, with its froth spilling over her, teasing her—there for her to master, to conquer.

Ninety fi-i-ive...she counted the seconds in slow sequence, holding her breath, as she had practiced, unconsciously, so many times. *Ninety si-i-i-x.* A smile crossed over her closed lips. She was coming close to surpassing her last goal, close to reaching 100. But in an instant her undertaking turned to utter terror.

A creature gripped her head, clutching her hair, dragging her, pulling her with great force in one direction. There was no way to stop whatever it was. Some of her hair was being stripped from its roots. *Maybe I'm stuck? A fisherman's trap?*

It occurred to her that she had lost count of holding her breath, that she would die now at the age of nineteen, without ever having reached her objective, her glory. The notion of losing her battle to the *water* was heartbreaking more than anything else. It was personal between the two of them.

She swallowed, choked, the salt stinging her throat, her eyes popping open, the burning pain, seeing nothing. *So, this is it. Oh, what irony. This is my nightmare. This feeling—pulling down—the confusion, slipping, twisting pain, loss of sense, heaviness, and then the feeling of freedom seconds after your trachea closes. Eyes blinking one last time, unable to see, to scream, you merely succumb.*

When in her mind, she saw Anna's limp body floating face down, something in Angela *snapped*, and she fought back. She wouldn't let the ocean swallow her, too. She wouldn't let her mother go through that kind of pain again. At birth, her mother counted her limbs and each of her fingers and toes. She kicked her legs in scissor movement and then bit her attacker's claw and sang out from the water—the cry of a sea lion.

There was her monster, face to face—a human's, not a monster's, with the bluest eyes—sky color, bringing her back into self. They stumbled back to shore as one...mangled limbs splaying in whatever direction the rough current took them.

Why is he swimming in his blue jeans? They were heavy on him, clinging to his body as he dropped her on the sand, like a wet blanket. He lay next to her on his back, half propped up on his elbows. She quickly became aware of her own body. In the tussle, he had broken one of the straps on her swimsuit. She tried to cover her top with her hands and he threw his shirt at her with anger.

Her eyes stung through the tears. Her long matted hair covered her face. Trying to regain focus, she lurched at the stranger and screamed. "Why'd you do that to me? Were you trying to k-kill me?" she hiccupped, something she always did when nervous.

"Wh-a-at?" He tried to raise his voice; it was weak. "I just saved your life for Christ sake! What did you *bite* me for?" He looked at the mark on his hand, but the skin was not broken. "Geez, even my *dog* doesn't bite."

He pointed to the camper at the top of the dunes with its door left wide open. The obedient dog was still waiting for him since he had yelled at him to "Stay." He stammered and hyperventilated through his explanation. "I-I-I," his voice was raspy and his breathing labored. "I was just minding my own business, on my way to get lunch at Uncle Miltie's...and that's when I saw you go under and you didn't come up for a long time, a long, long time. I pulled over to the side of the road and ran over the dunes and—"

He wiped the drops from his face and let out one more huff of air. "When I saw you—you weren't coming up, what do you think? What do you think I'm going to do?"

She squelched a laugh that *he* was the one out of breath. His lean and bronze body melded with *her* beach in his bogus rescue attempt.

"I ran into the water, scared to death I wouldn't find you, grab you in time...believe me, the last thing I was worried about was *pulling* your hair!" He looked at her, and his voice toned down. "Were you trying to, trying to *kill* yourself?"

"Kill myself?" she repeated. "Are you kidding? No! Oh no, my God, no! I was only trying to break my record. I'm sorry if— Where's Uncle Miltie's, anyway?"

"You're sorry? That's it? You're sorry?"

"Yeah, sorry." She rubbed her scalp. "You practically pulled all the hair off my head. What do you want me to say? Thanks for saving my life? You didn't, plain and simple. You're not a hero, okay? I wasn't drowning, although, *you* damn near drowned me!"

"Yeah, right. I should have let you drown, you ungrateful little..." He looked at her harder. "And what do you mean "break your record?""

"I was counting." She pouted. "I almost reached one hundred."

"Oh, really?" He let out a small chuckle. "What else do you do for laughs?" His breathing evened out, as if relieved for the blunder, relieved that the strange pouty girl sitting next to him with goose-bumps was there to argue with him. "It's a lunch place, Uncle Miltie's. What's the difference? And a hundred seconds, that's what it's all about? Why? Why the hell is that so important?" he finally asked.

She scrunched her stinging eyes and obsessed over the topic she had immersed herself in since she was a kid—*Asphyxiation: suffocation or unconscious condition caused by lack of oxygen and excess carbon dioxide in the blood, as in choking or drowning.*

The older she got, the more headstrong she had become. She was her own person, feisty and non-conforming. And brave. Very, very brave. At least, she wanted to believe that. And she wanted to be nothing like her mother, who suffocated her with her worrying. Angela had great plans of adventure and travel, and nothing was going to get in her way. She was going to work for an airline based overseas, far, far away over the seas.

Angela's relationship with the ocean was innate, unlike Anna's. If she had been the one swimming that day instead of her sister, she would have known better than to *fight* the riptide. She held back her tears and stared at the passing clouds, looking for the celestial vapor of the sister she had never had the chance to meet. It was gone. She turned to the sunshine that rained on his face instead. They both sat for a few minutes in their own silence.

He looked back at the dunes where his shoes were strewn on the sand, when he had run toward the *thing* submerged in the water, bobbing up and down with each crest of wave on an isolated beach.

"Why is that so important?" he asked again. "The counting?"

And again, she didn't answer him. Like everyone else, he couldn't relate. But when she looked into his eyes, she saw his soft side. She realized they seemed familiar to her. She knew those eyes from somewhere.

He was shirtless, unaware of her watching him. The six-pointed star that hung from his chain reflected in the sunlight. Her eyes followed him as he stood up and twirled his key chain around his finger. His shoulders were thick and his waist slender, barely holding up his soggy Levis.

He whistled. "Come on, Shadow. Come on boy." The caramel colored mutt jumped out of the van and ran to his owner's side, his tongue flapping with joy, nuzzling up to Angela who let him lick her face as she ran her fingers through his shaggy coat.

Michael smiled at Angela. She followed him as he walked.

His lips were sexy, Elvis-like. "You know, I'm sorry if I scared you. I never expected to come upon such a beau-tiful—"

Angela blushed.

"Ab-so-lutely, beautiful *horse*."

"Oh," she said, furrowing her brow.

"Hmm... how does that quote go?" he asked, placing his hand on the animal's withers. 'If God made anything more beautiful than a *horse*, he kept it for himself....'"

He's Robert Frost when he speaks. No, no, he's Mark Twain.

"What's *his* name?"

"Umm. Sea Horse. He's not mine. I wish. I only groom the horses a couple of days a week at the Ross Estate where my mom is working right now, as a seamstress."

She watched his large hands stroking the animal's neck as he spoke. "I rent a house right down the road," he said, pointing. "You can see it from here. It's the one with the red roof."

He turned around to the cry of seagulls behind them, circling above the waves. Then there was quiet and he squatted down, letting the sand sift through his fingers. They both looked out at the horizon. "I try to spend as much time as I can taking in the ocean."

"Me, too," she said, trying not to sound immature, polly-parroting him. She always knew she'd discover more than just seashells at the beach. He was her best find yet!

"I'm not from around here," she added. She felt her tongue swimming in her mouth. "I'm from Massapequa."

"Massapequa?" He laughed hard. "That's unbelievable! I grew up there. My mother still lives there."

"Really? Are you serious?" Angela's mouth hung open wide.

"Lately though she's talking about moving," he added. "Geez, coincidences are funny, aren't they?"

She looked at him and smiled. "Very."

"I've been living here in Southampton now because of school and all. I graduated from Southampton College. This area inspires me to write more."

"You're a writer?"

"Yeah. Mostly write about nature. But I go to Massapequa *all* the time. That's where I got my camper. I named it—" He inclined his head and laughed at himself. "Never mind!"

"No, what? Tell me." Angela pushed.

"I named it Mr. Doobie."

"Mr. who?" She laughed.

"Yeah, don't ask. You wanted to know." He smiled. "I'm getting ready to hit the road again . . . me and my dog."

Who is this guy? Now he's John Steinbeck and his dog, Charley . . . searching America. She gave her forearm a pinch as her heart entered a steeplechase.

He extended his hand. "By the way, I'm Michael Beckman. . ."

Michael Beckman. She repeated his name in her head.

Her face got hotter as she took his hand. "And *I'm* uh, Angela. Martino."

His hands were telling, as much as the words he used describing his journeys. It didn't take Angela long to know he was someone worthy of sharing the deepest of secrets. Each of his gestures suggested sensitivity that she had never seen in a male; well, maybe except for Perry Como.

She imagined the feel of his hand on top of hers, as he spoke. She thought of her mother's hands, looked down at her own, still smooth and unpricked from collected weariness.

She wondered what brought them together, two gypsies at heart, both on inward journeys. It was the *wondering* part that she liked. She tried not to gawk at him as he talked about riding horses in Montana; shooting rapids in Wyoming; hiking trails in Utah; climbing rocks in the Grand Canyon; watching shooting stars in New Mexico. . . .

"Sorry." He held up both his hands in midair. "I get carried away whenever I talk about the road."

"No. Don't stop." She dug her foot further into the buttery

sand, catching his eye, assessing him as a profound storyteller. "I enjoy hearing your road stories. You make life sound so unpredictable," she said, turning in a circle with her arms out-stretched and her hair flogging across her face.

She stopped turning and faced Michael. He searched her face as she searched his. "I want to feel that, too," she said. "What you *write* about—the unexpected. I suppose that's how life is when you're on the road, huh? "

Michael's eyes brightened as he watched her. She stopped to look into them.

He has the goddamn seascape in his eyes. We both have the same urge to be someplace else, but I don't want him to go. And I don't want to go, myself—oh no, talk about your timing. This can't happen. I won't let this happen.

"So, what are your plans?" he asked, not knowing he was breaking her spell.

"Traveling?" They laughed over having the same answer to the question.

Angela's voice exploded. "Oh my God, I want to go every-where, see everything. I want to go on country roads, like you. I want to hitchhike through Tuscany . . . and stand on top of the hills of Montmartre with my easel, run freely in the Alps where the air is so thin it makes you feel faint and—" She stopped and looked at him, feeling childish. "You think I'm giddy enough, don't you?"

"No." He shook his head. "Giddy is good. You're crazy, you know that?"

She liked the way he looked at her when he said that, as if there was nothing better than being crazy. As if that were something they shared.

Of course, her father's income as a printer could not send her around the world. She planned to work abroad for an airline as a stewardess. She had interviewed well for the airline of her choice, the one that would base her in Frankfurt, Germany.

She told Michael about the big interview for the job, sitting in the waiting room with dozens of applicants, watching one girl after another, come and go, until a giraffe-tall woman with a coiffed Pageboy called her name.

"I'm Miss McDowell. Follow me, won't you?"

She had tensely followed the interviewer into her stuffy office to the sound of the woman's stockings rubbing against her unending legs, thinking about how carefree her life was only a few days before when she had hung off the side of a dinghy, dredging for crabs at the mouth of the canal.

"Well, I've reviewed your resume, Miss Martino," she said.

Angela nodded. She noticed the photos staggered on the wall behind Miss McDowell, pictures of when Miss McDowell was young and pretty.

But, oh man, her fly outfit sure looks dated.

"I see you're fluent in French?" Miss McDowell said.

"Yes. I mean, *Oui.*"

"So, Angela, tell me, why do you want to be a stewardess?"

Angela said she loved meeting all kinds of people and working for the airlines would allow her to—"*Je ne sais quoi. It is joie de vivre* . . . it will be the joy in my life."

"Yes, all kinds of people, indeed." She tapped her pen lightly on Angela's application. "Do you have a boyfriend, Angela?"

"No, I'm not ready to commit to a boyfriend . . . yet," she answered, thinking this question was out of place.

The interviewer smiled. "That's good. When I started my career, I *had* a boyfriend—the love of my life. But he believed the generalization about stewardesses that they have a boyfriend at every port. I can assure you that's not how it is. To be perfectly honest, much of the time you can feel isolated. I think you should know that up front, before you waste your time and ours."

Would that be *her*, in years to come, a lonely woman? "I understand," Angela said, "and I appreciate your honesty, but I want this more than anything else."

Miss McDowell ran her finger down the resume, until she got to Angela's hobbies. "You ride, I see? Horseback riding was *my* life for many years." She took a long look at Angela who had worn a proper navy blue suit, not a hair out of place. As degrading as it was for Angela who had always thought of herself as "one of the boys on the block," when asked, she paraded herself around the room so the woman could check her posture and grace as she moved.

Would Mrs. McDowell hold it against her that her legs were too skinny to make the same swishing sound?

The interview finally came to an end, and she exited the interrogation room, arrow straight until she rounded the corner, where she let the imaginary books fall off her head and her shoulders slouch to their normal position. She had no idea if she'd get the job. If she didn't get it, she planned on going back to night school at the community college during the next semester and finish earning her credits toward a degree.

As Angela told Michael about applying for the job, she kneeled to sketch drawings into the wet sand with a seashell. "I see you're artistic," he commented.

"You think so?" She turned her mouth sideways.

A wave filled in her etched trenches, so she relocated to a clear spot, and liked that he was studying her every move. He gathered some different tools for her from a pile of discarded shells that were being picked through by a pair of gray spotted seagulls.

Angela's seashell collection at home consisted of dozens of scalloped-shaped, moon-shaped, and those that had been abandoned by snails. She adored everything about the beach, the feel of the sand, the sounds of the waves—everything. This had bothered her mother, who took it as a sense of betrayal. Angela should have felt the same aversion to such a place.

"Here, try this one," Michael said, handing her the largest of the mollusks. "A career, traveling? Hmm...sounds good to me. I write for a local paper. I've worked there all throughout college. One day, I want to be a travel writer...write for National Geographic."

"That sounds exhilarating," she said.

He blinked up at the sky. "The last time I *really* felt free was when I went on the road. I had just graduated high school, still a kid in a lot of ways. I couldn't get enough. The wild rivers and the mountains are thrilling. But it's the *stillness* that I miss. It's magical."

Angela looked at the sky too, as if the magic was present that moment.

He looked at her again. "You're a good listener," he said, and she smiled. He looked at her bare skin, not a sign of jewelry to detract from her simple beauty. "Anyway, it's the most fulfilling lesson I've ever learned. You know, I have to admit though, *home* to me, will always be New York."

Even though she had the *same* desire to wander much the same as a vagabond, she was satisfied to hear his last comment. Angela was a true New Yorker, too. She had always been grateful she lived by the ocean, even though she complained otherwise to her parents.

"I didn't forget, you know, that you never answered my question," Michael said.

"What question?"

"Why's the *counting* so important?"

She licked the salt on her bottom lip. "It's a long story. Maybe I'll tell you another time. Time? Oh my God, what time *is* it?" she asked, stumbling into her dry clothes. "I've got to get back to the stables."

"Must be about five o'clock, I guess," he answered, looking at the low sun.

"Oh man, I'm late! Gotta go!" she said in a rush.

He called after her. "Hey, Angela Martino. Come back and let's hang out sometime—you know where I live now—the one with the red roof. Okay?"

"Yeah, okay," she answered, tossing her hair, not sure of what she heard when she mounted the horse. She threw her foot into the stirrup and shifted in the saddle, taking up the reins with a sudden jerk. She could feel his eyes on her until she galloped into the distance and turned around to see him still standing there, a small dot in the sand, both of them aware of the ebb and flow of the tide—so familiar to them.

He had touched her, not in a physical way, better than that, better than the *other* boys. But he was one enticement she could do without. She flashed onto her mother's life of "doing without"—sharing a lipstick with her sisters and working in a one-room sweatshop, and her father working overtime in a tedious job, never fulfilling his dreams.

She had to ride fast—fast to get away from what could be a *trap*.

"No way," she told Sea Horse, as she pulled the bridle to the left toward the dunes. "So, he has nice blue eyes. Big deal."

Michael was no longer visible. Angela bounced hard in her saddle and looked back over her shoulder. One pure white cloud amid the blue scurried her along the desolate shore, reprimanding her for the forbidden swim. She wasn't entirely to blame—the waves were rolling in with perfectly ripe temptation.

Deep in thought, she was startled by Sea Horse's whinny and slowed him down to a steady trot, humming one of her favorite lines from Janis Joplin. Another song about freedom, as she prepared herself to meet the sermon on her mother's face, especially after her mother spent the day with Mrs. Ross, the slave-driver. She wouldn't mention meeting Michael. If she did, her mother would think her travel plans were all talk. Angela needed to prove how serious she was about her future, how different she was from her mom. She was tired of the arguments they'd had over her career choice, like when they had recently visited the Parrish Museum in Southampton: Angela skipped backwards with excitement in the grassy courtyard filled with reproductions of Greek and Roman statues. "Just think, Mom, I'll be seeing the *real* ones in Greece and Rome." She bit her tongue as soon as she had said the words.

"After all I've sacrificed, and you want to *leave*?"

Amazing. Her mother never said those words; they were written all over her face. Maybe if her mom were a screamer, she'd be able to let go of some of her grief. And let go of Angela.

Well, I'm sick and tired of protecting her from all her grief.

Anna—if you had only learned how to swim.

All the pain that washed up with her sister's body—pain that made her father a workaholic and her mother a Catholic fanatic, and pain that made Angela want to *fly* away.

From a distance, she could see her mother's lone figure on the beach, her hands on her hips. Still too far away to meet her mother's dispiriting mask, Angela practiced her apology for not keeping track of the time. It was going to be a long, tense drive home to Massapequa.

Was her hair still damp? Was it obvious that she'd been swimming? Was it obvious that she had just experienced the most romantic day of her entire life?

FOUR

DIEREN, HOLLAND
1940–1941

S ylvie had little recollection of her maternal grandfather since she was only four when he died. Her mother spoke highly of him, but it seemed she only did so in front of Oma. She talked about his sense of humor and his zest for life. Surely, she could apply some of those attributes to herself.

Sylvie witnessed her mother's behavior right before Oma came for a visit; she'd take off her rings and bracelets and stuff them into the corners of her lingerie drawer. Peculiar, how mothers and daughters could be so different.

Sylvie's mother, Helene, seemed more evasive and strained whenever Oma came to stay with them. Even though Oma didn't live far away, Sylvie loved when Oma came for a sleepover. She endured her grandmother's maudlin lectures because in the evening, Oma would come into each of the children's bedrooms and tell them about the old days in Holland…"long before you were born," she'd say, while brushing Sylvie's long golden-blonde hair, clipping it to one side in a wide tortoise comb she had bought for her.

"Now, let's get you out of this stiff organza dress," Oma said, making a disapproving face. "It wasn't long ago you wore the pinafores I made for you. Sylvie, why all the dressing up?"

Oma asked, covering her granddaughter with the blanket. "Just like your mother."

Sylvie frowned at Oma's gingham housecoat, her frumpiness.

"Tomorrow, I will teach you how to bake . . . something else your mother never cared to learn." She kissed her granddaughter on the tip of her nose and started toward the door.

"Oma?"

Her grandmother half-turned with her eyebrows on an upward swing. "Yes?"

"Thank you for the hair comb. I'll wear it forever and ever."

"Clip it to your heart, and I'll be forever happy," her grandmother answered.

Sylvie nodded, even though she did not understand.

When morning came, it was easy for Sylvie to find Oma in their big house. The tart scent of apple peels lured her into the kitchen. When she ran into the room, clumsily, her mother reprimanded her. "Sylvie, slow down. And be more graceful. An aristocratic lady does not walk pigeon-toed. She walks with finesse. Maybe you aren't paying attention at your ballet classes."

Unlike her own mother, her grandmother didn't say too much. She seemed content to stay put at the counter, chopping or stirring with the help. She smelled like the insides of the pantry, sweet and spicy, all at once.

Over the years Mother and Oma got in each other's way, more and more. Sylvie watched the two of them—defiant at the cutting board—Grandmother finishing off her plain apple fritters with a sprinkle of cinnamon sugar and grated oily rind of a lemon, while Mother defiantly smothered her store-bought French profiteroles in chocolate sauce.

The blade Oma used for making the fritters wasn't sharp

enough to put a nick in the tension between them; the tap-tap-tapping of the knife hitting the cutting board.

Soon, Mother put a stop to her extended visits. "Three nights is enough, Mother. I have things to do, you know."

Sylvie was angry with her mother whenever she made Oma leave, even though her mother would be less agitated once her grandmother was gone. She wondered if she'd ever have the nerve to tell her own mother to leave her home when she was an adult.

Sylvie had always taken pride in the fact that she was the only one in the family to inherit Oma's thick, wavy hair. But one day she removed the unadorned yellow-brown comb from her hair and replaced it with the glimmering one her mother bought for her. She had to—mother made such a fuss over the small diamond-studs that were fastened to it.

"Oh, don't you look superb, Sylvie. I must show you off to your friends' mothers." She laughed, pulling her by the hand, ignorant of the ache in her child's belly. Sylvie finally figured out how to get accepted into mother's world, and soon she'd be joining her when she'd go on her outings. She would have the prettiest clothes, and her mother would be *proud* of her.

Sometimes, on her loneliest days, she'd speculate where her mother went all the time...since Papa was always out, it seemed her mother competed with him by keeping busy with social events as often as possible. She wasn't the type to sit and fuss over wallpaper samples. Perhaps she was uninspired, since there were no more empty rooms to decorate.

In her adolescence, Sylvie systematized her garments, pretending this was still her biggest worry. She'd kept her clothes in meticulous order: the whites lined up together, short sleeves, long sleeves, perfectly pressed, and then came the colors, from pastel to dark. She had inherited her mother's flair for good taste. One day, with an increase in allowance, she would outdo her mother with her own purchases. And Mother would surely notice. She hummed, busy with excitement. *The showier, the better.*

As Sylvie matured, how she appeared to others mattered to her more than anything, and she found no greater joy than when she was stopped on the street with compliments from passersby: "Sylvie, what a lovely scarf" "Sylvie wherever did you get those shoes?" "Sylvie, *you* are the fashion plate of Dieren, aren't you, my dear?"

With teenage drama, she was aroused whenever she would be near her wardrobe and inhale the wonderful scent of cedar. She'd promenade before it with extended fingers, flipping the many price tags on all her new garments, making them dance like vibrant butterflies. New things made everything all right again.

Over time, there were fewer and fewer tags to flip.

Sylvie feared the cheaper shampoos would make her hair lusterless. And what of her shoes? They were losing their gloss, too, and she'd no longer be able to see herself in their shine when she looked down at her awkward feet.

Even years *before* the war, Sylvie recollected the sirens being tested in school. Routine drills were conducted, where students hid in the school basement. "Now class, remember to listen to the wail of the siren: when you hear one continuous rising and falling sound, what do you do?"

Marielle raised her hand. "You take cover," she said, confidently, tossing her curls.

"That's right, you take cover," the teacher said.

"And what does it mean if the whistle gets louder and louder?" a voice asked from the back of the room.

"It means you run like the dickens," Henrick answered, looking around the room for approving giggles.

"That'll be enough, Henrick."

The teachers rehearsed this on a regular basis, telling the students it was much safer where *they* were in the countryside, but their voices were unconvincing ever since the bombings in Rotterdam. Sylvie pondered, *how long will the eerie red glow remain in the distance?*

In the larger European cities, Air Raid Wardens went from home to home at dark, to make sure people had covered their windows and doors with black cloth, not to let any light show through.

The Rosenberg home still felt immune to what was going on in the big cities, but the house had lost some of its comfort. The halls where Papa used to pace seemed longer, and Sylvie could almost see her father's hair getting thinner and whiter by the day. He flicked more ashes from his cigar than ever before. She had always loved the smell of his cigar.

One rare day when Papa tried to relax, she went to lift the humidor to retrieve a cigar for him, but it was empty. He had told her that he no longer smoked cigars, and he didn't miss them. Sylvie didn't believe him. How did he expect her to believe him while she, herself, had missed the honeyed aroma that clung to his clothes like a honeycomb?

Did he also not miss the leg of lamb at the dinner table? Now there seemed to be a lot of spaetzle and other doughy concoctions offered in its place.

He'd always been so busy with work before, that one day

when her father called her to join him to chat, Sylvie didn't drag her feet at the chance. He tapped the love seat with his hand. "Come here, Sylvie," he said, his eyes fixed on her face. "You know, you look more like your mother every day."

Sylvie figured this was a good thing because her mother was stunning, an exceptional beauty, really. Maybe that was why he was becoming more attached to her than to Gretta . . . time was not being kind to her older sister, not softening her features.

Papa looked tired. She surmised the decline in the gallery's income must be devastating to her father. She overheard him saying to Uncle Nathan that they'd have to move much of the artwork, along with thousands of privately-owned works of art during the occupation. She no longer heard him whistling or humming a tune when he came through the front door. Gretta no longer took cello lessons; Wilhelm no longer worked on his coin collection, and Ruthie kept her doll in the same dress, day after day.

While Papa was trying to relax, she was thrilled he wanted to have a private chat with her. "Tell me again," she asked. "How did you start this whole art business, Papa?"

He looked at her with delight, as she was the only one in the family who showed an interest. "Well, I know you've heard the story many times before, Sylvie." He winked. "Since you ask, I will tell you again. My father, your Grandfather Benjamin . . . ."

"You called him Big Ben, right?" she said. "When you were a boy?"

"Yes, Big Ben, like the clock. And he was a punctual man when it came to selling. He would push that broken-down old cart through the cobblestone streets of Leiden."

"Where Rembrandt is from?"

"Yes, that's right. When your grandfather started, he was about sixteen, a shy young man with a vision. He was the one who created the business from bare bones. My brother Nathan and I give him all the credit for our success."

Sylvie's father's eyes looked far away when he spoke. "He was always pushing and pulling big carts down the road, going back and forth to grand antique markets. Back and forth all day, which was good for him. He was a pacer. Never could sit still. Like me." He smiled. "And you."

"One day, Opa, your grandfather, found an old painting tossed on the side of the road. Not knowing its value, he thought he could sell its frame. He knew he had to sell the furniture and objects he had collected in order to have enough guilders to feed his wife and children, your Uncle Nathan and me. He would sell it all before he returned home, days later."

"All except the *painting*," Sylvie said. Sylvie looked at the painting that hung in the hall, the painting that Ben found turned out to be a Rembrandt, "Portrait of Dirck Jansz. Pesser"

Sylvie's father had kept that one in memory of Big Ben, and promised himself never to sell it. It had become part of his bloodline. Sometimes, Sylvie believed her father loved that painting more than anything else in the world.

Sylvie smiled at her father. "Mother said people laughed at him, called him a junk collector."

"Is that what she said?" he asked. "Well then, I must remind your mother that if it weren't for this *junk collector* who passed his livelihood on to his sons, she wouldn't be surrounded by such luxury." Her father scanned the room, looking up at the heavy drapery climbing the twelve-foot high walls and back down to the plush velvet seat they sat upon.

Sylvie had to wonder if it was the mockery that made her own father so driven to succeed.

"Come, let me show you something I fell upon just the other day."

Sylvie followed her father into his office, and he opened

his desk drawer and took out a blue book filled with lined paper from an old shoebox.

"It's a list? Opa's list?" Sylvie asked.

"Yes, see, next to each item, Opa marked its value in guilders."

Sylvie read the items listed: "old milk bottle, glazed ceramic jar, brass door knocker, pewter tankard, porcelain tile, silver picture frame, decorated tin, cabochon-studded candlestick, jewelry, gunpowder pouch, musket from the 1800s, two sconces, Victorian door handle, tapestry, furniture, Oriental rug, old postcards, coins, engraved prints, and fine art."

"See," her father said. "Fine art. Where Opa left off, and where we started."

After Opa's heart attack, which he had suffered after losing his wife, Sylvie's father and his brother Nathan had acquired the growing business, and opened a small gallery in 1920. Josef and Nathan became powerful, thriving partners. Her father was good with numbers, and her uncle good with making deals. Before the war, they made many contacts and trades, worldwide, and ended up with more Rembrandts in their collection than anyone in Europe.

At first Sylvie's interest in her father's work was merely to get him to sit down long enough and talk to her, so she could rest her head on his shoulder and feel his voice vibrating through him. Over time, Sylvie was no longer acting. She had become genuinely interested in the history behind each painting he had acquired.

Sylvie and her father were talking about another painting, "Portrait of a Lady with a Black Cap," when her older sister entered the room. Gretta had been spending more time with her other siblings since Sylvie's and father's shared interest.

"So, where is the painting, now, Papa?" Sylvie asked. "Have you moved it to the other gallery? Or have you sold—"

Gretta interrupted. "Father, I need to—"

"Shhh. Wait a minute, Gretta." Her father held up his hand. "Ahh, Sylvie, you mean the one I purchased from the ten Cate Family? Part of a group of Rembrandts? Yes, we certainly celebrated *that* transaction."

Gretta locked eyes with her little sister, and Sylvie kept up with the staring contest.

Was that bump midway on her big sister's nose, growing? Maybe her once exotic looks were changing right under Gretta's own nose. Or right on it. For an instant Sylvie sympathized with her sister, until she saw the foul glare she was giving her out of the side of her eyes. In retaliation, Sylvie stuck out her tongue like she did when she was a child, pressing her head into her father's shoulder, so he did not notice.

Gretta pivoted on her heels and left the room in a hurry.

The winter of '41, Sylvie recalled as being unusually cold...would the winter of '42 be even colder? Or was it just the rationing? Jews needed coupons for purchasing items, clothes and gloves, hats and shoes. First, they had to register for the coupons in order to get them. Of course this was one of the ways the Germans knew where the Jews were, when they began rounding them up.

At the beginning of the war, the Rosenbergs held onto their decent clothes, like other Jews held onto scraps of bread. But Sylvie was crushed she could not keep up to par with her reputation for style. When she outgrew her clothes, she couldn't buy new things, so she had to take Gretta's prudish hand-me-downs, which almost killed her. Now, when Sylvie walked on the streets, no one turned their heads to look at her anymore. She felt unattractive and unlikable.

The corners of her mouth caved at the sight of her favorite

camel-hair overcoat with the black velvet trim. *Such a fine fabric, ruined, by the word inscribed in black—Jood, Dutch for Jew. How odd to see Mother with a needle and thread in hand. Mother had to sew the patch on because her personal seamstress left the country.*

Sylvie examined her double-collar coat with the big ivory buttons, now so unfamiliar in her hands. The rough embroidery...how ugly the outerwear had suddenly become; its stitching looked painful, fresh as post-surgery. Maybe when the star hardened into a scab, she'd tear it off, and watch it grow another arm, as a starfish does.

Morning drizzle spotted the windows over the kitchen table while Oma was showing her disinterested daughter how she prepared *poffertjes* on the stovetop. By early afternoon, the small pancakes soured in Sylvie's belly when she heard more horror stories that passed throughout the neighborhood like borrowed sugar. Maybe they should move to England where one of her unmarried Aunts—Aunt Chelley, lives. But that wouldn't be much fun, would it? She needed to be around people her own age. She was starting to feel like a prisoner, and Mother said she could no longer go to Hana's, especially because she's Jewish, and not a "protected" Jew.

When the Nazis first occupied the Netherlands, Sylvie hadn't paid much attention to world events or to people scurrying around to secure false identity papers from the Underground, something she'd heard about. The hum on the avenue had been replaced with something that didn't belong. At first, she disregarded the subtle changes around her, as they had little effect on her own life. Then everything on the streets started to have a different look and feel, even a different smell. Diesel. She became aware of the screeching sounds of motorcars from the police and the Germans, high-ranking officers riding in motorcycles with side cars.

One day the noise wasn't just *around* them, it was inside

their home. Father was away on another one of his short business trips, meeting officials with names their parents often
whispered under their breath. Again and again, Sylvie heard
her mother telling her father to use his connections, call the
duke, call someone important. "What are you waiting for?"

Sylvie and her brother and sisters clustered at the top of the
staircase in the middle of the night after they heard their
mother's bedroom door slam and booming male voices downstairs. Gretta put her finger over her mouth to shush the others,
as they peeked below at the men raiding their foyer. From the
children's view, they could only partially see the men, from the
waist down, wearing belted jackets that reached to the top of
their thighs. It was the Dutch police.

*How can that be? Have the Dutch turned on us, too? I thought
only the Germans are our enemies.*

A minute later, the captain came rushing through the door
that was left ajar. "What is going on here?" he demanded of his
fellow officers. "I told you, not *this* house."

He stood very close to our mother. *Why was he touching
her back?* Sylvie imagined her mother's heart skipping a beat,
like a rabbit with its foot stuck in a trap. Sylvie watched as the
men marked up the parquet floor with their big black boots,
the floor her mother had always insisted stay perfectly shiny.
"Oh no, the floor," Sylvie whispered, "Mother's going to have a
bloody conniption."

Gretta told her to shush, looking at their baby sister.
"Watch your language, Sylvie."

"What's a com-nip-son?" Ruthie giggled.

Wilhelm covered Ruthie's mouth and she started to make
a crying face.

The children sighed when the police apologized. "Yes, wrong house. Wrong house."

"Move on!" the captain ordered. "Have a good evening, Madame. Saturday, you will stop by my office to *complete* some business, no?"

"Yes," she muttered.

"Very well, then. Regards to your husband."

To the children's surprise, one of the officers stepped out in clear view and looked up at them. His eyes went directly to Sylvie. "What is *your* name?"

She could hardly hear her own voice. "Sylvie," she answered.

"Sylvie, you say? Well, Sylvie, you are as pretty as your mother. Another time, perhaps you will play a song for me?" he gestured toward the piano.

"I don't play the piano," Sylvie snapped and saw her mother's spine stiffen.

They scattered in different directions back to their bedrooms and never talked about the unwanted visitors again. Sometimes Sylvie would glance at newspapers or hear things on the radio that frightened her. She'd lie awake in bed thinking of the bombs, waiting... at dawn she listened to how the birds chirped on their tree branches, as if nothing had changed for them. "Stupid birds," she whimpered, even though she ordinarily adored animals.

It wasn't until years later Sylvie began to understand the relationship her father must have had with the Dutch police and why the German soldiers went to the homes of other Jews, and not theirs. The Germans, always so precise, surely wouldn't have made careless mistakes. Yet, countless times as she watched the Dutch police pass by their home as if it were invisible, she didn't entirely relax until they rounded the bend.

Mostly, Sylvie tried to overlook any of the negative news—the bulletin about the 600 Jews assigned to report for war-related duty in the East. And she tried to pay no mind to the Jewish males in the city being arrested and deported to Buchenwald, until her cousin Harry was one of them. She and Harry were the same age and they used to go boating on the canals in Amsterdam when they were children. It wasn't until her own Dutch Theatre, DeHollandse Schouwburg where she and Harry had imagined themselves on the big screen, was turned into a makeshift prison in the Jewish quarter that she could no longer pretend.

Many of the Jewish shops had been closed down and padlocked; swastikas marked them in devil's handwriting. Rabbis at the synagogues had to turn over lists of the Jews. Even the Catholic church bells no longer tolled.

She noticed the drone of airplanes becoming more frequent overhead. Sylvie feared being in her bedroom on the third floor...if bombs were to drop, wouldn't that be where they'd hit first? She felt safer curling up in a tight ball under Papa's roll-top desk, even though his study was supposed to be off limits. She was petrified that if found by the enemy, she would unravel like Oma's cylinders of yarn, like Oma herself who would eventually lose all her energy.

On other days when confined to her bedroom, it was the silence that was worse. Sylvie would peep from behind the curtains looking down at men who walked by in shiny helmets and hobnailed boots. Such a hard sound as they passed. She watched, stricken, as men took away bicycles of neighborhood children. Her bicycle, the one with the pink basked up front, was not taken away.

What's happened to my schoolmates? Miriam who lives on Spoor-straat? And Anna who lives on Prinsenstraat? Did they hear fists beating down their front doors in the middle of the night? Did the Germans burst into their homes and separate them from their mothers, and sisters and brothers? Didn't they have anything of value, like us, to trade for their lives?

Is that why we still have a radio? Why we still have enough sugar for our tea? Why the German officers turn their heads when they pass our home and not our neighbors'? How many times will they turn their heads? How much time do we have before we run out of "things?"

Then she worried that being a rich Jew wouldn't help them either. The Mendelsons are rich, and their house looks empty now...where'd they go? Did the Nazis take away rich Jews, too?

She confronted her mother. "Don't tell me the Mendelsons moved, too?"

"Never mind that! Please don't ask so many questions. Be patient and have faith in your father's plans, and we will be fine." Her mother walked away.

I know Papa has a connection to the art that Hitler desires, but there must be more to it. How could he trust them? After they get what they want, wouldn't they just do what they want with us anyway?

One dreary day, word came from other Jews in the small village that there may be a roundup. To take precaution, they agreed to leave their home and go into hiding until it was all over. The air had turned dewy and raw, an everlasting chill that froze Sylvie from that moment on into becoming someone else. Sylvie's mother had given her instructions to pack a blanket and a pillow because they may be forced to spend the night at a shelter.

Sylvie's teenage frame had stiffened as the wind howled through the shuttered window of her spacious bedroom. Not knowing the conditions that would soon be forced upon her while in hiding, she was more upset about leaving her *things* behind than anything else. Outraged by such humiliation and inconvenience, she stuffed her silk quilted bed jacket, heavy leggings, and her fluffy cashmere hat into the soft leather bag, until it bulged. Numb with excitement and denial, she didn't dare leave any of her favorite belongings behind, in case the Germans confiscated their possessions before they returned.

She'd heard of riches to rags stories before, but she dismissed them, trying to convince herself that she was unafraid. Sylvie's eyes wildly searched the wardrobe: *There are my high-button shoes...my good Merino wool skirts, and my fine stockings.*

Her mother opened the door to her room and hurried her along. "You don't think you are taking all *that*," her mother said. They had a nasty game of tug of war over her prettiest petticoat. "Put the petticoat away now!"

How Sylvie wished she could bring along her bath salts and her best eau de cologne. With another glance around her bedroom, she grabbed her rouge, her eyebrow pencil, her hair brush, and Oma's hair comb. Satisfied she had everything she couldn't possibly be without—she tugged at the zipper and headed for her bedroom door.

"Sylvie," her mother had said. "Stop fussing! I told you to bring your blanket and your pillow. That's all!"

Sylvie stomped her foot and dropped her bag.

"That's more like it." She pointed at her daughter's bed. "Now, get your pillow and your blanket. It's not like we're going on holiday—we'll return shortly. Hurry," her mother said, exiting.

With her hand on the doorknob, Sylvie had turned to leave her room that night, not really knowing if she'd ever return, when she remembered the most important thing of all—her solid gold Star of David which she had hidden because it was so special, and she thought she should be the *only* one who knows where it was kept. Papa had given it to her on her thirteenth birthday, even though she did not have a Bat Mitzvah. That was the year she had blossomed, as Mother promised she someday would—into a stunning beauty, from the scrawny girl she used to be. She stuck it in her pocket. *It's so small, Mother won't mind.* Eventually, she mused, this gold piece would go to her first child. He would be the perfect son with the perfect life. Of course, before the child was born, she'd have to be rescued from her castle and swept away on the white horse by a nobleman who would also be absolutely perfect...because *that* was Sylvie's favorite dream of all.

People were squeezed inside the damp abandoned building behind the new Jewish schoolhouse she had attended only weeks ago. In the one room, alone, which smelled of urine, there were maybe fifty or sixty Jews huddled together without heat. Babies were crying, children being quieted, and shriveled up old men, chain-smoking in the darkest corner. She concentrated on their hacking coughs and the tips of their cigarettes turning on and off like glowworms.

Sylvie dug the palm of her hand into the points of the gold star she had slipped into her pocket earlier, until she drew blood. But she stopped the self-mutilation when she noticed a crowd of people flocking around her parents, thanking them for everything they've always done for the community—especially the needy. *My parents—humanitarians?* She looked over at them through different eyes.

"See, I told you we'd be coming home again," her mother said
with relief as they walked into their house. "All that scare for
nothing."

Mother was right. They were safe. They returned home
from the shelter unharmed that night. She had recognized
almost everyone there around her age from the new Jewish
school she attended, but she noticed some of her school friends
were missing, including her best friend, Hana. Mother tried to
assure her that Hana must have been staying with neighbors.

Sylvie went up to her room on the third floor. None of her
things were missing. Her eyes were drawn to the dead insect
flat against the sill, the same insect that fluttered its wings at
her through the glass first thing in the morning. Again, she
wondered about Hana's family.

"It's difficult enough to worry about *our* family," her mother
had explained. "Worry about yourself right now, and then we'll
do what we can for the others."

Sylvie counted on her mother to know what was best. Why
should she have to worry about the others? She tried hard to
stop wondering about her school friends. Besides, Katrina
had told her that Joanna heard from Madelon, who heard
from someone else, that the Nazis made ovens for incinerat-
ing human corpses. Sylvie was upset with them for making up
such far-fetched stories.

There was one other day, one "topsy-turvy" kind of day, as Oma
used to say, that Sylvie believed they'd surely be killed. It was
the day they had to hide in the basement when her father was
away on his final business trip to secure the proper papers.
Mother had rushed the children in line, one by one. They
scrambled into a huddle, shuffling down the stairway that led
to the wine cellar and then squeezed through a dwarf-sized

hatch into the root cellar where they'd wait until the all-clear sounded.

Mother spoke softly into Ruthie's ear that it was like a game, but Ruthie didn't look as though she was having any fun at all.

She whispered in the dim light. "I think there's a spider crawling up my leg, Mama."

"Shush now, Ruthie," Mother scolded. "This is a very *serious* game, do you understand me?"

Ruthie couldn't comprehend what they were doing in the damp chamber, and could not read her mother's grim expression. "Are there mice down here?" Ruthie asked.

They were in a tight space with a low ceiling where they used to store parsnips, beets, potatoes, carrots, and turnips, and the scent still lingered.

"Shhh, what's that?" Wilhelm shuddered. "I hear someone upstairs. They're in the house."

"Who's upstairs?" Ruthie insisted.

"Silence," Mother said. "Wait until they go away, and I will tell you who they are."

They could hear the Nazis standing above them right where Rembrandt's painting of "The Rabbi" once hung over the sideboard. The heavy furniture was being moved and thrown over. They imagined the soldiers were taking as much as they could, plucking the walls bare, like petals off flowers.

Thank goodness Papa removed Opa's painting from the house. Goose-bumps covered Sylvie's arms as she wondered if he sent other works of art to another country. She held her breath as an all-consuming dampness filled her nostrils, and she thought she'd simply forget how to inhale. After a while, it seemed no one was breathing at all. Sylvie saw how tense her mother was holding the new infant in her arms. Baby Rose was only five days old. She hardly felt like part of the family yet, especially since mother didn't *show* until the end...No one knew. No one talked about it, except for the time Sylvie overheard Oma remark how "irresponsible" Mother was: "Now you'll be eating for two," Oma had said. Sylvie thought Oma was being irrational because her mother wouldn't eat for two when she knew we were rationing... "We won't mention this to Josef," Helene had said. "Maybe it's a false alarm. Besides, he doesn't need more stress in his life at this time."

The noises from upstairs, above the root cellar, stopped. Mother held Baby Rose to her chest and whispered, "We must wait a few more moments, but I think they're gone now."

"Oh, I was so afraid," Sylvie said.

"Don't be afraid. Soon, we will not have to hide anymore from the Germans."

When Sylvie asked *why*, Mother answered, "It's because of the Rosenberg name." She promised them the Rosenbergs would ultimately be safe since they were *special*.

FIVE

MASSAPEQUA, NEW YORK
1970

Sylvie filled the bathtub with hot water and checked the temperature with her big toe. Her bunion swelled with redness after a day of suffering in those five-inch alligator heels...but her neighbor had said the shoes flattered her so. How she missed the days of her youth in Holland when she was swallowed up in extravagance and loved by everyone.

Purposely, she added an extra capful of bubbles.

Before submerging herself in the tub, she looked in the bathroom mirror and considered her own value which seemed to be diminishing daily since she came to America. She imagined how the art could fill the empty walls of her world now. The art had always given her power, from her childhood down to her ex-husband. *Maybe Mitchell was right. What was stolen from our family should be returned.* She was glad though that the big payback hadn't happened while *he* was in her life. *Marrying me just for the notion we'd someday reclaim the art. Heh! I showed him!*

The last time he had slammed the door behind him, she knew she'd never see him again. The quiet of the room told her so. After the divorce papers were signed, she was relieved to know Mitchell would have no rights to any reparations from Holland for the 200 masterpieces.

Mitchell was nothing—a door-to-door salesman. He was

Jewish, but he was not a very successful Jew. He was good at selling his charm, however. He sold his goods to all the ladies in town. *The lonely ones, like me,* she thought. Sylvie hadn't been with a man for years after leaving the camp, convincing herself that all men were evil, but being companionless started to get to her after awhile. The timing was right. And she was stunned by his alluring, seductive, eyes and his charisma. He was adept at sweet-talk and flattery and he tempted her with flowers and gifts while they dated.

Then, there was the whirlwind September wedding, not exactly the storybook kind she dreamed of. *How could things have gone so wrong with the marriage? My luck, with one deaf ear, I had to hear his persistent knocking on my door that day?*

A hot day it was on the 4th of July weekend. Sylvie thought the banging was coming from one of the neighbor's delinquent kids setting off homemade cherry bombs. She was surprised when she opened the front door to the fireworks going off in the darkness of Mitchell Beckman's eyes. Good thing she just had her hair colored the day before, even though she was so sure she *hated* men.

She leaned back on the suburban front door, holding it open with the heel of her foot and squinted harder to get a better look at the stranger, much the same as watching an actor on the late night movie. The square of his jaw and his crisp attire made her thirst for more.

He stuffed his paperwork under one arm, wiped his sun-tanned neck with a handkerchief, and rolled up the sleeves on his white dress shirt. "Phew! Must be 100 degrees out here. As they say, you can fry an egg on the—"

"The sidewalk," Sylvie finished, with a lilting voice, watching him loosen his striped tie. "Not even the slightest breeze today." Her eyes jerked back and forth from the brilliance of his black leather shoes, to the brilliance of his toothy white smile.

The aroma from neighbors' barbecues that she hadn't been invited to wafted down Chestnut Avenue. "M-m-m, doesn't that smell good?" she asked, leaning her head sideways against her front door, closing her eyes to take in another long whiff.

"Yes it does. Enough to whet any man's appetite. And perhaps any woman's?"

"How long have you been banging away out here?" she asked.

"Oh, I apologize. I may have knocked a little too vigorously, but I can't seem to find the doorbell," he said, touching the doorframe.

"Don't have one. I try not to encourage many visitors," she said, wondering if his lips were full under his mustache. Was he looking at her finger to see a wedding band?

"Then I wish I sold *bells*, because I'd like to persuade you to invite *this* visitor more often. I bet you have plenty of gentlemen lined up, calling on you, am I right?" His cotton shirt stuck to his body, obviously sculpted by Michelangelo himself.

"What exactly are you selling, Mr.—?"

"Beckman. Mitchell Beckman. So, Miss? Mrs.?"

"Rosenberg. Sylvie Rosenberg. With a Miss in front of it."

"So, Miss Rosenberg, may I call you Sylvie? Maybe you'll be interested in what I have to show you."

"That depends." There was something about the look in his eyes. She hadn't experienced such strong palpitations in a long time. Better than a doctor's visit, she concluded. At least she knew her heart was still beating. She pushed the door open wider. "If it's imported chocolate, you've got yourself a sale."

"I detect an accent. Are *you* imported?"

"Dutch."

"Oh, now I understand your sweet cravings. A lady such as yourself deserves only the best."

"I appreciate a man who appreciates that. Why don't you

come in, and we'll talk about your—what is it you sell? Brushes? Steak knives? Vacuums?"

"En-cyc-lo-ped-ias. And I'm proud to say that I've read every volume in the set!"

Oh my, so full of knowledge, so full of curiosity. I hope that's all he's full of!

And so, the day went on under the guise of his sincerity. Sylvie and Mitchell had hit it off at the outset. He asked to look at the photo album on the coffee table. When she showed him the photographs of the family estate with the elaborate décor, the full waitstaff, and the gardens, he was impressed…but what finalized "the sale" for Mitchell was when she got to the photos of the family art. He looked smitten.

Thinking she was the main attraction, Sylvie patted her hair-sprayed beehive making sure there wasn't a strand out of place from which any old bee could fly out. But she got stung mighty hard by the love-at-first-sight bug.

Sylvie swirled her fingers through the bathwater and watched the bubbles dissipate.

"We're going *away* on a honeymoon," Mitchell had told her only a week before they left. "Guess where?"

Sylvie jumped up and down. "Hawaii?"

"No. Even better. We're going back to your homeland, to Holland, to revisit your roots," he had told her, while nibbling on her neck.

Sylvie said nothing.

"You don't seem that excited," he said, plucking the airline tickets from his shirt pocket.

Sylvie loved Holland, and loved the Dutch people, but there

were too many bad memories. *Not my idea of a honeymoon. Maybe I will feel differently when we arrive in my hometown. I'll contact my sisters and brother when we get there and ask them to meet us.*

As soon as they arrived in Amsterdam, Sylvie called her sister Gretta in England. All her siblings were living in London, not far from their lonely Aunt Chelley, who remained single. In a perfectly civil voice over the phone, Gretta greatly disappointed Sylvie, telling her that she couldn't have possibly visit at a worse time.

"Sylvie. I'm afraid I'm terribly busy with my social club. In fact, I will be heading the event this afternoon. It's a rather huge affair. Wilhelm and Ruthie are helping me organize, and well, anyway, next time you travel all this way, please give me more notice."

Sylvie couldn't believe the similarity to her mother's voice. "That's quite all right, Gretta," Sylvie said. "I didn't have much notice, myself. I thought I'd surprise you, but I guess it wasn't such a smart idea."

Sylvie swallowed, and hoped her sister couldn't sense she was upset. She had to wonder if Gretta was *still* jealous that she was "Papa's pet." Some things never change, she thought. And yet nothing seemed the same, especially the day before when she stood in front of the home she had grown up in near the railway station—the same station the Germans directed them to before their escape, the same station most Jews in her neighborhood went to with bars of soap.

A gardener opened the iron gate, and let Sylvie walk through the backyard behind their brick house. Nothing looked familiar, except for one statue, in the same exact spot under the first floor window—a trio of figures—a young man flanked by two women, one older and one around the same age as him.

The females were giving support to the male, whose expression Sylvie had never forgotten—an expression of sheer heartache.

"It's been so long. So, how are you? How does our old house look?" Gretta dutifully continued the conversation.

"Well, strange," Sylvie explained. "A doctor lives there now with his family. They've restored it, but..." Again, Sylvie pictured the new addition added onto the house to extend the already large kitchen. She envisioned the truck pouring the cement over the jewelry the servants were told to bury under the soil. "But, it's so strange, Gretta," she said, hoping to reach her.

"What's strange?"

"Seeing how everything has changed."

"No, I take it back. Don't tell me. I don't want to know." Gretta cut her off, her mood altering instantly...like in the old days.

"I'm sorry if—"

"Listen, if you and your new husband make the trip to England, please ring me. But as I said, we will not be coming to see you in Dieren."

"Gretta, be honest with me. I understand if you want to avoid our past...in fact, this trip wasn't *my* idea."

"Well then, to be perfectly frank with you, yes, it is too painful. I have no intentions of ever going back there. And neither do Wilhelm or Ruthie. Perhaps someday we will visit you in America."

Sylvie closed her eyes. She remembered how uprooted their lives were when the Germans took over. How heartbroken Gretta was when she abruptly had to forego her college plans. And Wilhelm was just starting his final year of school. How lucky her baby sister was not to know what was going on.

Before Sylvie opened her eyes again to respond, she heard the sound of Ruthie's little feet coming down the central staircase. And she also saw herself sneaking the cat up those same stairs into her bedroom. The cat's fur was soft and long. *What was her name? Oh, that's right. It was Katz, the Jewish cat.* She'd forgotten that she had a sense of humor at one time.

"All of you coming to visit us in America would be lovely."

Both sisters paused.

"Have you been to visit mother's gravesite?" Gretta asked.

"Yes, I've been there." Sylvie had gone to the spot where Mother was buried next to the headstone of Oma, even though Oma's body had never been recovered. Their mother insisted when her time came, to be buried next to her. How odd, the concept was to Sylvie, when sometimes they weren't capable of being in the same room together while alive, yet their spirits would end up inseparable for eternity.

Her mother's headstone looked lost among the others, like a row house on a street in Levittown. Moss covered part of her name, and only "Rose" showed through; beside their graves, was a smaller one. She had extended her hand to touch the monument, her fingers retracting at its coldness.

Sylvie dismissed her sister's inquiry, knowing where she was coming from, wallowing in the theory that Sylvie and her mother had never gotten along. Sylvie may have won her father over, but never her mother. She didn't mention that she visited their father's mausoleum in New York every year on his birthday because it would stir up old jealousy.

After the small talk, they had nothing more to say.

"Well, then. Take care. And give my love to—my brother and sister, will you?" Sylvie asked.

"Of course," Gretta answered before the final clicking sound.

Her ex-husband Mitchell had quickly become overzealous and preoccupied with Sylvie's past, and the realization that he hadn't married her for love, hit hard... *it's the value of my father's paintings he fell in love with, not me.*

The newlyweds spent almost the entire honeymoon at the galleries where he grilled the curator about the artwork. It sickened her, how he took notes in his notepad as he pored through archives of the Jokos Foundation, the Jewish Organization. He had scribbled the word "Restitution" at the top of the page. As if *he* should be compensated for anything.

Mitchell's eyes sparkled. "Your father and uncle's galleries were certainly an incredible success, weren't they?" he asked several times.

Exasperated, Sylvie looked right through him. "Yes, they were very prosperous back then, but it's all gone now, everything's gone. I told you, they were forced to sell to the Germans for Adolf Hitler's Fuhrer museum."

"Did they lose everything?" His questions were sounding more like an interrogation.

"I-I don't know, Mitchell."

"Why didn't your Uncle Nathan go to New York, too, like your father? Why did he go to Basel, instead?"

"Uncle Nathan had tried to salvage what remained of the business over in Switzerland. And my father waited in New York, where he tried to rebuild the business with whatever art could be saved. My uncle obtained permission to take his family to Basel with him, but soon after his escape he was taken ill...."

"Oh?" Mitchell said. "Did he conduct more business before his death?"

She raised her voice. "I don't want to talk about those days anymore. Isn't there anything else you're interested in?"

Mitchell was not interested in much else, not even in what was to come exactly nine months later back home in Massapequa— baby Michael.

Sylvie's belly grew, and so did Mitchell's late nights. He'd stay out for hours most evenings claiming to meet clients, while she remained queasy about his faithfulness. When their son was born, she was like her own mother—not a natural at nurturing, but she did the best she could, raising him alone.

Her deviating husband got used to her lifestyle and helped himself to money from Sylvie's account—the yearly allowance from her father's estate—a mere smidgen of the wealth she knew from her youth. That was bad enough, but when she discovered he was wining and dining other women with the funds, it was over.

The three of them, Sylvie, Mitchell, and Michael would spend one unbearable hour a week together at Sunday breakfast. Sylvie would fry up bacon and French toast slathered in butter and cherry compote in a large pan. And then she'd stir up her coffee with five teaspoons of sugar, clinking and clanking the teaspoon against the porcelain cup, to annoy her husband.

Mitchell, in turn, would sip his coffee with an extra slurp, and give her a "take that" look. "I don't know how you aren't 500 pounds," he said.

"I grew up on sweets. I *love* sweets, so shoot me."

"Don't tempt me, Sylvie."

Neither of them paid attention to the boy in the middle— their son. As if he didn't know what was going on.

"Come on, Michael. Eat. Eat up, Mikey," his mother would say. "And I'll buy you a new toy."

"The boy has no appetite," Mitchell would yell at her. "Take him to see a doctor. He's sick. What kind of a mother are you?"

"You're the one who should go see a doctor. A head doctor. You don't know anything about kids. They're fussy eaters."

"Fussy? How can he be fussy when you pour a truckload of butter and syrup on everything...."

"And you complain? I don't see *you* starving yourself."

Michael blinked sleepily at his parents, covering his ears with his sticky fingers. By the tone of their voices, he had the sense to know that by the time the thick syrup slid down his throat to the knot in his stomach, he'd never see his dad again after that day. At such a young age, he knew.

"Michael, drink your milk. I'll buy you *two* toys, later."

"Why don't you put sugar in his milk, too, for Christ sake?"

"Good idea." She took a plastic bottle of chocolate syrup out of the refrigerator and poured it into Michael's glass, staring at her husband the entire time.

Mitchell went into a beastly rage, grabbed the Hershey bottle out of Sylvie's hand, and squeezed swingy chocolate marks all over the tablecloth, the plates and glasses, the utensils, the flower arrangement, and Sylvie.

She screamed. "My hair! You got chocolate in my hair, for God's sake. I had it done yesterday. What's wrong with you!"

Michael tried to get up from the table, and his father pushed him down again in his seat. "Stop that crying, Michael!" Mitchell yelled at his six-year-old son who closed his eyes.

"Don't you talk that way to my son!"

Michael rested his head down on his messy plate while they continued to fight over him. Finally, the room went quiet, and the boy started to nod off at the table with one side of his cheek looking like a slice of Black Forest Cake.

Sylvie took a wet washcloth and gently wiped his face as he slept. She wept hard. "I'm sorry my precious son. From now on, I will never let anyone hurt you, not ever."

The loveless marriage had lasted six long years—"For Michael's sake."

From that day on Sylvie and Michael lived alone, and she tried unsuccessfully to spoil him with new things. Sylvie still dressed up and wore her expensive perfume, waiting for another impromptu knock at the front door. But no one charming enough, no prince, ever came by.

Sylvie looked up from the bathtub, singled out one of the roses in the busy pattern of her shower curtain, stared at its blurry petals, and remembered everything. Immersed in the tub for nearly an hour, she realized she was quivering. Her lips must have turned purple. She stood up and got out of the cold water, toweled her goose bumps dry, and applied soft talcum powder. She tried to shake off thoughts of the past; non-diluting images thickened at the drain. How cruel life had been to her with love and war. Sylvie hoped her son's fate wouldn't bring him bitter memories someday, comparable to hers.

She dressed to get ready for work, where she'd try to forget, not only her war, but also her son's. Vietnam. For the past two years, Sylvie was working part-time at May's Department Store, not because she *had* to, she told everyone, and certainly not because she was, what do they call it, a "social butterfly?" She mainly squirreled away the extra cash for her side trips to Vegas. Better to use the money for whatever pleasures were left, rather than debt.

Like her father, Sylvie suffered from heartburn. She shut her eyes and replaced the gurgling in her esophagus with the agenda of her next junket to a casino, a sure cure-all. She'd double-down on number 32 ... bet red on roulette. And if gambling wasn't in the cards, she'd have to settle for Bingo above Bohack's Supermarket with the old biddies. They all wore the same stiff hairdos from low class beauty parlors.

Sylvie sashayed past the pyramid of shoes on display and ignored her duty to align them out of their state of disarray. She disregarded two young girls seated before her, ooh-ing and aah-ing over shiny red pumps on sale.

That's all I need right now, two more shiksas.

She never could understand why her son had taken up with a gentile in the first place. At least they were no longer together. *So, why am I still worried?*

She heard the girls calling for assistance, but she turned away.

Now my Michael. In a hospital. I hope he's strong I hope…

Her heart raced. She wished she was capable of praying, but she didn't know how, not for many years, and not in the past 22 days since she had received the news. All she could do was hope. She was frustrated that so many details were kept from her, that she couldn't visit him.

My boy. My foolish, foolish boy. What luck, his battalion had to go on some crazy rescue mission. A war hero, they told her when she had called the VA hospital. Who needs such an honor? For a medal? For what?

The psychological report had disturbed her most: "Michael isn't as wounded as some of the others," the doctor had said, "but he seems to have less to live for—there's no fight left in him. Perhaps when he's transferred to recover in Germany…."

Germany? My son cared for by Nazi doctors? Ludicrous!

Again, Angela crossed her mind. Why did this girl keep creeping back into her head—worse than a case of head lice.

She wouldn't be good for Michael. Besides, she has nothing in common with us—with him. He must be over her by now, she kept telling herself. *He's probably already forgotten she exists.*

Sylvie had only met the girl that one night. Angela seemed enamored by the family paintings that hung on her sage green living room wall. *An artisan? What does she really want from my son? Does she have the same ambitions as Mitchell? How dare that girl keep invading my mind like this?*

Sylvie looked at the floor mirror across from the two teens, still holding the red shoes, yet only seeing her own high-heeled pink leather platforms—how very *en vogue* they were. She hadn't had a minute since her morning break to run a comb through her coarse bleached blonde hair or check the face powder on her cheeks. The mauve-colored rouge—perhaps a tad too purple? Were the folds in her skirt straight, did her silk blouse lay flat beneath her wide patent-leather belt?

The big shot, Mr. H., was nowhere in sight. She took out her compact and peeked at her multi-tiered eye shadow. "Aagh. What a way to see yourself—in bits and piece—"

"Ma'am? Can I please see these in a size six?" the less appealing of the two girls asked.

"Give me a moment. I've only got two hands." Sylvie responded in the guttural tone she saved for annoying customers. As if performing in a circus act, she exaggerated balancing the boxes left behind from her last customer. *Is this worth it? Getting close to people's smelly feet is bad enough.*

After smoothing out her clothes, she went back to the girls who were all-smiles as she approached them with her pigeon-toed gait. Sylvie believed that like everyone else, they were admiring her sense of style. She was good at overlooking her own imperfections and, made up for them, by flaunting her designer-wear imported from England.

"So, what is it you girls need? Did you say size six?"

"Uh, yes, six. Ma'am? I've been wondering, where's your accent from?" The girl with the acne-filled chin asked. "Is it German? You sound a lot like my grandmother."

Sylvie immediately took offense to the girl's inquiry, not to mention her attire, her pimples, and her audacity to compare her to her *grandmother. Her fascist grandmother, no less.*

"I'll go fetch the shoes," she snapped, her hands in tight fists. Under her breath, she added what she really wanted to say aloud—*I make* one *trip to the back room per customer.*

"Ma'am, can you also bring me another pair of these in the next size up, in case they run small?"

Sylvie grumbled, jerking her body in the opposite direction.

"Ma'am?" the girl called after her.

"I heard you," Sylvie said, without turning to face her. *And people tell me I'm hard of hearing.* She moved her slim body in quick motions and shuffled away. Both girls giggled. As usual, her loss of hearing was a blessing.

When she returned with the box she looked at the girls and made an annoyed "tsk" sound with her tongue against her palate. "Are you sure about these?" Sylvie ran her thumb along the inseam, and leaned in closer. "Look at the chintzy material they're made of," she said, curling her lip. "Why don't you try these, instead?" Sylvie held out a pair of the newest style.

"Wow!" The girl's eyes brightened.

"And they do come in red," Sylvie added.

The girl quickly read the price. "Umm, I don't know."

Her friend piped in. "Go ahead, you deserve them."

"Well, I have been saving all my babysitting money this month. Okay, I'll just try them on."

"Good decision." Sylvie winked. Her fine taste could be contagious.

In a short time, Sylvie's attitude turned around. She was anxious to see if they fit. "Well, look at that!" Sylvie yelped. "They fit perfectly."

The three females stood at the register with three smiles. What shoes can do for a woman's soul, Sylvie thought, as she removed the price sticker and put the shoes snuggly inside the shoebox.

The pretty girl put a hand on her friend's shoulder. "How is your grandmother, anyway?"

Sylvie stopped what she was doing, and listened, thinking of how she loved her Oma.

"Well, she's still in the hospital, and they don't know if-if she's going to make it." The girl dabbed at the corner of her eyes, and Sylvie noticed her cheap mascara running down her cheeks.

"Oh my. Look at that!" Sylvie's voice boomed. "My records show that *you*, young lady, are the 100th customer. And do you know what that means?"

The girl stared at Sylvie.

"It means *you* win a free pair of shoes today, that's what. Well, how about that? This is your lucky day."

"Are you kidding? Oh my, gosh, that's great. Thank you, thank you so much. You are the nicest lady I've ever met."

Getting such a compliment was rare for her when it had nothing to do with showing off. "Well," she said ill-at-ease, "I only hope you get to go dancing in those shoes." She reexamined the girl's unsightly blemishes when she handed over the shopping bag and had to restrain herself from advising her to buy some Clearasil on the way out. Sylvie wiggled her fingers to hurry her off before the words would come out. "Bye-bye, now."

As soon as the girls left the shoe department, Sylvie went into her own wallet and counted out what she thought the value of the shoes were with her employee discount and placed the cash in the register drawer. She slapped her hands together. "I can't help myself. I'm just a do-gooder, that's all."

Sylvie sensed someone looming over her shoulder and turned around to see Mr. Hudson, the store manager. "After you close out your register, I need to speak with you, Sylvie."

When she punched out her time card, she headed for the back exit toward the parking lot, and ignored his request. She would tell Mr. Hudson that she hadn't heard him. She had used that excuse countless times since she was a child. Besides, she was pretty sure what he wanted to speak to her about—her lying to customers that shoes were out of stock or telling customers that the shoes were inferior. As a backup, she could explain how people misunderstand her accent. Or had she used this alibi one time too many?

"Idiot," she said, making her way between the parked cars. *He should only know how lucky he is to have employed me and my fine taste.* She felt for her key chain at the bottom of her bag. Sylvie had resented her boss since that first day when he interviewed her. It was his mustache, thin and prematurely gray—it reminded her of her ex-husband's, the way it twitched when he articulated his words.

Sylvie had been much happier when she was in Gloves or in Lingerie, but when the store was unexpectedly short-staffed, she was chosen to cover in Shoes for that dowdy saleslady who had called in sick with walking pneumonia.

Not much longer, hopefully. I'm only replacing her and her matronly clothes, temporarily. Poor thing…come to think of it, maybe I'll pick up a little something special for her next time.

Turning the key and starting the car, Sylvie hummed the Dutch tune she remembered Oma singing one day while the servants were preparing *Banketsaaf* for a special event. Sylvie could still smell the sweet *amandelspijs*—almond paste that filled the house.

After work, Sylvie pulled into her apartment complex, and was stopped by the mailman who had a large box for her. Even though she'd expected the package, she gasped at the return address—China Beach Hospital. She showed no expression. She hadn't taken a breath until the mailman carried the delivery right up to her front door. After she placed the bulky cardboard on the Formica countertop, she opened the kitchen drawer, and looked for a sharp knife. Then she stabbed at the box top and opened the two flaps and saw Michael's belongings. One at a time, she went over the contents, mostly what she had sent him over the past few months: unopened gumdrops, a Yankee baseball cap, a new calendar, a book of poetry...she held his T-shirts and other personal things up to her cheek, hoping she'd smell Michael.

When she reached the bottom of the box, she was taken aback by a cheap, feminine fragrance and quickly covered her nostrils with two fingers. There was a satchel of sealed letters tied tightly with a lavender ribbon. She loosened the knot and released the envelopes from the stack. She turned the sealed letters in her hand and walked into the living room where she could sit and slow down the quick puffs of air escaping her mouth.

Gracing the face of each envelope, she saw the girl's name Angela, written in Michael's distinct handwriting. *There's no address on any of them. Good. He never mailed them. He respected my wishes after all, came to his senses that mother knows best.*

She fanned the deck out like a Royal Flush on the glass coffee table. *I guess he's gotten over her by now.* She pictured how Angela looked when they met, wearing her paisley hemp tank top with the embroidered peace sign and a pair of army pants.

SIX

MASSAPEQUA, NEW YORK
1970

It had been the end of the summer of '69 when Sylvie and her son had that terrible argument and Angela's name came up again. Michael stormed out of the house. She feared he'd go out on a drinking binge. *Jews, we don't make good drinkers.* She had a feeling he'd get himself into trouble, and sure enough, a mother knows these things... his bed hadn't been slept in. Early the next morning he had enlisted in the Army— the United States Army—closed-minded patriots, high-ranking military men taking orders from smart-looking men in dark tailored suits, men with thumbtacks and maps.

Sylvie could hear doorbells all over the country ringing in her ears—*always two men in uniform at the front door, delivering grim news to mothers who were in the middle of hanging laundry on the clothes line or scraping leftovers off dinner plates.*

And she could still hear the doctor's prognosis, how over time Michael could possibly recover with surgeries and more therapy. How they were doing the best they could for him, and how Michael was in God's hands.

God's hands? Like the millions of Jews in God's hands?

She had pleaded with the army physician. "Let me talk to my—"

"I'm afraid that's not possible, Ma'am." The doctor went on

to tell her that her son had to recuperate somewhat before his debriefing, "And then perhaps—"

"Perhaps? You listen to me, and listen to me good, Mister Doc-tor. Who the hell do you people think you are? You tell my son—"

"Ma'am, this conversation is over!"

"No. I'm sorry. Please. Please give Michael the phone."

"As I said, Ma'am, he's not talking."

"Tell my son it's his *mother*. He'll talk to me."

There was a pause. "Don't expect too much," the doctor said in a more gentle tone.

When the nurse went to his bedside, she held the receiver to his ear, and Michael and half the ward could hear Sylvie's blaring voice, "Michael, Michael darling...are you there?"

The phone line went dead and his mother wept until no sound came out of her. Even after the burning in her throat subsided, Sylvie was unable to speak. She still wanted to open the letters, *had* to open the letters. Should she? Of course, she should. Too many days had passed since Michael had lost his will to go on. Sylvie knew she had to make a move soon. She would do anything, anything at all, to get him back. Besides, her curiosity was overwhelming. She closed her eyes and sat in silence without moving from the same spot, without following her usual routine of turning on all the lights throughout the house.

When she opened her eyes again, she was sitting in the dark. She became alarmed at her loss of time. She stretched her lean limbs over the arm of the overstuffed chair she had napped on and twisted the knob clockwise on the table lamp, its grooves digging into her fingers. The light beamed directly onto the untouched arrangement of Angela's letters, inadvertently positioned like an enchanting Oriental fan.

"No. I can't open them. Maybe tomorrow."

Tomorrow came and Sylvie moved in slow motion. She had to persuade herself to put her left foot into her left shoe, her right foot into her right shoe. Helpless, she dragged her body out the front door, barely finding the energy to lock it behind her. The keys fell to the ground and it was an effort to pick them up and find the keyhole. She fumbled and locked the door, double-checked the knob and made her way downstairs without taking a breath, until she settled on her car seat.

With nowhere to go, she wasn't conscious of driving down the road. She simply had to remove herself from what she left behind at home and somehow ended up at *the* most extravagant beauty parlor in town. She busted through the double doors, startling everyone in the salon to jump up and take notice.

"I don't have an appointment," she rushed the words at the receptionist, "but I must have my hair done today."

The receptionist looked at her without saying anything.

"Please?" Sylvie asked.

"Umm ..." She rolled her eyes, tipping her head toward the frenzied woman. "Susan, can you do this woman's—?"

Sylvie couldn't wait for an answer. "Oh, thank you, thank you, thank you," she said, plopping herself into a salon chair. "Cut, color, the works, okay?"

Susan eyed the receptionist, and they both shrugged simultaneously.

Susan draped the smock around Sylvie. "Emergency?"

"You could say that. I promise I'll make it worth your while." She winked.

She closed her eyes and let the girl comb through her thick hair. She let out a big exhale and half-listened to the other ladies talking around her. At first they talked about the restaurants they frequented with their husbands and the shows they had recently seen, which was bad enough, but when the conversation switched suddenly to the war, Sylvie was relieved it was time to sit under the hair dryer.

Again she thought of the letters, and how hard life could be for Michael. How hard life could be by making *one* wrong choice. Her mind went back and forth.

Just what is the truth with those two? Are they really still in love? God only knows.

She squeezed her eyes tight, trying to concentrate on the potency of bleaches and dyes.

"We're a lot alike, Angela and me," Michael had once told Sylvie on a night when he was unusually talkative. He shared this over his dinner plate of brisket with onions and cranberries—his favorite meal.

"She's got big plans," he had said with far away eyes. "Angela...she daydreams, like me, Ma, about travel and adventure, and..."

Angela, Angela, Angela.

Sylvie asked him to pass the potatoes. And that was that.

All at once she felt closed in. Her face was burning up. "My hairdryer. It's on fire!"

Susan let go of the broom she was sweeping up with and hurried to Sylvie's side. Her face was red and moist with perspiration. Susan frowned and quickly lifted the dryer hood.

"I'm sorry." She turned the dial. "Is that better?"

Sylvie attempted to read her lips.

She put her hand on Sylvie's shoulder. "Ma'am?"

"Huh?" Sylvie looked up at the girl and patted her hand as if she'd saved her life.

"Yes, much better. Thank you. You've been more than kind."

The next morning came with a lot of rain. She barely lifted her new hairdo from the pillow when she remembered her series of dreams.

Crazy… two, no three men were chasing me. Running, without moving, screaming, without sound. The dream had to be about the three men in her life and how she had suffered from their abuse: the emotional, the physical, and the one she ended up marrying, who wanted nothing more than to exploit her.

It was the emotional abuse of *real* love that was most painful. For years it was too difficult to say his name out loud. Michael's infatuation with Angela reminded her of her own zest for falling in love the "first" time. *Perhaps Angela's not the same as* him… she thought of *him* with the same old pinch in her chest that she relieved with her fingertips. His name was Samuel. Samuel, oh, how he had once made her feel inside.

The day had finally come when her past would catch up with her present and when her whole purpose was to protect her son from the same hurt someone like Angela could bring.

The rain had subsided by the dinner hour. Sylvie greased a small pan and sautéed leftover pieces of liver. She liked meat on the raw side. Her faded placemat sat alone on the dinette table, still sticky from breakfast.

Sylvie rubbed her hand along her cheek, the way Samuel had touched it… it was difficult to hold back her true feelings. *Once I was sweet like Angela, like candy. My skin has toughened, like dried fruit. How I hate dried fruit.*

She made up her mind that her misery was due to what everyone else did to her—*they* were at fault for stealing her joy in life; she couldn't let the same thing happen to her son. Trying to recall when she was once happy, a pleasant memory slipped through the window of Sylvie's mind like a wispy draft: a divine image of Holland, a special occasion, an elaborate affair held at their family estate. A lovely group of well-dressed women stood outside on the terrace near their tulip garden with parasols. Not unlike paintings in her father's gallery...and then almost as suddenly, the window slammed shut. How quickly things could change—a surge of uneasiness swept over the faces of the partygoers when one guest arrived and whispered something into her father's ear. The atmosphere had been buzzing with people speaking in undertones.

Why are they excluding me? She asked herself.

"Papa, what is it?" Her eyes probed his sullen expression. He waved her away, and she knew better than to keep asking. She dared not question another adult, either, not with the looks they were giving her. Sylvie detected the mood as threatening; all the glory she had ever known came to an obvious halt along with the music.

She was insulted that she was being overprotected from the politics. One day Holland was a glorious place, and the next, a felony to sing "*Wilhelmus*," the national anthem.

There was something very final when Mother closed the heavy front door behind the trail of visitors. After the last few guests left, Sylvie was told that it may be the last of Papa's parties for a long, long time.

She cut the liver into small pieces with her knife and fork, but she had no intention of eating. It occurred to her—what if the *same* door closes on Michael's life? What if he never feels joy again? She didn't think she could take that. She had to find out more about Michael and Angela's love for one another—maybe she should have listened to her son when he spoke of the girl.

Michael told me to give her a chance. He'd said, "Angel" is in her name for a reason.

Sylvie reluctantly relived the night she met Angela—a

plain girl, not modern to look at. I saw no makeup and no jewelry. And, I certainly saw no halo above her head.

Wait a minute. Didn't she go away to work for the airlines? Her flitting all over the world . . . what kind of love can she possibly keep for my son? Her throat thickened. Sylvie noticed how red the meat looked. She stood abruptly, her shoulders squared.

No. No. She's not the one for my Michael. Absolutely not good enough.

The meat looked like it was starting to bleed heavier. Her fork fell to the floor and she didn't bother picking it up. Sylvie recalled being adventurous when she was Angela's age, wanting to travel the world. "How can that be? We're nothing alike."

She sat back down and rubbed her palms over her throbbing eye sockets. "Is it time again for my pill?" Michael used to call valium, "mother's little helper." He said the same thing to Sylvie that Sylvie's own mother had said to her many years ago—that she was always running away from something. Sylvie *wanted* to run now, to *travel somewhere far away. . . .*

She remembered Michael's travels, his cross country trip before he had met the girl. *Was he running away from something, too? Oh, how he used to go on and on about his expedition.*

She pushed her dish to the far side of the table as if someone else would take the plate away and wash it for her. Her eyes filled thinking of him packing his camper he had named "Mr. Doobie." *After some character from Romper Room, I think, the kid's television show.*

She recalled all the odd jobs he had, working to pay off the camper, until he got full-time work at the local newspaper as an editor. She was amazed how he always managed to make his payments on time for his car loan. He was much better at budgeting money than she was.

The morning he had left for the purple mountain majesties—"to find himself," he had explained, she watched from the window as he rearranged things in his van—his typewriter, carbon paper, and a sheaf of blank white paper which he would later fill with words about the quiet of the woods.

"How that boy can write so many words about *nothing*." She no longer liked the quiet, herself, because that's when she thought too much about bad things. And yet, when he talked so anxiously about the American Bald Eagle soaring over the Snake River—she was hypnotized. *A regular Hemingway he is, my son.*

I used to write, too, about fulfilling my dreams. That extravagant calligraphy set her mother had given her for no reason at all. Maybe another one of those gifts to make up for lost time together. She had dipped her nib into the ink bottle and wrote her name in showy squiggles and strokes—*Sylvie. Sylvie Rosenberg* inscribed in her journal, now the color of English tea, the feel of its leather binding and cold metal clasp under her fingertips, before she had hid it under the floorboard for the duration of time they spent at the Internment Camp in Jamaica in the West Indies. Sylvie would look over her shoulder to see if anyone was coming and wince every time the floorboard creaked.

She sighed, giving in to carrying her own dish to the kitchen sink. She rested the plate with one unsteady hand, and with her other hand opened the cabinet door and pushed her uneaten liver into the trash can with her utensil.

Dizzy, Sylvie made her way into the dimly lit foyer and kneeled at the base of her father's antique secretary. The old furniture kept the book and old secrets waiting to come out of hiding if a small brass key taped beneath happened to turn clockwise in the rusty keyhole. But there was no turn of the key. The very notion paralyzed Sylvie who held the key's familiar shape in her clenched fist. With a long sweep of her free hand, she stroked the fine cherry wood on the side of the cabinet. "Yes. Still as rich as ever," she said, lovingly touching each little pigeon hole, each tiny knob and drawer, with visions of her father sitting there writing letters to whomever, trying to plan their escape from Holland.

As she closed the glass door, she was confronted by her reflection as if for the first time, by the deepening furrows buried in her image. Wandering through the empty house, she was almost floating like a drowsy skeleton until she gave in to exhaustion, again avoiding her roomy bed. And as usual she awoke with a falling sensation, not knowing where she was. She still had nightmares whenever she found sleep, but when she was awake, Sylvie was no longer a dreamer.

Her eyes blinked open. Her back ached from falling asleep on the living room couch with the bar jabbing into her ribs. She lay beneath four small heavy-framed paintings by a notable artist, the minute details of hound dogs with droplets of blood at their jowl.

"The hunt." She looked away from the grouping. "Poodles, they're not."

The morning sun attempted a cheerful path across the kitchen floor where Sylvie paced. She still had no appetite, even without dinner the night before. She had hunger pangs, yet food went through her for some time now, since she had received that terrible phone call with the news that Michael had been hit. Subconsciously, she knew, even before she got the call, before she heard the words, she *knew* he was hit. Her fear was similar to the shivers that ran through her body years earlier in the midst of her *own* war.

"I'm a survivor," she repeated, going from room to room—closed-in cages. She looked at Michael's college photo on the mantel, forcing a grin back at his jocular expression."And you will be, too, Michael. Do you hear me? You will get through this!"

As maddening as this was, she asked herself once again...*Should I rethink this about the two of them—together? What should I do? How hard can it be to find an angel?* she scoffed.

SEVEN

SOUTHAMPTON, NEW YORK
1970

After Michael had rescued the girl on the beach that day, he stood alone for a long time in the same spot, kicking the sand with his big toe. Then he looked up at the sky. For an instant, he viewed one of the clouds as taking on a seraphic shape.

"So, she has nice brown eyes. Big deal."

He had to keep on track with his plans which he had already mapped out for another cross-country trip. This was all he had wanted to relive, since the first trip he took right after high school graduation. And now, after finishing up with college and saving his money, he had waited long enough for another taste of freedom. Almost five years later, he desperately needed to get back to that simplicity—brushing his teeth and bathing from a cold water creek or roasting a hot dog and watching a can of stew boil on the open fire. Even more than that, he needed to break away from the materialistic world his mother forced upon him. In his mind, he saw his mother's heavy rings on her fidgety fingers. More than ever, Michael needed to be among what was unspoiled and the spontaneity of nature. Another trip would be the best remedy for what ailed him.

He recalled a blazing hot steamy day, melting him into the lifeless log he sat upon. He didn't know what time it was or what day of the week it was, and Mr. Doobie didn't have any answers. Time to put life on pause.

Thinking about those first excursions put a smile on his face. That cute baby bear he had spotted outside his tent meant that Mama Bear wasn't far behind, so he rigged up some ropes over a branch and hoisted his food up a tree away from his tent.

The environment filled the hole within him. He'd rip the knapsack off his back and quickly write about the soft rush of air that lured his eyes to a mother deer with her fawn barely old enough to walk. They appeared like statues with unblinking eyes, staring right back into Michael's. Their yellowish-brown fur was groomed to perfection by God's hand, ready to be placed in the storefront window of FAO Schwarz.

The trio observed one another for a long time, and Michael had to wonder if the deer were in awe of him, as well. He filled his journal with words meant to remind him someday of what he really needed to fill his spirit.

He'd awaken to the fragrant mountain laurel, the tranquility of the forest floor shrouded in dew and the gurgle of the brook in rhythm with the rapid chirping of birds—Michael's heaven.

While on the road, Michael read the old plantation stories told by the character Uncle Remus. He had immersed himself in Georgian history until it was time to head out onto the Freedom Parkway. He met all kinds of folks, labeled as beatniks, bikers, boozers, rockers, hippies, educated bums, and local yokels; it was their *differences* that made his entries into his daily chronicle come alive.

An old van with an abundance of black people wedged inside and handmade lettering on its sides—"Highway Boys Gospel Singers" came cruising by him one damp and hazy morning. Michael watched them as they got out of the vehicle and marched into the small white gospel church, laughing and smiling, oblivious to his presence. The writer in him made him grab his pen and pad and shuffle in behind them. He could see the story in his head, hear the sound of the clicking keys, the ringing sound at the end of each sentence when he'd pull back the carriage on his manual Royal.

He caught up with the last person entering the church's door.

"Would you mind, Ma'am, if I join you today?" he asked, coming up behind the woman at the entrance. She was heavy-set, a dark woman in a flowing white nightgown of a dress. And she had a dazzling smile.

"Why, everyone's welcome here, sonny."

Not seeing any other white people in the crowd, he sat in the last row, observing the informal, yet impassioned homily. He enjoyed the musical dialogue between pastor and flock. At some points, the people howled. They were euphoric while they worshiped, stomping feet, clapping hands, and shouting "Hallelujah" and "Praise the Lord," jumping with their arms swinging in the air. He had never seen such celebration of life.

Michael found himself slapping his own thigh and bopping his head to the crooning of *Let it Shine,* and it occurred to him that he was probably the only Jew that had ever entered the wide-plank doors of the old church with the peeling indigo-blue paint. This inspired him more. His soul joined hands with their wisdom.

He found his way to Route 55, New Orleans. In the French quarter, he went overboard on the Creole cuisine, not the right place to have bigger eyes than your stomach. In between each forkful of crawfish and gumbo, he gulped down glasses of water and was scolded by a diner.

"Oh, yo'll be payin' now for yo' tourist hankerin,' all right," she said. When she laughed, her whole body rumbled the floor.

A bony trumpet player balancing on a corner stool seemed

to know everyone who passed. With his belly churning, Michael nodded at him, as he made his way out the door and he wandered through the streets in the softness of the night air. Above him, he saw moss-green flowerboxes, coupled with yellow wooden shutters and decorative scrollwork adorning ebony wrought-iron balconies.

Michael mapped his way in and out of each state. One hot afternoon, his van gave up and had to be pulled over to the side of the road. "Now don't you go overheatin' on me, Mr. Doobie."

Michael threw the map to his side as a dust storm blew out of nowhere, bringing hundreds of tumbleweeds before his path, like bizarre-moving animals. He waited it out, until the hot steam rising from the winding pavement had dissolved and Mr. Doobie had cooled down.

After driving for seven hours, Michael left behind miles of yellow weeds. He got out of his bus, walked along the side of the road and stretched his body much the same as a long-legged tomcat. He walked a few yards to where he had stumbled upon some abandoned cabins.

"Old ghosts," he said. "Wonder if Kerouac ever slept here."

On to Route 10, to Roswell, New Mexico, where the aliens supposedly landed in the 40s. Then Michael headed west toward Tucson, Arizona, one of the oldest towns in the United States, to an Indian village called *Stook-zone*, which means *water at the foot of Black Mountain*.

Michael had pulled up to the convenience shack to clean his windshield and saw an old man sitting out front on a splintered bench. His features adapted to the stone mountain background behind him. He watched Michael dip the squeegee into the water bucket and slowly raised his crooked body from the bench to get a closer look at the Volkswagen's license plate.

"New Yawk," he said, as if telling Michael where he was from. "Long way from home, son. How'd ya like it here?"

Michael looked at him, dog-tired, as he wiped the front window. "Excuse me?"

"I said, how do you like it here?" he articulated the second time around.

"Oh, it's hot as—it's great, sir."

"Come on in outta the heat and have a drink with me," he offered, his head hanging low, as he pointed to a Coca Cola machine inside the gas station.

"No thanks. I just had a drink, and filled up the car, and now I'm headed out to Sedona." Michael saw the man's face fall, so he slammed Mr. Doobie's door shut, and said, "Sure. Why not? But, the drinks are on me, sir."

The man picked his head up as giddy as a schoolboy and hurried into the place with short steps and the tapping of his cane. "When my legs was betta, I used to collect hubcaps 'long this road." He motioned with his walking stick. "Still have 'em, hundreds of 'em in my barn."

"Really? Well, I sure would love seeing them," Michael said.

The man knocked over his bottle of Coke with excitement, his eyes turned young right on the spot. "Follow me," he said to Michael. "Yep. My son used to help me collect 'em," he said, showing Michael one after another. "Oh, enough 'bout me. You're going to Sedona, heh? I was there many years ago with the family," the man said with his unused voice.

At first, Michael had envied him for his timelessness, living among nature, then he quickly realized what a curse that could be when there are no signs of family in the backdrop.

Michael's memory of himself together with his dad and mom was distorted. Did they do anything together? Sit on the couch, all three of them, laughing at cartoons on television? Lay on the living room floor, sorting out pieces of a jigsaw puzzle? Build a sandcastle in the summer or a snowman in the winter? Rake leaves? Plant flowers?

What? What did we share?

They didn't have a grandmother or an aunt or an uncle come for a visit. Where were all his cousins? What was the meaning of *family* to him? He asked himself that question often. Somehow, Michael understood the meaning of a whole family, even though he never had one. He witnessed family life in his friends' homes.

After his big post high school trip, he soon returned to New York to start college, where he buried his head in books—until the day he'd ridden along the beach road and happened to drag a girl by her hair, kicking and screaming, out of the sea.

EIGHT

DIEREN, HOLLAND
1940–1942

Sylvie was aware of changes in the art world because of the war, but when her parents seemed to hold back the details, she grew suspicious. *They're still keeping secrets.* One day Sylvie and her father were sitting on the divan in the front parlor, and her father's voice sounded removed, as if he were talking to a business associate. His eyes looked past his daughter's, past the window pane, past the clouds beyond the window pane...he mumbled while in deep concentration. He did not blink. He did not blink at all, not once.

She had to wonder. Is my father afraid, now, too?

"Are you all right, Papa?" she asked.

He cleared his throat and straightened his posture and his bowtie. He spoke with a straight gaze, "One of the paintings Hermann Goering is interested in is for Hitler's birthday. His God damn birthday!" Her father rubbed his chest with the palm of his hand, his usual sign of heartburn when he was upset.

"Who?" Sylvie asked. "One of Hitler's men?" Sylvie was shocked he had let this information slip out as if it wasn't the first time he was being coerced.

Has Papa been forced to give up paintings before for Hitler and his henchmen?

"Hitler's birthday?" she repeated.

Her father found his focus again, looked squarely into Sylvie's eyes. His hand went from his heart to the side of her cheek. "Oh, never mind. There's nothing to concern yourself about," he answered.

In spite of troubled times, her father tried to comfort the family. But Sylvie could see right through him. And over the weeks and months that followed, the security she had always found in her father was gone. So fragile she could have picked him up with one finger and placed him on the shelf next to one of the porcelain figurines in mother's sacred collection.

It would soon be well-known that the German art historians stole the property of their victims, and the most distinguished masterpieces would be moved to secret places on special trains. The Fuhrer had grand plans for his Linz Museum. Hitler would send off art specialists to take thousands of artworks by force from around the world; Dutch art was sought after because the Nazis did not consider Dutch art degenerate.

Since new developments were rarely shared with the children, the always-curious Sylvie, strained to hear many hushed conversations through door cracks, about "big trades." Apparently, her father had leverage in certain areas. One day she overheard her parents talking. Her mother suggested they leave the country. "Why wait?" she had asked. "Let's go now. Maybe to America."

But her father kept putting it off, appeasing her with another trinket he had brought home from his trip to Switzerland—items that were hard to come by. He said something about "frozen assets," and then their voices faded. Gretta walked by Sylvie in the hallway. "What are you doing?" she asked. "Snooping again?"

"Just buckling my shoe," Sylvie answered, quickly squatting down.

At the Rijksmuseum, the Lange Lanz collection was brought out of its long time storage to fill up empty walls. Museums would slowly reopen with whatever remained.

The day would come when her father would have to give up some of his own collection of paintings by Flemish and Italian artists and 17th century Dutch masters. Among them: Gerard Dou, Nicolaas Maes, and Jacob van Ruysdael.

She tried desperately to control her mind of the reality she did not want to accept, but every night she'd toss in her sleep, trying to ward off the nightmares. She'd think of earlier, happier days:

Ahh, Grand Opening Day—a perfect sunny morning when the whole family gathered outside the new gallery Papa and his brother opened in The Hague—another one of Papa's dreams. We all dressed for the occasion: Papa wore his best Italian suit with diamond-cut cufflinks and his two-tone oxfords; Wilhelm wore a monogrammed patch on the pocket of his pin-striped shirt; Mother, her sophisticated ecru dress with wide-padded shoulders nipped in the waist, enhancing her hour-glass full figure. Typical of Gretta, she looked smart in her plain white blouse with a high, stiff Peter Pan collar and an a-line skirt to the knee. I wore my new spring black wool coat with matching soutache collar and cuffs and my floral cloche hat. And the little Princess, Ruthie, with her ribbon-adorned hair, wore a blue-fitted basque bodice with full circular skirt she twirled the entire day.

Oh, how I wish we still lived father's dreams.

Soon, though, Sylvie had dreams of her own. And bad timing or not, one of Sylvie's dreams was coming true, too. His name was Samuel.

"Hmm...such a noble name isn't it?" she asked Katz, her tawny-streaked cat, after sneaking the feline into her bedroom one day. The cat had been banned from coming upstairs ever since she got the two lovebirds in the tall gilded cage that stood in the corner of her room. Lately she had been sneaking Katz into her room to talk about her fears, but after meeting Samuel, her fears were pushed to the back of her mind.

She stretched out on her roomy bed and rubbed her bare toes through the cat's fur. "So, pussy cat, how are you faring through all this bedlam, lately? To tell you the truth, one day I think the world is coming to an end and the next day, I think the world is a wonderful place."

She picked up the cat and gave her a hug. "Today, Papa let me tag along with him after Sabbath to the Dieren gallery to tie up some loose ends at work. And do you want to know what happened while I was there? If you insist, I will tell you. Well, you know that boy Samuel I always talk about who works at the gallery on weekends?"

The cat purred and walked in circles around her feet, sneaking looks at the birdcage.

"He's a little older than I am, but so what. He's finally noticing me. I admit it was agonizing at first, the way he stared at me. I think it disturbed Papa a bit. But he really likes Samuel. Says he's an honorable lad. And I must say, this "honorable lad" has the bluest eyes I have ever seen. Gentile blue. I don't care if he's a gentile. We're not that Jewish. My parents say that we're liberal Jews because we don't follow the traditions of Judaism.

"Anyway, I wandered off to my favorite roomful of collections, and Samuel followed me. I stood beneath my beloved painting of a young girl in a white ruffled blouse, her long blonde hair tied back in a midnight-blue velvet ribbon. When I heard him enter the room, I pretended not to notice. But my heart did a flip. Then a flop." She giggled, stroking Katz's chin with her fingernails. "He asked me if I could come along every Saturday with Papa, and of course you must know what I answered. He said he will teach me a lot about art.

"When he told me this, his hand was resting over mine on the ezel (easel) holding a smaller schilderij (painting) of poorer quality, but I knew his *words* were absolutely priceless.

"Call me selfish, but I don't care about what is happening in the rest of the world at the moment, now that he's a part of *mine*. Samuel and I talked about the future. We'd both like to run our own galleries someday. Can you imagine that?"

After Sylvie had accompanied her father to the gallery enough times, she crossed out all the other boys' names that were faintly scribbled on the back cover of her schoolbook. On the front cover of her notebook, she inscribed "*Sylvie & Samuel*" in bold letters and drew a red heart around them.

"I've been seeing so much of Samuel at the gallery lately, Katz," she whispered. "I was right, you know. He's not like the other boys in my school. Most of the time we sit in the broom closet where we can talk, privately."

The cat meowed.

"But today our fathers were busy, tied up in a meeting, so we sat under my favorite portrait again. Samuel actually noticed I was wearing my best white blouse—what's left of my best, anyway, since we cannot shop anymore. It's with the flouncy trim. You know the one. I felt my face heat up as he made comparisons to *her*, the lovely girl in the portrait. He said I was blushing, and pushed my hair back from my face, ever so softly, exposing my likeness to her. We both looked to see if our fathers were anywhere nearby. Every minute alone was heavenly.

"This art must be worth a lot of money," I told him, proud of Papa's collection. He said his father is grateful that Papa has been so generous and gave him such a fulfilling job. "You know so much about art," I told him, "I bet someday *you* will be the curator."

"We looked at the same portrait for what seemed like hours. He said she was breathtaking, but he'd rather own a portrait of me. Oh, how I adore every word that comes out of his mouth. I was ready to faint when he put his arm around me. I nearly did and had to lean on him, so not to keel over. I've never felt this way about anyone before. And no one has ever felt this way about me. Is this what love feels like?"

The cat jumped off the bed and up onto the windowsill, and yawned.

"Hey, Katz, I'm not done talking yet. I've seen you hanging out with that alley cat, you know. Can't you give me any advice about love? It's not something I can talk about with the rest of the family, although Papa did mention how cheery I looked as we walked back home to Stationsplein 10. Even though Jews are only permitted to walk on the shady side of the street, the sun shines on both sides for me now."

Her hands cupped to the wall, Sylvie eavesdropped outside the room where her parents listened to BBC radio. She heard the familiar sound of the stations changing and the static, as her father turned the plastic radio dial, until he settled on what he needed to hear on a Dutch station. Almost immediately, she heard her mother's gasp with the news: "Queen Wilhelmina is leaving the country."

Sylvie heard part of the Queen of Holland's address: "I wish those left behind the very best," she had said, before she bid her people farewell.

Sylvie could hear mother's cherished sideboard crack under the weight of her father's fist when it pounded the cabinet. "Those left behind?" he mocked.

There was more talk between her parents about "the art," more details Sylvie couldn't make out. She heard the clinking of glass. Father was pouring whiskey from the leather and crystal set. She heard her father say, "Because of the art, *we* will not be left behind. *We* have something the Germans want. As I've said before, I will have to go through certain channels, get permission to travel...."

The click of the radio, and then there was silence. Sylvie panicked about getting caught with her ear to the door and dashed down the hallway and up the stairs, taking two steps at a time in her pigeon-toed way, until she hit the top landing.

She slipped into her bedroom and quickly closed the door behind her, and leaned against it with her back; she thought how life might change for them and closed her eyes in thought. *Why is the Queen abandoning us?* She shook her head. "No!" *I will not let anyone ruin this for me! I've been so happy about Samuel lately. I must only think of how lucky we've been. We've entertained royalty. Our butlers took coats of dukes and earls, and other noblemen at the front door, while serving girls on duty special evenings wore starched white aprons and ruffled caps. They'd bring wee fruit tarts from the Maandag Bakery on real silver trays with imported teas and chocolates.* Tears fell from her cheeks as she bit the ends of her hair, a nervous habit. She denied it all.

Then she licked her lips. She could almost taste her favorite dark chocolate. Satisfied with what she allowed in her mind, she shut off the light and closed her mind to the conversation she imagined her parents were still having downstairs.

How different life was before the Nazi occupation when her father used to talk about the art industry with such pride, especially when business was flourishing. Even as a child, she was aware that her father was *all* business and never left much time for anything else. Yet, he was lighter on his feet when he walked. And once in a while, he'd stop for a moment, scoop up one of the children and playfully toss them into the air, before locking himself in his office.

In the days following Queen Wilhelmina's somber speech, Sylvie noticed her father being more distant, as if he couldn't face her with the truth. He no longer took the extra time to share what was happening outside their home, but much worse, he no longer took the time to show his affection. It seemed one more pleasant memory was being replaced by an unpleasant one, every day.

Sylvie had become more reclusive, while trying to hold on to the jubilant times—ice-skating with her friends on the canal in Amsterdam; baking *Speculaas* in the oven with her grandmother; Uncle Nathan playing the grand piano; and cousins from all over Europe coming to visit their home country during the winter holiday.

"Those left behind." Sylvie had to fight off the Queen's words that remained vivid in her mind upon wakening each morning. How angry her father had sounded after hearing the Queen's announcement. She walked back and forth from her window to her vanity table. Then she bounced down the stairs to where her father was in his office.

Sylvie's cavalier attitude made her father furious; she said something about her wardrobe looking a little bare...but she soon found out by her father's reaction that she said the *wrong* thing. "Which do you like better, Papa, my emerald-studded dress or my black velvet one?" she asked, holding up both of her old party dresses that still fit.

Her father, always a gentle man, grabbed her by the shoulders and shook her like a cloth doll. She didn't recognize the hard look in his eyes.

"I don't give a damn about your wardrobe."

"Papa, you're hurting me," she said with a shaky voice.

Her father sat down, burying his head in his hands. "I'm sorry," he said. "I forget sometimes that you're still a child."

"No, I'm not. That's the point. I'm *not* a child." she cried. Sylvie crossed her arms over her chest and rubbed both shoulders with her hands.

"Sylvie," Her father's tone was frighteningly calm. "You're right. It's true. You have always been my confidant."

She didn't look at him as she spoke. "I-I have nightmares, sometimes."

Her father stood and wrapped his arms around her. "I know. We all do."

She looked into his eyes. "You are worried about what will happen with your art?"

"You have always shown an interest in the art, so I will tell you: as you know, the Rosenberg name has been a conduit for major works of art which the Germans could only obtain when our safety was guaranteed. But now, well, now, negotiating has gotten complex. It is difficult to explain."

"What will you do next?"

"Special arrangements have to be made. There's a financial agent of Goering's, a German banker. He gave me his word, Sylvie."

"Is he your friend?" she asked.

Her father hesitated. "Not exactly."

Sylvie really didn't understand any of the politics. *What special arrangements?* "What does it all mean, Papa?" Her eyes narrowed.

"I must wait for further instructions after I complete business with the Swiss Consul. But I have complete faith in them. I will let you know when I learn more."

Sylvie waited each night to hear her father tap on her bedroom door, and the distinct sound of his bulky gold ring. But she heard nothing. Night after night, nothing. He had already told her too much, she thought.

Day by day, their home had become more unpredictable. One of the Rosenberg servants, the one they had employed the longest, left without saying goodbye to anyone in the family. Sylvie thought that was strange, until she discovered that persons of German "blood" were no longer allowed to work in Jewish households. *I didn't know she was German.* Sylvie wiped her tears and told herself the servant was evil and she would not miss her. She would not miss how the woman had crushed Sylvie's body up against her bosom with hugs since Sylvie was little.

After *all* the servants were gone, Sylvie was lonelier than ever and spent much of her time in the sanctuary of her bedroom. She thought about how the oppression sneaked up on them, how anti-Jewish orders had come into effect one after another, forbidding them to ride in their own cars or on trolleys; to shop between certain hours of the day or to be on the streets between 8 p.m. and 6 a.m.; to attend theaters; or any forms of entertainment; to use swimming pools, tennis courts, or any athletic fields, and eventually, any activity at all in public places. Every day another fraction of freedom was stripped away under Nazi rule.

All along Sylvie had presumed she was privileged. That is what her mother and father had always impressed upon them, but was soon, loosing that confidence. They were told—"when out in public, go along with what the other Jews are doing, not to stand out. People who are jealous can become vicious, you know."

Sylvie found a folded up newspaper—the Haarlem Courant—in the wastebasket of her father's office that he had brought home after one of his trips. Her father had circled a small headline: "Over 200 Jews Massacred in Poland." She immediately refuted the article and dropped the paper back into the trash. Later that day, she came back to his office and picked it out of the trash to find out more about what was going on elsewhere. She wished she hadn't.

It wasn't until Jews were banned from visiting Christian homes that Sylvie felt personally affronted. Many of her friends were Christian. She had mixed feelings of pride and shame over *who* she was on that day. Could her Catholic friends have pitied her? The same friends who had always envied her? Pity would have been worse than death.

"Well, I certainly won't miss them! How could I? They aren't the *same* now. And that's what they must think of me."

Tears of rage stained her pillow when their troubles became too big for her to ignore.

She could not find solace anywhere. And she could not pray to a God she was never sure of. It had taken a while for Sylvie to mistrust *everyone* though. The gradual draining of humanity and the closing off of people from one another happened slowly like an infectious disease.

Once in a while, the mean-spiritedness of Gretta would come out and she'd taunt Sylvie about what could happen to them. "They will take everything," Gretta told her. "Soon it will be us."

"Liar!" Sylvie yelled at her sister, shivering at the thought of bare walls and empty drawers in her own home. "I don't believe you! Why are you lying to me? Why is everyone lying? Has everyone gone completely mad?"

Sylvie threw a book at Gretta's head, missing her by an inch, while her sister quickly exited her room. Then Sylvie flung herself on her bed and dug her head deep into her pillow. *But, we're "special". Papa said so.*

NINE

DIEREN, HOLLAND
1942

One of the first signs of the family's despair was how unapproachable they had all become. Mother no longer wore her favorite perfume and Papa no longer had his shoes shined. Gretta had bitten her fingernails down to the quick; she had always been so fussy about her nails. Wilhelm got more withdrawn and muffled his crying whenever anyone came near him. And Ruthie kept her rubber doll attached to her side like a third arm. The bemused expression on her baby sister's face is what Sylvie most avoided. How could such horrid things be happening around her in such a short life? Was the world ending?

The Rosenbergs kept their fears deep inside with a lack of conversation and connectedness, making the days drag on, turning into weeks, then months. Alone in her room, Sylvie woke many times in a panic, her dressing gown soaked in perspiration. For a long time, she hadn't asked what had become of the other well-to-do Jewish families, like the Janssens, the Kaufman's, or the Mintzners. She didn't want to know.

The time came when Sylvie had to turn in her bicycle, too, like the others had. But she couldn't get over it...her bike was so much fancier than the other bikes in the neighborhood, a special gift for her. She thought back to when she'd ride it with

her steel blades swung over her shoulder. She was "Queen Sylvie" sitting tall on its cushy leather seat...the wheels rolled
her dreamily over crested bridges for a skating date with Samuel. She could still feel Samuel's strong arm around her waist
as he guided her in circles on the thick ice of the broad canal.
Still, Sylvie knew better than to talk about what happened to
her bicycle. How could she bring that up so soon after Oma
had vanished? Her grandmother was taken right off the street
one drizzly morning. A neighbor of Oma's pounded on their
door with the news. Helene and Josef told the children to hush
while Mrs. Van Kloppen described what she saw from her second story window.

The crinkly old woman dabbed at her tired eyes with a han-
kie as she spoke. "I picked up your mother's brown paper bag,"
she said, looking at Helene. "It was ripped at the bottom, but
I salvaged some pears and apples that hadn't been run over. A
long dark car whisked your Oma away," she said, looking at
each of the Rosenbergs. "All four doors opened at once, and
the next thing I knew, the crows were picking at what had
been squashed into the cobblestone. She was gone and I just
watched—"

"Now, now, Mrs. Van Kloppen," Helene ushered the woman
toward the door. "We will do everything we can to get my
mother back. Thank you for telling us. Please, you keep the
fruit. And take some of these biscuits, too," she said, grabbing
them off a tray. "I'm sure we will get to the bottom of this just
as soon as possible."

She quickly closed the door behind the shaken woman
and turned to her husband. He held his wife as she sobbed.
Later that night, the Rosenbergs were contacted by officials
that Grandmother was at Westerbork Camp. They were told
the camp was for Jews who deserved preferential treatment. At

least it wasn't Auschwitz, where she'd have to get a number tattooed on her left forearm.

"Tell me my mother will be safe, Josef."

"I'm sure she will be safe," he said, not directly looking at
Mother.

"We have connections for the masterpieces that Hitler
wants for his collection, which the Germans can only obtain
through our survival. Do you understand? Through our
survival."

Sylvie did not like that her father had to repeat himself.
She listened intently to every word, especially when he said
that Hitler's men intended on using Grandmother as a *pawn* to
make certain barters within the art world. Sylvie let go of her
breath. *Ohh, Oma.*

A letter arrived from Oma from Westerbork. From Block 27.
Sylvie could tell from her words that she tried to make things
sound better than they were. Oma described the little boys and
girls there who only got to play with sticks and stones in the
yard among the purple heather. Sylvie wondered if the children
liked the way her grandmother smelled like allspice and ginger.
But then she realized that smell was probably gone by now.

The guards would call out block numbers during roll call.
She'd wait until she heard the command, "Clear," before moving a muscle. Oma wrote how she stood perfectly still in the
shoes four times her size—shoes for a clown, "grappenmaker,"
she said, purposely trying to make light of the situation—for
the children's sake. Sylvie knew no matter what, her grandmother was still sacrificing.

There were days she got a half liter of soup and a hand-
ful of bread. Oma joked in her letter that she needed to lose
a little weight, anyway. She boasted that she hadn't suffered

a scratch, but she was forced to listen to the Germans mock the less fortunate Jews, an underlying threat if the Rosenbergs didn't cooperate when dealing with art.

She also said that every Tuesday, the deportation trains left Westerbork for worse camps. In between the waiting, most of the other Jews were given senseless jobs to do—moving sand from one place to another or cleaning pig sties. But she said that she was lucky, being a seamstress, and her worst physical wounds were being stuck with her own needle.

Once again, Sylvie stood outside her parent's bedroom and could hear their conversation.

Papa was telling her mother they had to be strong. "For the children." His voice came from a true heart, but his words sounded fraudulent to her ears. And probably to mother's.

"But, I keep thinking of the Jacob family. They're gone now, too. And they'll be coming for us next."

"Don't talk like that, Helene. I'm sorry about your mother. And about the others, but please trust me, I will do whatever it takes to save the rest of our family. I'm working this out. I beg of you to *trust* me."

Sylvie went back to her own room trying to convince herself that she could trust her father. But in the dark of night, she grew more petrified; she wondered if Oma was as scared as she was. Sylvie would open her nightstand drawer and retrieve the silver thimble that Oma had given her to play with a long time ago. She turned the small cap between her fingers, feeling its many indentations like the pores in her grandmother's skin. Without her softness.

Night after night sleep would not come. After a while, Oma's letters didn't come, either. Sylvie couldn't shake the bad thoughts away and screamed under her pillow.

God, how I loved that pink bike.

She trapped Katz in her room, forcing the cat to listen to her fears, once again. "Lately, Papa and Uncle Nathan have been away a lot after getting special permission to travel, which I think is having a dreadful effect on Mother. Haven't you noticed she's acting like a different person? She must be terribly nervous about Oma. I'm afraid it's having an impact on her health. In the morning, she doesn't join us for breakfast, anymore, complaining she's queasy. And sometimes, no one knows where she is...she simply disappears for a while, maybe she needs time to think things out, or maybe she wants to be alone to *pray* for Oma...although she comes off as a non-believer, I believe she prays in her *own* way."

Too much time had passed without Oma's words, so Sylvie turned to writing in her journal on weekends. She wrote obsessively. She wrote until her wrist hurt and her heart didn't. She didn't know where so many words came from, sometimes jumbled up like the days of the week.

One day, quite by accident, Sylvie was eating her breakfast cake, and she overheard her mother and Gretta discussing something in the pantry where they were sorting through what was left of the canned food. She felt the sky shift with their words—"We can no longer stay in our home...." When they came out of the pantry and saw Sylvie sitting at the table with her mouth filled with cake, Mother quickly added "Don't worry, Papa may be able to make the *big* trade soon—possibly for 25 exit visas—we would go on to Spain where there will be a boat waiting."

What is Mother saying? Why is she talking such nonsense, as if delivering good news? What will happen to us? What will happen to Katz? We will lose everything. But even worse, I cannot bear to lose Samuel. No, I will not leave him behind. I'll refuse, that's all.

"NO. *I WON'T GO! I WON'T! I WON'T!*" Sylvie screamed, running from the room.

She was anxious for Saturday when she would see him again. *Surely, Samuel will have a solution. He is my Sir Galahad.*

Sylvie's father warned her that it may be the last time she could come with him to the gallery because being on the streets was getting too risky. When she saw Samuel and told him her family would have to leave Holland soon, he kissed her teary eyelids. *A salty first kiss I will not forget*—she wrote in her journal. *Oh how I wish I could see my friend Hana again and tell her... she would say, 'That sounds so romantic!'*

"Hmm... I wonder where Hana is?"

Samuel told her that everything would be all right. There's a secret area in the barn near his farmhouse in the countryside that he played in as a child. He would ask his family to hide them there. He promised Sylvie that the last time they were together in the broom closet at the gallery where they shared a final embrace, and then it was all over.

Helene slapped her daughter across her face—something she'd never done before, and Sylvie used words she'd never used before, not in front of her mother, anyway. It was when Sylvie insisted again that she wasn't going anywhere without Samuel. "Because Samuel loves me," she told her mother. "That is why," she said, squeezing her mother's hand that had slapped her.

"You are being ridiculous!" her mother answered. "See, this is why we have to hide things from you, Sylvie. You are too immature and self-centered."

I wanted her to know that I was old enough to fall in love. I wanted to ask her if she remembered what that felt like when she was my age. But I didn't.

As warned, Sylvie was forbidden to join her father at the gallery the following Saturday, as he was meeting with German officials and last steps were being taken. She cheered up when her father came home with a sealed note from Samuel for her, which she quickly tucked into the front of her blouse, concealing it from her mother. She ran up the stairs to the privacy of her own bedroom, her heart beating faster with every word that she read.

"No-o-o! How can he?"

She tore up the note into small pieces and scattered them onto the floor. "Today is as bad as the day Hitler was born!" Her two love birds twittered and twitched inside their gilded cage.

Samuel's short letter started with an apology: "I'm sorry to share this news with you, my Sylvie. I don't know how to write these words. We will *not* be able to help your family hide after all. Our lives would be at stake if we do. My parents told me to tell you that we will pray for you. You probably doubt my feelings for you as you read this, but always remember that I will never stop loving you."

All along, I thought he was my knight but he's just like the rest of them. He and his stupid anti-Semite family. He may as well turn us in to the Nazis. I will never forgive him, not for the rest of my life!

Sylvie's pen dropped from her hand. The tears came, but the words did not. She could not release her anger as she paced back and forth in her room and yelled at the four walls: "I don't care about him or anyone else, for that matter! We Rosenbergs don't need their God damn help!"

"After everything my father's done for his father, how can

he do this?" She saw his clear blue eyes in her mind turn a muddy blue—into eyes of a traitor. "That's what he is. A God damn traitor! Traitor! Traitor!"

She plopped herself down on the edge of her bed, overcome by waves of emotion. Her love for Samuel turned around, did an about-face right on the spot. She watched her own heart break, falling downward from her chest, slapping against her thigh, bouncing off her knee, sliding down her shin to her feet... she watched its slowing pulse dying right there on the floor.

She blotted her puffy red eyes with a wet washcloth and managed to pull herself together. When her hysteria turned into a small sigh, she told herself how much she hated him. "I hate everyone!" she said, looking into the vanity mirror. "Now I'm like everybody else, filled with nothing but hatred. I suppose that makes me a grownup, too."

Feeling dazed, she wished she could call down the stairs in revelation: "I'm almost ready, Mother," as if ready to go to the symphony or to the theater and life would go on as before.

The day came when she simply surrendered. *I'm ready now... to run away with the rest of my family.*

One more time, she looked at the rosy-faced lovebirds, and wondered if she should throw the cover over their cage for their last sleep. She scooped up the cat and ran downstairs, and opened the back door. "Go, Katz! Go to the alley and find your mate. Now, scat!" she cried, and ran back upstairs, grabbed her journal, and headed out the door with the rest of her family.

CAMP GIBRALTAR

Well, we've stopped running. We've escaped and are living safely in a British internment camp in the West Indies where we may have to stay until the war is over. We are "free" although there are bars on our windows. I still don't care about what day of the week it is, but I am marking the pages in my journal so I can someday tell my grandchildren about our whirlwind liberation.

The last thing I recall, before we were forced to flee our home—I was upstairs in my room and listened to people herded past the house and then, harsh voices in the foyer. Mother instructed me and my brother and sisters to move quickly. We grabbed only small items we'd be allowed to take with us that day. We filed outside as if we were made of tin; some of the other Jews Papa was trying to save followed. I had already accepted our fate. I dragged my dead heart inside my dead body, and moved involuntarily…dead weight that blended with the others on the street.

I kept Papa's "forever words" inside me, the words he had taught me when I came home from school the very first time asking him why some kids said bad things about being Jewish. He told me to always walk proud as a Jew, as if I "belong" wherever I am in my own body. From that day on, while we waited for the train, I'd think of those words, straighten myself out, and walk with my chin up. Years of ballet, the hundreds of plies to straighten my crooked feet hadn't mattered one iota; it wasn't until Papa gave me those words that I could stand tall like a ballerina. His words were not hidden under a big bow or wrapped in sparkly tissue paper like Mother had always given me. They were pieces of Papa I always knew existed, underneath. I knew him better than anyone. I was the one everyone had called Daddy's little girl.

Hours before we had left our home, we received a telegram telling us in code that Spain would accept affidavits in lieu of passports with the prominent German signatures.

Papa assured us we'd be all right once the Rembrandt passed hands. I was reminded of when I was seven years old, turning in circles before Rembrandt's self-portrait in his gallery. How extraordinary, the dark painting seemed... even in the shadow, the artist's eyes were telling me something about life.

The image of a giant swastika on blood-red, chased me as it once had when I was a child in the park, bullied by the Christian kids. I recalled seeing the birds flying overhead in the sky that day, giving me the strength I never knew I had. I closed my eyes, trying to convince myself that I no longer needed my nest, allowing my arms to become my wings.

Our father handed us "the papers." He said he had to go somewhere else, with a marshal. He then informed us that he will not join us in the West Indies, in Jamaica. He had to separate from us. "I must go on to America," he said—words of betrayal to me. Why hadn't I noticed before that he was the only one carrying a suitcase? He told us it was easier this way for him to go alone through Canada to New York, rather than be a burden with 25 people... he'd set up business in New York, and then he'd send for us. He said he wouldn't be long.

I grabbed my father's coat sleeve, as mother pulled me away in the opposite direction. I had never seen her eyes begging before, so I let go of Papa, not knowing it would be forever.

Then there were dozens of Germans, all wearing earthy-grey uniforms. "Achtung!" they shouted at us. I was sure they would kill us right there on the spot, shoot us down, like I'd heard about in school so many times. At the station, one of the police dogs growled at me as I passed. The officer who held the dog back was so amused by this,

*that he—a grown man—growled and snarled at me as
if he were a dog, too. I could see the beast's big snapping
teeth, but what frightened me more, was the mean-spirit of
his master. I will never forget his one gold tooth in front, as
the man laughed. I looked at my mother who had always
had so much to say. She said nothing.*

*Like Ruthie, I hid my face. Someone pushed me up
from behind into one of the cars. I was immediately overcome with the smell of fear. The doors shut with a bang,
and I heard the bolt click. The whistle screamed and I covered my ears with both hands. I felt the vibration of the
train moving forward. I had even lost faith in Papa's promise that we'd be safe. Where are we going? Where are we
really going?*

*Frail, filthy people crowded around us, and I pinched
my nostrils. They wore rags and dirty brown shoes, some
mothers clutching their children. Everyone in the boxcar
turned into small whimpering animals. The train made
a stop and some people were told to get off and board
another train, but our family was told to remain on the
train. The guard had a list and he'd call off names. In the
pandemonium, we were shoved about.*

*Wilhelm was no longer standing next to me. I pan-
icked. I had to fight my way to the front of the car and I
shouted at a guard. "Please, my brother! He should not be
going on that train. His name is Wilhelm Rosenberg."*

*"Get back," the guard ordered, checking his list. Then
he seemed to notice something pleading in my eyes.
"Rosenberg?"*

*The whistle started blowing, announcing the train was
about to move when I saw the back of my brother's head;
he was being transferred onto another train that was going
to Belgium . . . with a final destination near a camp called*

Breendok, which I later discovered was one of the smallest camps and one of the worst. There was one guard at that camp for every ten prisoners—who continuously endured endless beatings because they had refused to collaborate or they organized the underground press.

Mother and Gretta saw what was happening and jumped up as the other train moved a few feet.

"Halt!" the guard shouted, stopping the train, with his checklist still in hand.

Wilhelm was roughly grabbed from the train headed to Breendok . . . where trucks waited.

He rejoined our family and I knew how much I loved him.

Later, Gretta shared a portion of her food with me that she had in her pocket, as if paying me back for saving our brother.

Strange, how there was a certain peace inside the dank boxcar, lulling us as the wheels thumped along the track. I consoled Ruthie with a story I made up on the spot. I called the fairytale "The Train That Got Away."

Ruthie's small chest stopped heaving as I stretched out the words . . . "and then, Ruthie, the choo-choo train came out of the long dark tunnel, into a bright light where people stood in a meadow filled with colorful flowers . . . .

I finished the fairytale with the happy ending, and watched Ruthie as she dozed.

Gretta looked at me and smiled. This was one of the few times my sister Gretta had showed me tenderness. She squeezed my hand, a gesture I treasured and feared all at once. In the corner, my mother held up Wilhelm, cuddled at her side after giving in to exhaustion. His long lashes decorating his swollen eyes as he slept, standing up. Never *before had I seen the family united in this way—surely a sign that we would die very soon.*

We passed a field with grazing sheep and another with wildflowers swaying in the breeze.

After a while, I stopped counting the many stubble fields I spied through small holes carved in the horizontal slats of the wooden cattle car. Gradually, the terrain changed. I had never seen such astounding scenery, never knew there were so many shades of green. I nudged my little sister to wake up. "See, Ruthie, just like in my fairytale."

Finally, our train came to a stop and the doors opened. We jumped down, covering our eyes from a bright sun. There were others jumping down from cars, too—twenty-five of us in all—the twenty-five visas Father had negotiated in the trade.

For a moment, I felt Papa's hand on my cheek. And I understood.

Although fatigued, we followed a Spanish man with fatherly eyes, who led the way. We ate a few scraps of bread and potatoes, and traipsed through olive groves and saw spectacular mountain views. A soldier was walking alongside a girl on her bicycle, so intent on flirting, he didn't even notice us.

After some time, the man guiding us brought us further into the forest to his relative's tavern where we were treated to a dish of paella and where I drank my first glass of wine. I let it make me dizzy and wanted more. A few in our group of 25 looked weak, and I worried they would fall ill and simply give up before we reached the boat.

On our trek from the tavern in the forest to the boat at the coast, a storm kicked up and we had to hold onto one another to stay on our feet. We were relieved to board the vessel that had waited for our arrival—a big cargo

ship that smelled of fish...not quite the luxury liner I had
wished for. Along with the foul smell was the foul mouth of
the crew members who did not seem happy to escort us to
our freedom during the rough weather. It was the rockiest
boat I had ever been on, and I was told to keep my eyes on
the horizon.

In such close quarters, with no privacy, along with the
filth and constant nausea, I feared my paella would be
making a return trip...there were moments I thought we
would all die at sea. But when morning came, I looked out
at the turquoise sky and water that shimmered magically
in the sunlight. The landscape and seascape took away our
breath. Funny, how small I felt, as if I was standing on a
blank canvas, waiting to be captured by a famous painter.

TEN

MASSAPEQUA, NEW YORK
1960–1963

At first, Angela's mother, Jean Martino, had loved living by the water. She and her husband, Anthony, had moved to a 33 square-mile community called Massapequa, named after the original native population. The neighborhood was a melting-pot, a paragon of suburbia in the '50s, made up of other families who had moved from small cement stoops to spacious front yards... the American dream. Then the tragedy. Anna was buried along with the tribal spirits.

After that first tragic summer, Jean felt stuck in the middle of fish-shaped Long Island like a mangled piece of ingested bait. For almost a full year after her second child was born, Jean remained bedridden, keeping everything she needed on her nightstand. She made her sedated world small and safe.

One day her doctor made a house call when she told him that she couldn't get out of bed because she felt as if she'd fall right through the floor and be swallowed alive. Jean's sister, Tana, cared for the new baby as if she were her own for most of the first year, while Anthony worked long hours. Everyone was thankful Angela was such an easy child, so independent. Maybe a little too independent.

Along with Angela's baby steps, when Mrs. Martino was well enough, she became obsessive about keeping everything clean and orderly: making the bed the same way every day, tucking in the corners just so. After her chores were completed she'd stand on line at the pharmacy, behind all the other resourceful housewives, waiting for their Demerol. Until one day, she just threw the pills in the garbage.

She took on small sewing jobs for well-off people and watched Angela as she sat content on the floor going through her tin of buttons for hours, lining them up, all shapes and sizes; individuals with personalities. Some were dark and seriously bulky, others delicate drops of pearls, and then there was the royalty of buttons—the rhinestones. She was pleased one day, when Angela was about eight or nine, when she turned to her and asked her how to sew.

"Make your stitch long when you baste the hem," her mother instructed, talking with the pointy part of the straight pin sticking out from tight lips. Angela sat by her mother's side for many days, sewing ricrac on the pockets of her smocks and on the potholders with orange and red and brown roosters.

Over time, Angela began to judge her mother mending strangers' carelessly ripped hems and pieced-together scraps of material to make matching napkins and tablecloths. Before long, she silently ridiculed her mother's favorite apron; the one with rows of cherries nestled between checkered red squares, the one her mother had wiped her hands on countless times.

Her mother looked tiny as she stood at the counter, scouring the sink with a Brillo pad so hard that Angela thought she'd rub the enamel off. She didn't want to end up like that, stuck her whole life behind a black machine embellished with gold letters—*Singer*. Her mother had always told her she wanted more for her daughter. But Angela thought life would have been easier if she had been born a boy.

For years, Angela accepted women being locked away in the house as normal, wondering if that was the reason her mother was sick on the inside. It wasn't until Angela was ten that she found out what *really* made her mother sick. Angela hadn't confronted her parents about the *discovery* for a long time—not until after the lump settled in her throat.

The lump in her throat would always come back, though, whenever Angela thought about the day she discovered the newspaper clipping dated 1950—the day after she was born— in a corner of the attic placed among her mother's possessions in a threadbare box. Her first instinct was that it was a piece of overlooked litter. That's when her own last name popped out at her. For an instant, she was flattered by the bold letters—MARTINO, until she saw the name preceding her surname, was that of a total stranger: *Anna.*

The *Massapequa Post* mostly stated the facts of the frantic attempt of saving a young girl who was carried out with the current. With her finger, Angela followed the words carefully, not knowing what to make of them. She stopped short at: *The daughter of Anthony and Jean Martino. That can't be. I'm the daughter—their only daughter—this isn't real, then. It's a mistake. Why doesn't it say Angela? It should say Angela!*

Unaware of her trembling in the drafty attic, she held the torn obituary stapled to the article in her shaky hands, as if an actress reading a part in a play about *fake* people, not her family. Angela sat in the quiet, staring blankly, until she heard the shuffle of feet on the stairs. She quickly tried to refold the paper back up exactly how it was with her clumsy fingers.

No! No, it didn't go like this. She reopened and refolded the article in the opposite direction. Her eyes were drawn to the rocking horse's glazed eyes in the corner and then to her doll's old wooden high chair. All of a sudden, it occurred to her that maybe she wasn't the *first* one to use those toys. She dropped down to the splintery wood floor to crawl out on her hands and knees, fearing if she stood up, the creaking would alert her parents to her whereabouts.

Now she knew why her mother always warned her not to go into the attic. It wasn't because she might fall through the eaves, after all. Angela realized her mother didn't want her to find this article hidden over a decade ago, neatly folded into perfect squares by her hands and tucked into the bottom of a cloth covered case beneath tangled costume jewelry.

As she closed the light switch, dots of sunshine speckled through the slanted slats in the roof, like bouncing balls on song lyrics, dancing on boxes marked Books, Games, Christmas, Boots, Toys. Not a single box was tangibly marked with the word "Sister," but the word weighed heavy on Angela's shoulders like a yoke, and she assumed she had done something wrong by discovering her existence.

I have a sister . . . had a sister.

She had found her mom in the kitchen. She kept her eyes fixed on her mother, as if she were someone else. Angela watched her as if for the first time—magnified—the way she picked up the knife and methodically chopped the onion into small pieces like fragile shards of glass. Without saying a word, she seated herself next to her mother at the table and helped to chop the onions, giving her an excuse for teary eyes.

A long time passed, when Angela in her early teens, confronted her parents about the big secret. Her mother begged her forgiveness. "I'm sorry. It's my fault, entirely. Don't blame your father. He wanted to tell you. I insisted we wait until you were six or seven, but when the pain didn't go away, I didn't want you to have to go through..."

Angela bit her tongue until it hurt, until she was able to speak. "What was Anna like?"

Her mother stared too long while she spoke about Anna, as if reading from a fairy tale...until she reached the part "when the water swept her away."

After watching her mother weep like that, Angela swore she'd never question her again about her sister. Sometimes she'd ask her father. He only cried invisible, manly tears.

She wondered if her parents had moved to Massapequa because of all the glorious *water* surrounding the homes there— the hundreds of canals channeling from the Great South Bay that led to the ocean beaches. She'd always been drawn to the water, herself, like a tadpole. When Angela was eleven, she went down to the docks across the street from her house and studied a nearby fisherman. At first, he was oblivious to the girl wading in her pedal pushers.

"Where's your pole?" he asked, noticing her.

Angela gave him the once over with a slight smile, then shifted her eyes down again at the line of water that marked her ankles. She could hear her father's lecture in her mind, "Don't shake your head, speak to the man." And she could hear her mother's lecture—"Don't talk to strangers." She waded further out, getting her pants wet above her knees, until he drove away in his pickup truck, and she plodded over to where he had been.

She saw what he left behind. "You poor thing," she said, spotting a small fish gasping for air, its gills opening and closing, frantically. She scooped it up and tenderly slipped it back into the water, watching its silver body reflect in the sunshine.

"Swim for your life," her voice quivered after it.

The salt water thickened her hair. She pushed back a few

strands from her eyes and scratched her itchy nose with her green-stained fingers, wondering if she left seaweed marks on her face. She was always coming home a mess, wearing her adventures on every piece of clothing her mom had made for her. Her mom was always forgiving, no matter what.

As Angela matured, she wondered if her parents were capable of making reasonable choices for her and soon she started asking many questions about their life—safer questions. "Mom, why'd you and Dad move to Massapequa, anyway?" Angela asked as they drove past the two-story wooden Indian Chief constructed on Sunrise Highway—a popular landmark and meeting place.

Her mother's grip on the steering wheel tightened, as she prepared herself for cross-examination. "I don't know. I guess I always had a soft spot for Indians. It's a funny name, isn't it?"

"Yeah, I'll say." Angela giggled. "Out-of-towners can't pronounce the name: 'Wha did ya say? Massa-wha?"

Her mother joined in. "Or where ya from, Massa-Pee-ka? You're from where? Mass-A-Packa?"

"Massa-Quee-ba?" Angela laughed, childlike.

Her mother's hands relaxed on the steering wheel.

Angela liked to think there was something magical in the drinking water where she grew up. That's what everybody in school had said, anyway. She remembered the stifling smell of her classroom—thick chalk. She'd wait for the springtime, when the custodian passed under the open window with the mower, and she'd inhale the sweet smell of freshly cut grass and the promise of what was ahead.

They used to say that in the early 1920s, when William Fox, the movie producer got into real estate, he was attracted to the many canals and waterfront of the Great South Bay. He had built a number of southern Californian Spanish style houses with stucco walls and red tile roofs. People said Massapequa was destined to be the "Hollywood of the East," until the stock market crashed in 1929 to the dismay of many little girls who had dreamed of stardom in their future.

In junior high, while sitting in Mr. Midura's Social Studies class, the teacher finally managed to pique the interest of Angela and her best friend Katie Iverson, with the lesson of the local Marsapeque Indians, and the famous Joneses of the 1700s. The girls' first stop after school that day would be the burial ground of the Marsapeques, behind The Old Grace Church—where they were to smoke their first cigarette.

They were enthralled by the romance of a major in the English army by the name of Thomas Jones, also known as "Pirate Jones," who met "Freelove" Townsend, the daughter of a Quaker. Thomas and Freelove fell in love and were married, and received several hundred acres of Townsend's estate as part of the dowry, which was land her father bought from the Indians.

"Freelove?" Katie raised her brows. "What was she, a whore?"

"No way! I bet she was pretty, with long black braids."

"And Thomas Jones was probably a real hunk," Katie went along.

"Not like the nerds in our school. They're so into arm-farts and spitballs."

"They're so gross. Never ever go into the kissing closet with Kevin Simpson. He has the breath of a carp."

"Yeah, but he's so cute, like Paul McCartney in the Beatles."

The two girls giggled behind the old walls of the large church. The legend of Pirate Jones went that he had been buried with some of his treasures, and 135 years after his death, a disappointed digger etched these words on his gravestone:

BENEATH THESE STONES
REPOSE THE BONES
OF PIRATE JONES
THIS BRINY WELL
CONTAINS THE SHELL
THE REST'S IN HELL

They read the poem aloud as they stuck their tongue in the end of the recessed filter of their Parliament cigarettes and puffed and choked.

"Hey, I think I inhaled," Katie said.

They nodded their heads in unwavering approval of how *cool* they looked, until they gratefully put out the butts with the twist of a heel.

Angela looked at the dirty cigarette and then up at the old church's steeple, wondering if she was sinning at that very moment. A few days earlier, she'd been rooting through her bureau drawers looking for a hat to wear to Sunday mass while her mother waited for her downstairs.

"I'm coming, Mom," she yelled down as she scrambled around her bedroom looking for something to stick on her head for church. *Not* wearing something on your head must certainly be a sin. She opened one drawer after another. When she opened her underwear drawer, she thought about her and Katie hanging their training bras off old Mr. Swenson's bumper, and how hard they laughed when he pulled away in front of neighbors scratching their heads.

Leaving the drawer open, with her underwear hanging out, she ran downstairs, empty-handed. Her mother grabbed a doily off the arm chair and placed it on top of her daughter's scalp. Angela couldn't believe she was as God-fearing as other Christians to wear that thing on her head.

"Hey, Angela, look at this headstone. I think this is it. I can't make out all the words, except the name Jones, and the year 1713. Just think, there are *skeletons* under our feet."

"You think their souls are in heaven or hell?" Angela asked her friend with a serious expression.

Katie gave her a look. "I don't think either. I think after you die, you go back to what you once were."

"And what's that?"

"Dust."

"Really?" Angela considered this. "I don't know. I'm kinda hoping for more. So . . . what's it like to be Protestant?"

"Why, you thinkin' of converting?"

"Hmm . . ." She looked at Katie, then at the cloudless sky.

Angela had sat her skinny rear end on the hard rosewood pews every Sunday. The high stained glass windows depicted saints and sinners, a distraction from the mere mortals seated around her. Most were familiar faces to her, as the daughter of a woman who never missed mass on Sunday, sometimes went on first Fridays and during the week, made novenas.

She closed her eyes and then opened them to the back of a young mother seated before her who lovingly lifted her infant up like the sweet baby Jesus. Like a magic wand, sunrays made way inside the church, tapping sunspots on heavy shoulders— friendly colorful handprints of angels. Funny, Angela thought, she never saw her sister's spirit *inside* the cathedral, always on the outside, always down by the beach.

But, why only as high as the clouds? Why not as high as the stars? She'd heard Anna used to love to wish upon a star. Said it was lucky.

Katie interrupted her reflection. "Ange, you still listenin'? You know religion is nothing but fear and guilt. It's such a load of crap."

Angela mentally put herself back in the wooden pew sitting next to her mother, as Katie spoke. Her mother was holding her missal and a string of cheap pink rosaries. She grasped each pink fake pearl like the knots on a lifeline suspended from heaven. There weren't enough plastic jewels on earth for her mother to redeem her soul for the loss of Anna—and all the summers and winters, all the fallen leaves and the birth of seeds her first daughter had missed.

As usual the priest on his pulpit was going on and on—he said something about how fortunate people were to be born Catholic, as if it was the only right religion. "Do not weaken! Do not let non-Catholics weaken your beliefs. Do not let anyone taint your conviction . . . let us pray."

Had she heard correctly? The contradiction? *How do we think we're better than our neighbor and love thy neighbor at the same time?*

The obligatory basket attached to a long pole jutted out in front of them. Angela's coins fell to the floor, clanging and echoing off the highest point of the cathedral ceiling . . . spinning like tiny tops, spinning her back to the memory of when she was a shy little girl waiting on line for confession. One of the nuns in her long black witch dress pulled her to the front of the line and practically pushed her inside the dark box. Angela panicked at first and forgot what she was supposed to say to the invisible man behind the black curtain.

He spoke first. "What do you have to confess today?"

She recognized his voice right away and wished she could use a bad word right there on the spot, because he was the priest that all the kids feared, and she was unlucky enough to get him. Why couldn't she get any of the other priests that were so nice, like Father Bill?

She answered in her most earnest voice, "Umm, nothing. I did not sin this week, Father" even though he wasn't *really* her father.

Her answer angered The Great Oz. Her only recourse was to deliver what he wanted to hear, no matter how dispiriting that may be. "Yes, umm...forgive me Father, for I have sinned. I lied to my mother and umm, talked back to my father?"

Yes, this seemed to have pleased the priest. In his mighty voice, he commanded her to say ten Hail Mary's and ten Our Father's. He was powerful, the way she imagined God would be...but not kind. Not kind at all.

"Let's have another cig," Katie said.

Angela smiled at Katie who was still on the same subject about religion being a load of crap. "Cause you know as well as I do that people are just afraid of dyin'. They hold Hell over our heads, 'cause without it, religion would crumble. It's brilliant. Theological abuse, if you ask me. Think about it."

Angela had thought about it. Plenty. And she had to admit that local history was much simpler than theology.

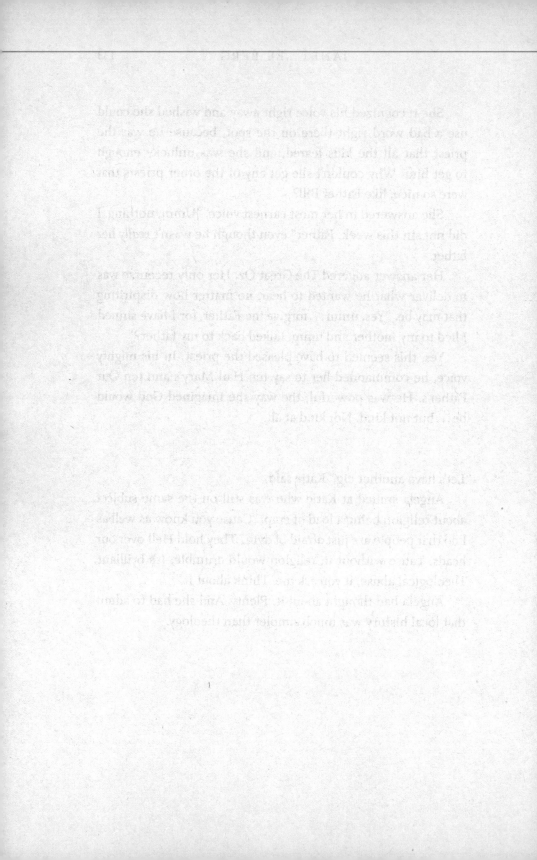

ELEVEN

QUEENS, NEW YORK
1971

Sylvie was relieved to finally get out of Shoes and into the Book Department. She meditated there in the world of readers and writers. On her lunch break in the cafeteria, she was in a trance, delicately dunking her glazed doughnut in her extra-sweetened coffee. She hated when the cake broke apart and left crumbs floating on the top of her cup. The decaf had a bitter taste, but she had to sacrifice.

"More palpitations I don't need," she had told the clerk with the face mole.

She sat alone, avoiding co-workers, pretending to be engrossed in the romance novel she had grabbed off the shelf. This would keep her mind off other things like the news head-lines. She'd already lived the casualties of war, why did she need to relive such unspeakable acts with this war in Asia? She looked at the cover of the paperback. A young couple was embracing on the cover, rolling onto the sandy shore. She liked reading about shallow characters in meaningless love stories. What other kind of love is there?

Sylvie moved three days later.

Sylvie grabbed at her throat, feeling parched. "Air. I need fresh air." Since her move from the house in Massapequa to smaller quarters in Queens, her restlessness multiplied. She'd been shut in for the entire weekend. Her back was stiff from five sleepless nights in a row on the living room couch—or was it six? She rolled off the couch onto her feet and shuffled to the window, peeking out from the edge of the dark curtain.

She shed her pajamas like a layer of skin and slipped her fragile body into the gray sweat suit she had worn the day before. She went back to the window which dared her to lift its shade. She gently pulled the cord. It was stuck. She yanked harder, springing the shade into action, the sun spontaneously bursting into her squinty face. Covering her eyes with the back of one hand, she tried to open the window to let in some air.

"Doesn't anything work anymore?" She pounded at the wood base with both hands. "Damn!" she said, breaking a nail. She chewed at the ragged edge of her fingernail and spit it onto the floor next to the opened envelope that had put her in such a state. This was the *only* one of Angela's envelopes she had the nerve to open. And it would be the *last*, she decided, after reading the crushing words that weren't meant for her to read:

"I've got to tell you, Angela," the letter said, "After spending a day in boot camp, I admit it's still not as bad as spending a day with my mother…"

Sylvie stuffed Michael's letter addressed to Angela back into its holder, a tear slipping out of the corner of her eye.

Despite her pigeon-toed stride, Sylvie walked fast. She needed to clear her head, not simply stroll. Maybe she'd figure out what to do about the letters, but every time she thought of that girl and her son together, she'd think about her own past, and cringe. Sylvie couldn't let Angela hurt Michael the way Samuel had hurt her.

A co-worker had once told her to butt out of her son's life because she obsessed too much over him. *No such thing...I'm a good mother, that's all,* she thought, breathing in the fresh air, while commending herself.

She was distracted by the noisy chatter of a nearby bird. Mid-step, she came to a halt and, pointed her face up at the mighty oak. A blue jay perched on a branch pecked at a sparrow's nest. She had heard about blue jays. They're the nasty birds, the kind that eat other birds' young. Sylvie studied its white crest and blue feathers on its back. So exact. Like a uniform.

"Stop that chirping now! Do you hear me? Before I climb this tree and pull your feathers out, one by one."

A little girl stopped to stare at Sylvie talking to a tree. Sylvie didn't see the girl's inquisitive freckled face at all—she stared at the child's fancy bicycle with the tasseled handles. Fancy, yes, but certainly not a *Gazelle* bike—the one she had in Holland, personally measured by the factory owner to fit her body.

She came out from behind the tree, and watched the bike's wheels as they rolled down the sidewalk, and turned the corner, disappearing behind St. Rose of Lima, the Catholic Church.

Sylvie walked closer to the church, tucking her hair behind one ear, to better see a gathering of people making their way out of the arched double-front doors. They were soon followed by a bride and groom in a shower of rice as they descended the front steps. One big sanctimonious Christian family—she growled at the sight.

Ah, they're told to marry their own kind, just like the Jews.

Hadn't she survived the Holocaust for one reason? To pass the experience down to her Jewish children, who would in turn pass the same down to their own children? Jews had to stay with other Jews so they wouldn't become powerless. That's what made the tragedy possible in the first place.

Her father's *forever* words always came back to her, "Have attitude in your posture, as if you accept *who* you are."

The bridal party lined up with their tacky carnation bouquets. She wished she could blink and turn them into the abundance of flowers she knew in *her* country. Even in the early winter, their backyard garden was filled with bold amaryllis along slated paths of ivy, where shy sculptures peeked out behind the bushes.

Was her imagination coming into play or, did she in reality, go to church once with one of her Catholic friends? Sylvie paused to think. *Yes, yes, her name was Sofie. She came from a warm, loving family.* Sylvie didn't realize she was smiling at the memory. *It was Christmas time. And then after church we came back to my house . . . Those were good days, when there was actually dancing in the house, especially, on December the 5th, St. Nicholas Eve.*

Years later, and it seemed surreal—not so much the legend of St. Nick, but the idea that people of *all* faiths used to celebrate the euphoria of the season together in her home. There was such joy and laughter. People greeted one another with three kisses on the cheeks.

She was envious of her non-Jewish friends when St. Nick came by boat from Spain, dressed superbly in his long red robe on his white horse riding down the streets. He went to each home where the children left wooden shoes on the hearth of the fireplace. Down the chimney he came, filling the shoes with many presents.

Sylvie turned around and started walking back home when she saw something move on the sidewalk before her. "What on earth?" She looked down at a baby bird. "Oh no, that damn blue jay pushed you out of your nest!" She looked up at the tree.

"Where's your mother? Guess you need me to give you a hand, don't you? That's all I can give you, I have no wings, you know."

She gently picked up the sparrow and found it to be as light and delicate as the eggshell it came in. In her bare hands, Sylvie enjoyed its warmth and the pleasant cadence of its heartbeat, and raced to take it to her home. Before she entered the apartment building, she found a clean shoebox on top of someone's trash can and placed the bird inside. Then she filled it with grass and twigs. She listened to its faint tweets, studying its face. "You are kind of cute. Are you a boy bird or a girl bird?"

The bird remained silent, opening its beak with its eyes closed.

"What's the matter, cat got your tongue?"

The bird chirped, stretching its neck closer to her voice.

"I'm sorry. That was a bad joke. I bet you're hungry, aren't you? Hmmm. Well, I have some nice chocolate truffles, would you like some? No, I didn't think so. Hold on, and I'll be right back."

She remembered all the worms Michael used to dig up as a kid. But that was in the suburbs where it was easier to find dirt. Even though the idea repulsed her, she went for a spoon in the kitchen drawer and headed out the door in a hurry, looking for the darkest, richest soil.

"Oh, this is so disgusting," she said out loud, hoping no one would see her behind the complex, as she scooped up the fat little squirmers and cut them into smaller pieces with a stick. She turned her face in the other direction. "Uggh!"

She returned to her apartment, her face streaked with some mud and called out to her new little friend. "It's okay, I'm back. I'm coming, Chirpy. I hope you don't mind if I call you that."

She looked down inside the box. The bird didn't look good. It wouldn't eat the worms no matter how hard Sylvie tried to get them down its unyielding throat. "Oh no, don't tell me. Are you sick? Do you have a temperature?" She rested her pinky finger on its little head. "You are feeling rather warm. What am I going to do with you?

"I know! Dr. Stern. Of course, the doctor will help."

The doctor, a retired podiatrist, lived about a dozen or so doors away; she would go to him. Sylvie cried the entire time while running with the box to the old doctor's apartment. "Please, don't die on me, Chirpy, please don't die."

Dr. Stern opened the door to her incessant banging. He had no choice but to quickly come out of retirement when he saw the look on Sylvie's face.

At least Chirpy wouldn't have to worry too much about survival in his short life.

Sylvie's foot was heavy on the gas pedal as she drove all the way from Rockaway back to her hometown Massapequa. The satchel of Angela's letters tied in the lavender ribbon was on the passenger seat next to her. Her glossy black Lincoln Continental allowed her to own the road. She surged forward, while reapplying her Power Red lipstick in the rearview mirror—its main function was for her makeup. She ignored the occasional toot or honk of a horn, until she heard a long blast and hit the brakes. She looked back at the street sign—South Bay Avenue and attempted going in reverse.

A gruff man ten years her senior in a plumbing truck, blasted his horn and rolled down his window. "Hey, you wanna get yourself killed? What the hell are you doing stopping short in the middle of the-road? Where'd you get your license, Sears Roebuck?"

"Mister, where's South Bay . . . Lane? I think it's Lane." She was holding her map flopping in mid-air, rotating it to the street guide, and tilting her head this way and that.

"Whaaat? You kiddin' me, lady? Now you want directions? You want me to tell you where to go? I'll tell you where to go, all right..."

Sylvie couldn't hear what else he said as he left the scene. She pulled the car to the curb and put it into park. She slid out of the driver's seat and walked along the cracked sidewalk, trying to avoid stepping on the ants, especially the little ones.

"Hmm...I think the street ends here. Could it be South Bay Street? Unless it's South Bay Drive?"

She knocked on the front door of a house with fake geraniums in the window boxes. The elderly woman opened the door a crack. "Are you selling anything?"

"Oh no, please!" Sylvie said, thinking of her ex. "Please give me a minute of your time."

"Well, okay then." The woman opened the door all the way, and Sylvie did her best to ignore her white cotton anklets and lime-green polka-dot housecoat, playing the part of private investigator with her inquiry about a girl named Angela.

"Angela? I think I know who you're looking for," the frumpy woman said, scratching the roughness on her elbow. "From the Martino house?"

In a flash, it came back to Sylvie—the night she had met Angela and asked her her last name.

"Yes, that's the one." Sylvie smiled.

"Oh, if it's *who* I think it is, they've been living here maybe twenty years now. Maybe more. They moved here from Brooklyn. Such a shame, you know, with the family tragedy 'n all."

"Tragedy?"

The woman narrowed her eyes at Sylvie and stuffed a soiled tissue into the pocket of her housecoat. "Ahhh, my memory— you know, it's not what it used to be."

"You were saying...the tragedy?"

"Something happened to the first child. I can't remember

the details, exactly—that poor woman, Jean, or is it Joan, was ready to give birth to her second child, what's her name? Oh yeah, Angela, sweet thing. I think she's living in France now. No, no, it's Germany."

Germany? Sylvie felt her neck get hot.

"Anyway, I heard the mother was in a bad way after the incident. I can understand, since my husband passed last year—"

"So, which street do I turn down?" Sylvie rushed her.

The woman pointed to the street before she closed the door.

Sylvie stopped dead at the garbage pail sitting at the curb in front of the woman's house, where she retrieved an empty juice bottle and looked back at the artificial geraniums decorating the frumpy woman's house. Without hesitation, Sylvie made a quick detour to a neighboring garden, plucked a variety of fresh flowers, hydrangea, day lilies, and roses, and arranged a lovely bouquet in the bottle, which she left on the woman's doorstep.

"Yes, you've been extremely helpful," Sylvie said to the closed door.

She muttered to herself as she opened the car door on the driver's side. "I knew all along there was something funny about that girl. I'm sure she never even told Michael about this so-called tragedy. She's probably withheld many things from my son, which means she's been deceiving him all along. She's a hypocrite, a liar and a—"

Sylvie didn't know where her anger was coming from. She revved the engine, and made a U-turn without looking over her shoulder and headed further south toward the water. She slowed as the numbers got higher...67, 69, 71, ahhh...73."

She stopped the Lincoln across from the yellow-shingled Cape Cod and stared at the empty mail basket with hand-painted flowers that hung from a stainless steel nail. Sylvie sat in her car for a long time in front of the plain house with the handmade dotted-Swiss curtains that hung in the bay window.

Just like I thought—plain people.

A rusty-bottomed Dodge sat in the driveway. Nothing satisfied her curiosity. Nobody came out, and nobody went in. Sylvie got bored quickly, but then she had an idea. The letters remained on the seat next to her. *This will have to wait a little longer,* she thought, and pulled away with an ashy flicker in her eyes.

Sylvie followed a stern-looking librarian to a cozy spot in the reference room. "What did you say it's called?"

"Microfiche," the librarian answered with her finger to her lips, reminding Sylvie where she was.

Just as the lady in the housecoat remembered, the article was dated May of 1950, the same year Angela was born. Sylvie used to read the *Massapequa Post* on a regular basis, but she purposely stayed away from the obituary section.

She carefully followed the words on the blurry microfiche with her finger:

In a tragic accident on Thursday, May 25, 1950, Seven-year-old Anna Martino, the only daughter of Anthony and Jean Martino of 73 South Bay Road, Massapequa had been wading at the shore while her expectant mother watched. When a current swiftly carried her out to sea, Mrs. Martino, who does not swim, screamed for help. Lifeguards at Jones Beach had gone off duty at 5 p.m. that day.

Quickly, some good Samaritans rushed into the surf to rescue the fair-haired girl.

"The water was rough," Ryan Gunderson, 46, one of the would-be rescuers said. "The waves were messy. I had

such a bad feeling. I couldn't believe how the water pulled
me, and I'm 6'3" and a strong swimmer."

Another man, Andrew Grady, reached the girl at the
same time as Gunderson, about 40 yards from shore. "She
was like a rag doll," Mr. Grady said later. Mr. Gunderson
placed an arm under her body towing her to shore, while
Grady buoyed the two up, when the current pulled Mr.
Gunderson and the girl under.

When the two men made it to shore, Grady, an off-
duty firefighter, immediately began mouth to mouth resus-
citation while Gunderson restrained the distraught Mrs.
Martino. "With every breath, I thought of my own kid," Mr.
Grady said.

When efforts at the beach were not successful, the two
men carried Anna and helped Mrs. Martino to Mr. Grady's
Plymouth, as the police arrived. At Massapequa General
Hospital, Dr. Donald Serpe pronounced Anna dead of
asphyxiation at 6:06 p.m.

After the last word, Sylvie stared at the poster on the wall
across from the microfiche machine. The words on the poster
posed a question to parents in bold colorful lettering: "Did you
read a bedtime story to your child last night?" Sylvie wished
she could go back to the days when she could sit with Michael
on her lap reading him his favorite book. *What was the name of*
that book he loved?

"Excuse me, librarian, how do you turn this thing off?"

A woman who had been sitting nearby the entire time
engrossed in her thick book, looked up with a scowl. She
looked directly at Sylvie. "Shhh."

"Oh, shush yourself!" Sylvie said. Her skin heated up around
her neck and ears. She was angry about the drowning. Could
these be pangs of pity? *There's no comparison. I lost family, friends*

and neighbors. Cousins and aunts and uncles…I lost so many—
what did she lose? One life—that's all—she only lost one life!

Sylvie's mind turned to when she and 24 others had boarded the boat. As soon as they had walked the crude gangplank, the smell of bait made her feel trapped. They sailed away promptly on the rocking vessel, afloat in an endless ocean packed like itsy-bitsy gray fish in a tin can. Gray fishes with eyes frozen open, floundering on deck, all scarred in some way. Fishes without color. And to Sylvie, who had once so adored the spectrum of colors on the walls of her father's world, believed this was the end.

The weather was vile, and people became seasick with the first wave. It was heart wrenching to watch an elderly couple who had made it as far as the escape boat, curl up in each other's arms, near death. Many of those who came on board along with their group of 25 had suffered more hardships than the Rosenbergs, and the frail eventually succumbed to dysentery or typhus.

Sylvie met up with some of her older cousins on the ship who came from other locations in Europe: Alma and Abraham, Hertog and Jeffrey, Emanuel and Vogeltje—who still looked clean and wore fine clothing. The sight of them comforted her eyes. She would focus on them and not concern herself with the others. The others were all one and the same—each with lackluster expressions—such a contrast to the rosy complexions in those old portraits Papa owned. These were cheeks of simple dread and desperation. They did not exist. If they did, she would become one of them.

On the second day out, a young woman, perhaps in her early 20's, stood on the upper deck and locked eyes with Sylvie's, right before she boosted herself up with tattered shoes onto the pitted iron railing. Without a sound, the woman was gone. Had the woman thrown herself overboard? Maybe Sylvie had imagined the whole thing. *Was she ever actually there? Was the woman really* gone?

Sylvie pointed and tried to scream. What came out of her sounded like the cry of a sick seal. "What is it, young lady?" the deck hand asked. He ran to the railing. He could only see white caps below, splashing the dark water like a fan brush.

The whistle sounded, and Sylvie covered her ears. Someone yanked her by the collar and pulled her away from the commotion. It was her Uncle Bey, the one who swallowed diamonds right before he joined them at the train station when the situation had become lethal and the Nazis stormed and looted homes. Sylvie's mother never could have swallowed all *her* jewelry; she left the gems buried in the backyard, three feet south of her favorite rose bush.

Throughout the duration of their voyage, whenever Sylvie pictured the drowned woman's hollow expression under the water, eyes unblinking, her scuffed shoes no longer kicking, Sylvie would clutch the railing, fighting the queasiness.

Who was she? Her mental picture nagged at Sylvie. For days after, she would ask the crew several times, "Have you figured out who the woman is? I mean, was?"

"She's the woman with no name. One of many," the deck boy answered, "that's who she is." Sylvie felt a flutter in her chest wash over her as she ran from his words. Still gripping the railing, she heaved over the side of the boat, thinking she'd spit up her guts. Why did it bother her so much? She didn't personally know the lady. She was one of so many . . . one life.

Like Angela's sister.

The boat, sailing further and further away from home, is what truly made her sick, she guessed. They had reached the point of no return. The air over the land behind them, smelled like death, and the air over the sea before them smelled like sorrow.

TWELVE

MASSAPEQUA, NEW YORK
1969

Typically, Angela's mother didn't raise her voice. It had been much worse than that. It was a Sunday morning when Angela had set the breakfast table to soften things up about not going to church again. Her mother flipped the griddle cakes as only she could do and served her husband and daughter without saying a word.

"Mmm, Mom, these are dee-licious."

"You're not trying to butter me up for missing mass again, are you?" Her mother handed her husband the jug of maple syrup and gave Angela one of *those* looks. Angela rolled her eyes and stuffed her mouth with a forkful of blueberry pancakes, so she wouldn't have to answer.

Her father over-poured the syrup and put the jug back on the table with a thud.

Angela tried to think quickly of something of interest to change the subject. "Oh yeah," she said, absentmindedly, "Guess what? I forgot to tell you, I met this really cool guy on the beach, and he wants me to come see him soon . . . his name is Michael Beckman."

Silence. She could hear her mother blink, her father swallow.

Angela looked at her parents, totally perplexed. Her dad made a face, and her mom looked solemn. "What's wrong?"

"He's Jewish?" her mother said as her face paled.

"Jewish?" Angela asked, confused. "I dunno. Who cares? We talked forever about surfing, traveling and—so what if he *is* Jewish?"

"Umm, I'll clear the dishes," her dad said, standing up, pushing the chair out with the back of his knees.

"Oh, there's nothing wrong with being Jewish, of course. And there's nothing wrong with being Catholic. If you still *are* one, that is. What are you not telling us, Angela? Are you and this boy serious? Is that why you stopped going to mass? Because the church doesn't accept another religion when you marry—"

"Marry?" I hardly know—he's practically a total stranger. Mom, think about what the church is doing, what *you're* doing..."

Come to think of it, there was a chain Michael wore around his neck. A Jewish star? She was sure of it now, but the ornament held no meaning at the time. She had only noticed the softness of the sand between her toes...and the softness in his eyes.

Angela pushed aside her plate and rushed from the kitchen table, nearly taking the tablecloth with her. She flew up the staircase and slammed her bedroom door, deciding it wasn't loud enough and slammed the door a second time. The picture of the Hawaiian Pipeline above her headboard, shuddered. She could almost hear the wave roar through the framed glass—the same wave that had replaced the picture her mother had once hung there of The Last Supper or some other meeting of saints that used to teeter over her pubescent head.

Damn her! She's such a holy hypocrite. She lives by the bible, but she's afraid of living, afraid of everything, even afraid of people like Michael. Why can't she show her anger when it matters? Like with her elitist boss.

Angela hated the way her mother kept her head down,

especially around Mrs. Ross, who talked *at* her, not to her.
Over the past year, the same scene was repeated between her
mother and "Ross, the Boss:"

"B-ut, Friday?" Mrs. Martino would stutter. "Can't the curtains wait until Saturday?"

"Oh no, I'm afraid not. My clients, notably important people, are coming on Saturday. So, I can count on you, of course?"

"Of course," her mother would answer.

Mrs. Ross had grabbed her tennis racquet and brushed
past Angela. She gave her a wink and Angela stiffened. At that
moment, she had to wonder. If she were in her mother's shoes,
would she have had the nerve to stand up to the woman?

*Oh my God, I have to get out of here before I am in the same
shoes!* Angela thought.

Her mother was always hunched over the sewing machine
behind an Everest of work...calloused fingers from years of
puncturing herself with sewing needles, an endless humility
that sickened Angela. She threw herself across the bed and
looked at her four walls. The giant poster of the Beach Boys—
the three brothers, Brian, Carl and Dennis Wilson, cousin
Mike Love, and Al Jardine, whispering about a world inside a
room filled with secrets.

Their voices got louder inside her head. Angela reached
over the side of her bed to pick up one of her sandals and threw
it at their unbroken expressions. She had to get out of this
room. Out of this house. Out of this town.

The sun's rays shimmered as they filtered through the fine lace
of the ecru drapes. Through the mirrored armoire's reflection,
Angela watched the sculpted shadows playing across her cheek.

She pushed the white eyelet blanket off the bed with her feet in one long stretch and forced herself to rise. Barely reaching the phone, she toppled the base to the floor, with a ding and a thud, quickly yanking the cord upward, not to wake her parents.

She murmured, looking at the clock. "Ugh! It's 6:45."

One eye flashed wide open and the other remained locked closed by sleep, as she dialed Katie's number with the tip of one fingernail. "You ready?"

Katie moaned into the receiver. "What? Ready for what? That depends. If I have to go to work today, then I *ain't* ready." Since they had graduated, Katie worked four days a week at the Farmer's Market, saving money before heading off to an out-of-state college.

"It's your day off, you goon. And ain't ain't a word."

"Oh. Then I'm ready. Where we going?" Katie yawned.

"To the beach, remember? You're borrowing your dad's car?"

"You mean the woodie?"

"I mean the station wagon, but if you want to call it a woodie..."

Angela was still scrutinizing the dings on her board, when her friend pulled up to the curb in a jolting screech. She stuck her board in the back of the *woodie* and hopped into the passenger seat when Katie hit her instantly with "surf lingo."

"Katie, why are you talking like that?"

"Why? 'Cause I was a Girl Scout once, and we have to be prepared."

"Prepared for what?"

"You know, all those cool surfer dudes down at Gilgo Beach. We have to know the terms before we can *talk* to those guys. Or else they'll think we're a couple of ho-dads."

"A couple of what?"

"You know, 'anti-surfer types.'"

Angela took out her hairbrush and brushed her hair in long strokes. "Katie, I want to *surf*, that's all."

"Oh yeah, then why does your hair look so perfect today? You've been ironing it again, right? Anyway, I've been studying, so listen to this: 'Hey, why don'tcha grab your big gun and we can go hit the surf down by the jetties, 'cause I hear there's a lot of hot doggin' where there's some real heavies, and we can shoot the tube—"

"Uh, Katie, you're kidding, aren't you? You didn't even *study* for your high school finals."

"Yeah, I know," Katie smiled devilishly, smacking her gum. "Priorities, Angie, baby. But wait, there's more—we can do a couple of spinners, walk the nose, fer sure, and if they turn into crunchers, we can always back down or cut out—"

"Stop! It sounds ridiculous! Maybe you should concentrate on the sport."

As they drove over the Robert Moses Bridge, Angela could hear the *silence* of the beach—what had always lured her there to begin with, but whenever she was with Katie and they belted out songs of their favorite record albums, she could practically break the sound barrier purely from the joy.

They circled the Jones Beach Tower and headed east until they rolled into a parking spot. The two girls clumsily maneuvered their boards out of the wagon, carrying all their beach gear, trying to look natural and cool.

"Watch me. You carry it under your arm, like this," Katie demonstrated.

"No, I can't. My arms are too short, or the board's too wide."

Angela squeezed her beach towel between her knees and held her beach bag by her teeth, until she balanced the board on top of her head. As they meandered their way barefoot over the dunes, concentrating on where to step, they reached the top in synchronized awe. Angela looked at the shapes of the clouds, meditatively. She shook the image out of her head, dropping her load to the ground. "Oh, man," Angela breathed in a subdued voice. "Will you check that out?"

"Yeah," Katie agreed. "They're gorgeous!"

"What are *you* looking at?"

"Those guys surfing, what else?"

"Not them. I mean the waves. Aren't you excited? I mean, *stoked?*"

"You're so into *Mikey boy,* lately," she said in high-pitched mocking. Then she perked up. "Guess I'm on my own. Maybe I can get one of them to teach me how to surf."

"Surfers are interested in *one* thing—catching a wave," Angela said.

"You do have sugar water in your veins, girl."

They grabbed the corners of the beach blanket and parachuted it onto the sand. Katie pulled off her T-shirt and stood there posing in her hot pink two-piece, swinging her dark hair against her pale skin. "Ooh, it worked. I think one of them is coming out of the water. Yes, he is. He's coming this way—Oh my God, look at those deltoids!"

"Looks like you really *have* been studying your vocabulary." Angela pursed her lips.

"I can't believe it. He's trying to get our attention. Look, he's smiling at us, and waving. Act cool," she said dropping to her knees, nonchalantly waxing her surfboard on the *wrong* side as he walked past them and straight to a suntanned girl coming over the dunes in a miniscule, skin-color crochet bikini. "And I thought *my* bathing suit was skimpy," Katie complained.

Angela walked toward the water, dragging her board,

leaving Katie standing behind with her mouth still open. "Hmmpf! I bet she can't even *surf.*"

"She doesn't have to. Hey, wait up!" Katie shouted after her.

The girls straddled their boards for a long time, trying to catch one wave after another. "This is so hard. We'll be lucky if we get one good wave out of a hundred," Katie griped, drifting further away on her *Bunger.*

"Yeah, I know. That's what makes that wave so special. It's such a rush!"

"You think we actually *look* like surfer girls?" Katie furrowed her brow.

Angela didn't answer, lying patiently on her board, waiting for the right moment to paddle and become one with the water as each swell lifted her body into weightless exhilaration. When they were exhausted enough, they both got out of the water and headed back toward their beach blanket.

"Ummm, Ange, something's happening to your hair, uh, something un-surfer like!"

"My hair?" Angela felt her smooth curls, frizzing up. "Oh, no. Not that!"

"What's the matter? Didn't you bring your *iron?*" Katie chided.

Angela dropped her board on the spot and chased Katie down the shoreline until they were out of breath, laughing hysterically, finally plopping themselves down onto the blanket. Even though the temperature was a mere 75 degrees, they applied another coat of suntan oil on their legs.

The transistor radio played "Paint it Black," by the Stones, and of course, they'd memorized *every* last word and sang along—about girls dressed in their summer clothes.

"It doesn't get better than this," one said to the other, playing imaginary drums with her knuckles.

"Hey, look what's still in my bag—the paint marker." Katie

crawled up to Angela, who was lying on her back with closed eyes and, without asking, started drawing a flower on Angela's face. "You must be so psyched about going to work for the airlines, heh?"

"Yeah. I can't wait." She didn't mention any of her misgivings. "Hey, don't paint a clown face on me, whatever you do," she warned, behind closed eyes.

"Don't you trust me by now? We've only been blood sisters since we're what, nine?"

That's what Angela loved about Katie. She knew her better than anyone else. They could read almost all of each other's thoughts. *Almost.*

"I never noticed. Does he have a big nose?"

"Who?"

"Michael," Katie said. Angela gave her a look. "Not as big as your *mouth*! Why'd you ask, because he's Jewish?"

"I'm kidding. You should know that. My old man kids that way. You know, about people in Massapequa—or should I say *Matzoh-Pizza*—home of the Italians and Jews."

"Amazing, isn't it? That people have such misconceptions and all stick to their own kind." Angela shielded her eyes from the sunshine, pointing her chin upward. "Ow! Don't press so hard."

"They *just* put a man on the moon, and they can't get these markers to...there, there it goes. Is that better?" Katie eased up on the pressure.

"Anyway, I suppose everyone hides some prejudice," Angela said wistfully. "You know, there's *something* about Michael's eyes. I was aware of it the minute I met him. Maybe it's because of what I read in *Anne Frank* that I'll never forget. When Anne Frank looked at Peter's face, she said she could see how lonely he was. I was about Anne's age when I read the book. I mean, what she did with the *time* she had left...her ending was kind of, you know, fulfilling, don't you think?"

"Angela, are you falling in love? Talk about bad timing, huh? Just when you want to go away. Where's that free spirit in you? Before you know it, we'll be middle-aged and grow warts and all sorts of ugly stuff." Katie blew the loose strands of hair out of her eyes and examined her artwork.

"I don't know. I've been thinking a lot about *life* lately," Angela continued. "Seriously, don't you ever worry about the future? Vietnam is so scary. A lot of boys we've graduated with ended up there. I'm so glad Michael's got a high draft number."

"Yeah," Katie concurred. "Did ya hear Danny Meyer's brother is over there right now?" Katie pressed harder still on Angela's cheek.

Angela sat up. "Society's changing. Remember when we had to read *1984* in Sophomore English? The whole human race at the end of the 20th century is supposed to become dehumanized—soul-less."

Katie pushed her back down so she could draw a peace sign on Angela's other cheek.

"Ouch! Easy! Miss O'Brien said, 'Man will destroy each other or die out of sheer boredom.' We'll lose our individuality, become like, like machines."

"Does this have anything to do with you not going to church anymore?"

"I don't know. Maybe. I wanna think for myself. As much as I care about Michael, I'm ready to leave. I'm so sick and tired of being treated like a child at home, so tired of waiting for life to begin."

"I'm going to miss you. I hope you and I never lose touch." Katie tapped her heart with her closed fist.

Angela mimicked her with teary eyes. "Never."

"Hey, I'm starved. How about you?"

Angela nodded. "Ready to split?"

"Burgers at *All American?* I can almost smell them sizzling."

"Mmm...and those crispy fries." Angela's tongue slid across her lips.

Katie put her arm over Angela's shoulder. "Can't figure our lives out on an empty stomach now, can we?"

THIRTEEN

MASSAPEQUA, NEW YORK
1969

Angela and Michael were inseparable all summer, refusing to believe their romance was coming to an end; they spent one of their last days together on the lawn of the Massapequa Town Park, trying their hardest to pretend it wasn't true.

"Hey, look what's in my pocket," Angela said, while lying on her stomach with the back of Michael's head on her backside.

"What's that?" Michael responded, sleepily.

"My ticket to Woodstock." She unfolded it. "I wore these jeans there. They went through the wash. But, you can still read what it says." She examined the red letters: Woodstock Music and Art Fair. Friday, August 15, 1969. 10:00 A.M. $8.00. Good For One Admission Only. No Refunds. Ticket #02009."

"Mine's tucked safely in the back of my sock drawer," he said with closed eyes and let out a laugh. "That was certainly a memorable weekend. I think it was the funniest thing ever when you smoked your first joint."

"Shut up!" She smiled widely.

Michael opened his eyes, sat up and turned to face her. "Especially when I asked you where the "roach" went to, and you screamed your bloody head off."

"All right. Ha Ha. I thought—" She laughed at herself.

"I know what you *thought*," he teased. "Smokin' pot's not your thing."

She gave him a look as he settled down again.

"We had a great summer, didn't we, Ange?"

"Summer's a bummer when it's over," she responded dreamily.

They both turned quiet, their smiles lingering. Angela kicked her feet back and forth in scissor motion. Michael moved and snuggled up to her side, still lying on his back, looking up at the veil of clouds. "What were you thinking about?" she asked him.

"I was trying not to *think* at all," he said.

"I know what you mean."

"What about you?" he asked.

"Well, I was thinking about how you used to tell me my hair smells like honeysuckle."

He leaned in and grabbed a piece of her hair. "Hmm . . . still does."

She beamed.

He looked around them. "I was wondering how they get the grass to look so green at the park."

"And the sky so blue. Look at the shapes of the clouds . . . see the one with the wings?" She let the words slip out.

He squinted at the cloud. "Yeah. Yeah, I do."

And she believed him. Someday she would tell Michael about her dead sister but, not quite yet. It was the first time she understood why her parents had waited to tell her. She could see Michael's eyes getting heavy, like the sinkers she'd cast out on the end of her fishing line.

The easy days of summer were moving further away, and life was changing. Summer days like when she was a kid and simple things meant so much . . . the crinkling sound of the wrapper when she opened her favorite piece of salt water taffy, cherry red; the sight of the grandma she could hardly remember, stirring a big pot of something yummy for their Sunday dinners in the screened-in porch; or the picnics at the park every Fourth of July where mothers pushed their children on the rope swings.

Michael pressed his closed eyes with his thumbs, which meant he was having another one of his headaches. He'd told her that lately he'd been getting a lot of grief from his mom. Angela surmised it was because of dating her. His mother could get intense at times over the Jewish-Catholic thing. Over her being "different." He'd rationalized that soon their lives would divide, anyway, and that Angela would leave to start her career in the air. They didn't want to talk about separating, so they avoided it. His dreamy head lay beside her on the lawn as she twirled a blade of grass between her fingers. Angela observed how the varying greens of the lawn blended together so beautifully around Michael, as he slept.

Each blade of grass comes from different roots. Life should be that simple.

Angela thought that lately her mother seemed a bit more relaxed on the interfaith topic, but she wished her mother could realize who she was now—no longer the scrawny neighborhood tomboy, who wore smudges on her face like first place ribbons. She wished her mother could see how she'd grown into someone who could make the right choices for herself. She wished her mother could see into her *heart*... how good Michael was for her.

Michael's mother was a different story, however, a more complicated one.

Angela wondered when life had become so perplexing... she missed simplicity: She was about eight or nine when she had sprawled her small body out on the sidewalk in front of her house, just watching the ants go in and out of the cracks in

the cement. There was always one ant that seemed more confused than the other ants, moved faster and more erratically in
circles, joining them and then going off in its own direction.
She picked the insect up and let it crawl between her fingers
and around her hand, tickling her. After she had risen to her
knees, she brushed off the loose pebbles stuck to her elbows
and carefully tiptoed, not to step on any of "the little people" as
she liked to call them. The ants made her feel like a God.

A gust of wind picked up, and Michael stirred in his sleep,
his cheek now on Angela's lap. She thought of one breezeless
summer night when she and Michael sat talking for a long time
in the backseat of his camper. All the windows were cranked
fully down, and the air was as thick as a jar of *Hellmann's*. The
flimsy straps on her sundress had fallen from her shoulders in
the stillness.

"Your skin is on fire tonight," he told her, his lips lightly
brushing her hot cheek. She could tell by the look he gave
her that he was ready for her—it was the same night he had
called her Angel Face, for the first time. She'd fanned herself.
She never had such an intense craving before, certainly not the
craving of an *angel*. Angela replaced the strap back onto her
shoulder. She wasn't ready then.

Am I ready now? She didn't want to regret making either
choice.

They left the park when the sky dimmed, and they could
hardly see one another.

Summer wasn't officially over, and there were still a few cars in
The Beach Club lot when Angela arrived. She tapped her steering wheel to an imaginary beat. "Where *is* he?"

She played with the lavender ribbon and inhaled the scent

of lilac writing paper on the passenger seat which she planned to give Michael on their last night together.

Her thoughts back to their first date had always given her the chills: he'd borrowed his mother's '61 Corvette, leaving her oversized Lincoln in the garage. She remembered how the gravel here was spinning under the car's wheels as the Corvette made its way through the two columns of The Beach Club's entrance, and she knew it was too late to turn around. "I've gotta tell you," she hesitated. "I don't know how to dance very well."

She appeared daintier, prettier, in her peasant blouse fastened with so many intricate buttons that her mother had patiently sewn.

He led her into the prominent stucco building. "Well, we make a good couple then, because I'm not such a great dancer either." He took her hand and they went into the courtyard on the bay side where there was a crowd of her friends, and she immediately introduced them to Michael.

Katie was dancing with a lanky guy Angela had never seen before and, when Michael's back was to her, Katie looked Michael up and down and dropped her jaw. She shook her hand in the air, "*Mama Mia.*"

Angela mouthed for her to shut up.

Despite being non-dancers, they danced the entire night, doing the Jerk, the Mashed Potatoes, and Angela's favorite, "The Stroll," when the guys and the girls form two lines, facing each other. Then the couple at the top of the line strolls down between the lines, a kind of hobbling step done with feet alternating behind each other, until everyone goes.

After a short break, the band tuned-up and played a slow song. Michael put his arms around her. Angela talked into his ear above the music. "My friends are staring at us."

He'd pulled her closer to him. "I can see that. I told you we make a good couple."

She loved the way he kept his eyes on her the rest of the night.

Angela grabbed the going-away gift meant for Michael and hopped out of the car. Leaning up against the door, she put her Timex to her ear and flicked the face. *Still ticking.* They hadn't seen each other for a couple of days because she had to pack and get ready to travel for her new job. *Hmmm. The last night we'll be together, and he's late.*

She sighed as his van came racing around the corner. He got out of the van short-winded and ran up to her. "Oh man, sorry. Sorry I'm late"

"Are you okay?" she asked, handing him the box of stationery without any explanation.

"Yeah. Yeah, I'm okay, but I have something to tell you that I've been putting off for a few days now—"

"What—what's the matter? Have you been drink—"

"Ange, I uh, uh, I enlisted in the army."

"You *what*? Stop kidding. That's not funny! That's not one damn bit funny!"

"Angela, don't ask me why." He grabbed her arm, and she shook him off. "I don't know why. I-I had a fight with my mother. You know. It was a bad one. I stormed out of the house, went drinking with the guys, had a wicked hangover, and I went down to . . . ."

Angela stared for a second, her eyes spilling over, the tears running into her mouth. She buried her face against his left shoulder, pounded her fist into his right shoulder. "You son of a bitch. You son of a bi—"

"Angela, I'm sorry." He let out a deep moan, a hurt dog. "Believe me. I wish I hadn't—the minute I—Oh, Jesus, what a mistake!"

She had never seen a guy cry.

Angela lowered her head and placed her hands on her knees, gasping as if her oxygen supply was suddenly cut off. There they were like the two lightning bugs she once kept safe in a jar, dancing around each other in flight like the night of the dance, the first time their bodies had orbited each other under the moonlight. They held their breath much like the two fireflies. Only someone had forgotten to punch holes in the lid.

"Ange? Angela, are you okay? Take a breath."

"I won't leave tomorrow," she said pointedly.

"Don't be ridiculous. You've been fantasizing about this since—since forever."

"I can stay for a while. I can help you get out of this mess."

"Angela, that's absurd. This *mess* is the United States Army we're talking about. Not the Boy Scouts." He must have realized the impact of his news and shifted his tone, his voice deepening. "It's too late. Don't be naïve."

"Naïve? You're calling *me* naïve? What you did was plain stupid!" she sobbed.

He raised his voice. "Listen, you're going away, and so am I."

"On the back roads, Route 66—*that* was where you were supposed to go, Michael. How'd this happen? What is this honestly about? An excuse, so you won't have to stand up to your mother? About *us*?"

He turned away. "No. Maybe this is what I *need* to do right now."

"Bullshit! Who *needs* this war? This war is immoral! It's unwinnable!"

"Angela, listen to me. We need to grow up. Our lives are just beginning. You know we have a whole lotta shit to go through in our lives, and now's your chance, Angela, run free. Fly. Maybe forget me for awhile—"

"Forget? Forget?" she hit him in the arm so hard, the box of lavender stationery fell on the ground between them and their two cars. She didn't want to meet the seriousness on his face. She kneeled to pick up the blank sheets of writing paper. "I've got it. Go away, Michael. In fact, go straight to hell. And bring your mother with you!"

He kneeled down next to her and helped her put the paper back neatly into the cardboard box. "Is this for me?" he asked, his voice gentle again.

She didn't answer at first, and then she spoke slowly. "*Was* for you," she said so low, Michael had to lean closer to hear her. "It was for you to write me about rock climbing and hiking trails, and, and shooting the rapids. Not anymore. Don't ever write me. Not ever!"

He looked at her with his sorry face. "Oh, Ange, can I take my gift, anyway? I promise I won't write you, okay?"

She didn't answer him.

"Angela. I want to give *you* something, too." He slipped the chain over his head and folded the jewelry into Angela's hand, patting her fingers closed. His eyes misted over, and then he pulled her body forcefully against his by the small of her back and kissed her hard, not like all the other kisses.

He couldn't shake his anger, thinking of his mother, how she looked when he told her he had joined the Army. The more he looked at Sylvie's large diamond "S" necklace that weighed heavily on her chest, the sharper the tone he had used: "Mom, I told you a hundred times. I joined because I *wanted* to... I'm going into the army. That's it. You can't stop me!"

Before Michael was to meet Angela at The Beach Club, he

had spent the last couple of days driving around alone in Mr. Doobie, smoking pot, listening to the *Grateful Dead*. Until he could convince himself that he'd better make amends with his mother in case anything should ever happen to him. He was always a sucker for her tears and was easily persuaded when she pleaded with him... "Michael, come with me to Vegas for a little bit—just the two of us—a quick get away for a couple of days before you have to report to Boot Camp."

She bawled so hard that the veins in her forehead bulged.

"Aw, mom, not again." He had to shut her up. Her kvetching hurt his ears. "Okay. Okay, Ma, I'll go with you." He knew she was a gambling addict, and once they got there, she'd soon forget he even existed and they'd go off in different directions, stay in different rooms, maybe different hotels for Christ sake, which would be fine with him.

Angela looked at Michael after the long, hard kiss, as if he were someone else. She wavered a moment longer, opened her clenched hand and threw the star onto the ground. She kicked the goodbye memento into the dirt.

When she heard the van door slam, she spun in disbelief and watched as he drove off.

"I hate you! You bastard!" She hopped into her own car and peeled out of the lot in tears. She made it to the corner before she turned the car around with a screech and, sped back to the spot where they had danced under the moonlight, a million moons ago.

She threw open the car door and fell to her knees, feeling in the dark for the chained star. She was hysterical, wiping her tears on her face with her dirty hands. She held the Jewish star in front of the headlight and looked closer, straining to see the numbers on the back—1940.

"It's his mother's," she whispered. "Why would he give me his mother's star? What kind of a goodbye memento is this? What is he trying to say?" She hated him for it, yet lovingly slipped the necklace around her neck.

Angela's packed suitcases were lined up in size order at the front door of 73 South Bay—the only home she had ever known. She wanted to be able to grab them without thinking the next day when the taxi pulled up. She didn't want to think about how scared she really was.

Once in bed, though, that's all she *could* do—think. She lay awake almost the entire night searching the glass eyes of the childhood stuffed toys that lined her shelves. The hundreds of pages she'd taken out of the binder from her airline employee manual to read in bed the night before had become her cover. When the alarm finally rang, its shrill sound made her bolt, and the paper blanket flew off her bed like a fleet of mini-aircraft.

With her jump start, a horse came to mind wearing blinders—they could run, but they couldn't see. *And she's off!* Out of the paddock—she was about to be swept off on a fast track...she heard the horn of the Sunset Taxi cab in front of her house, and she stepped outside, letting the blinders fall off her. A wild mare.

In the cab ride on the Long Island Expressway to JFK, Angela thought about what freedom would really mean to her. She rehashed her relationship with her mother. Her father said her mother couldn't get up to say goodbye; she was knocked out after being up all night, worrying sick, and that she had finally given in to taking a sleeping pill.

Angela was fully cognizant from the start that her mother had dreaded this day for a long time. Besides, they had said their goodbyes the night before. "Tell Mom I'll be fine, and give her a goodbye kiss for me." She dropped her suitcases back down and hugged her father for a full minute.

The cab pulled away from her home, and she rubbed her eyes. *If only things had ended better with Michael,* she thought. Angela could see the cab driver looking at her in the rear view mirror and covered her face, embarrassed that she was unable to hide her emotions. She made herself think of the good times before she'd fall apart right there in the taxi . . . that day in the park together, when they talked about Woodstock.

Funny, how radical we thought we were that day, driving up to Bethel. Then, Michael lost his wallet. The big jerk! She smiled. Aside from the clothes on their backs, they had taken a duffel bag with a pouch full of pot and a few snacks. When they looked at each other, totally free of possessions and burdens that would have weighed them down, they laughed silly until they ran out of gas. They ended up pushing Mr. Doobie into a rundown *ESSO* station where they helplessly read the sign: 34 cents per gallon.

A mangy-looking kid, wearing a perpetual grin and grease under his fingernails, came out to help them.

Lord help him, he only had half his teeth, yet made us the offer.

"Woodstock, huh?" the boy said. "That's gonna be so boss! I hear it's gonna be the event of the century! Joe Cocker, The Dead, Crosby Stills, Nash and Young, The Who . . . sure wish I could go, but I gotta work. It's my Pa's station, and he has no one else to pump. So, I'll tell ya what—I'll trade you some gas for some weed."

"Yeah, okay. I can dig it . . . I think we'll get high enough on the music, don't you, Ange?"

"Hell, yeah." She laughed, getting back into the camper, shaking her hair free from its tie.

When they got to Route 17B, they were hit by a heat wave and a traffic jam. People flew out of their cars and jumped on the front hoods, crawling along bumper to bumper, hoping for a breeze. A sole voice was joined by others in the middle of the highway, chanting lyrics of Credence, Hendrix, and Santana, getting louder as they turned up a dirt road into Max Yasgur's farm. Mr. Doobie bumped along on the sloping property, passing kids who were tearing down fences that closed in the festival grounds. Everyone was going in for free. Once they found a good spot, they pitched a tent. They were ready for the "wildest party on the planet." An old school bus pulled up next to theirs, painted in psychedelic shades of orange, green, and purple. Blankets were being handed out to strangers during the night, among other things, like black hashish.

"Who's that on stage?" Angela asked.

"I don't know," Michael answered. "Some Indian guy playing a sitar..."

"This is too cool," she said, observing others around her dropping acid, and offering her some. "I want to have *some* control. Just a little grass'll do me."

Michael laughed. "You sound like a commercial for *Dippity-do.*" He looked at what was left in his pouch and they lit up. Soon the rain came and never seemed to stop. Angela stood in puddles with other girls wearing long braids and flowers in their hair, dancing barefoot in their granny dresses, turning in dreamy circles.

One group of kids carried a long sign made out of a sheet. "Over 500,000 troops in Vietnam. Bring our boys home!" was written in marker. Other signs said, "Come to a love-in." Another, "Make love, not war," and "Hey, Hey, LBJ, How Many Kids Did You Kill Today?"

There were people everywhere, half a million, and still more trying to get in; they had unprecedented *power*, yet they were all about brotherhood and peace. Through the static of the transistor radios, they listened to the news about the event. Arlo Guthrie officially announced over the microphone, 'Hey, far out man, they just closed down the New York State Thruway.'"

Country Joe and the Fish got up, and almost everyone recited the words in unison, blunt words about war, words asking what they were fighting for... the rain came down harder. There were wall to wall wet blankets covering the ground, not an inch to walk between them in the mud. Everybody seemed to love the whole fiasco.

Saturday, The Dead tried to perform in the torrential downpour, but they were having so much difficulty, they couldn't pull it off. It rained more on Sunday afternoon, and the concert came to an abrupt stop. A bunch of people were throwing their naked bodies in the mud. The craziness continued, and nothing seemed to faze anyone.

Grace Slick woke them up the next morning at 7 a.m. when she yelled, "Good morning, people!" She started singing "Volunteers of America." Everyone roared in waves—a musical crescendo—where the surf was definitely up.

Hendrix did things with his instrument that blew their minds. He played the *Star Spangled Banner* on his guitar with feedback that sounded like bombs exploding—the antithesis of freedom.

FOURTEEN
LAS VEGAS, NEVADA
1969

Descending rapidly, the plane seemed to be free falling out of the sky. Michael contemplated the definition of freedom at that moment, and how he may have taken it for granted before he screwed up...the wheels on the plane joined the ground ever so lightly. Sylvie and Michael had reached Fantasy Land.

As he predicted, the minute his mother heard the bells ringing and coins dropping out of slot machines, her eyes doubled in size, and she walked away from him without looking back. He was elated to see his mother's troubled expression turn to one of euphoria. He knew she had a serious gambling problem, yet he couldn't deny her that wide-eyed kid-at-an-amusement-park look. A few hours without worrying would be good for her.

He started thinking about the favorite book he had as a kid, called *The Very Worried Mother*. Thing is, even at the age of five, he always made his mom read it to him, hoping *she'd* be the one to learn the lesson...no matter how many times he'd scrape his knee, he was always okay, like the boy in the book.

Even when Daddy left them, he was okay. He ran and caught up with his mother. She already made it to a roulette section and took a seat at the end of the table.

"Mom? I'm getting my own room, okay? Mom?" Michael wasn't sure she heard him. "I'll meet you in the lobby at ten tomorrow morning and we'll go for breakfast."

"Yeah, sure darling. I'll see you at ten."

He certainly wasn't about to complain and was grateful that his mother's preoccupation allowed him a surprisingly romantic interlude.

Touching her was a miracle. There was no other word for *finding* her, lying next to her body in the king size bed at the Sands Hotel. He had embraced her as if she might slip away at any moment if he opened his eyes. How could he have run into her *here*? She was just *waiting* for him. A coincidence?

In his mind, he went over the sensuous night like an unmarked road. He saw her at one of the blackjack tables, her dark and deep eyes, her shoulder-length auburn hair touching her bronzed shoulders, her skin delicate and velvety, as he remembered.

He was pained by the tormented look on her face. He had to fix that. He had to be with her, love her, make it up to her. He wanted her, and he could no longer wait.

You don't just *run* into someone like this.

"Don't put another card down," he offered. "When the dealer has a six showing, he usually busts."

She trusted him. The dealer drew another card and placed the card next to his six—a nine of spades. Then he drew again. Ten. Twenty five.

"Yes!" She screeched, and scooped up her winnings. "Thanks!"

He bought her another gin and tonic. Then another. They carried their drinks away from the gambling table, sucked them dry and, went out onto The Strip under the illuminated marquee that flickered above the grand entrance. So many intimations of Lady Luck flashed around them.

They returned shortly to the casino rotating as one through the revolving doors, going through the motions buying more chips, pulling the one-arm-bandits, betting on the Wheel of Fortune, and placing money on craps and roulette. They were both stalling—waiting for the big pay off. The time would be right when they were both besotted by liquor and lust.

She followed him into the elevator, their drink glasses refreshed, up to room number 46. "Look," he said, "The maid left a chocolate on my pillow." She smiled and took him by the hand to the couch where they sat and continued to sip from their glasses. One lamp in the corner was dimly lit, giving the room a hazy feel. Michael blinked wildly, the ceiling, walls, floor, all in motion. Neither of them said anything before they started kissing, slowly, then more eagerly.

"Wow," she sighed. "You're lips are burning hot."

"Yeah, yours too," he said softly. "I like that."

"Me, too," she whispered.

He felt her warm breath on his cheek. He spoke with his eyes tightly shut, "Phew, it's getting *way* too hot in here. Should I turn up the air?"

She walked to him while he fidgeted with the thermostat and leaned against his back as he lowered the temperature. He heard the distinct sound of her zipper coming down on her red knee-length dress, suddenly aware that she had her own idea of cooling off. She let the chiffon fall to the carpet in soft folds. He turned to face her with the room spinning around in one direction and her in another. She pulled him close to her by his belt buckle, and she stood dainty on her toes, wearing only a pair of white lace panties. He didn't want to stare, make her uneasy. "You are so beautiful," he whispered in her ear.

"So are you," she said. He dropped his head back, breathing

heavily, as she unbuttoned his shirt. She put both palms on his smooth chest. In one blundering move, he unbuckled his belt, and tripped over his pants, falling onto the king size bed on top of her. They both laughed nervously, lying naked under the sheets while they kissed with hunger. Her nails dug into his shoulders.

With his forefinger, he traced the length of her lean body, caressing her roundness, breasts and belly, the top of her thighs, working his every move with growing intensity. With one knee he pressed himself into her but then hesitated. He saw his mother's glower. *You can't stop this from happening, Mom.*

"Are you okay?" she asked.

"I'm *more* than okay, damn it."

Giggling, and rolling over on top of him, now, she wet her lips and with her tongue, slid down his body and then inched upward until they were face to face. She opened her mouth, wider, kissed him harder and he returned the favor, kissing her in return. They prolonged it, savored it, and fostered it.

The morning after, one eye open, he smelled her hair, and knew something was amiss. *No honeysuckle? This isn't right.* He moved his arm beneath her neck. Her hair fell away from her face. He inhaled deep into the back of his throat. *This isn't Angela!*

What took place came back to him—who he was—army-bound, drunk, irresponsible, swept away in the moment. He deserved to feel shame. He was sure this girl didn't deserve the aftermath of his downfall. But she wanted the same thing for different reasons. She told him she loved someone who didn't love her back.

"We *had* to get married," she told him. "After the baby was born, he left me. I had no idea that he'd take off. It should never have happened. None of it," she said, staring blankly at the busy pattern on the carpet. She told him of her suicide attempts—a failed overdose.

Michael watched this total stranger as she pulled her red dress up over her hips and placed each foot into her tall shoes.

"I still love my husband," she said.

Michael touched her elbow. "I'm sorry about—well, you know."

"*I'm* not sorry. There were never any commitments between us," she said, touching his cheek. "I bet you believe in promises 'til death do you part and that kind of thing, right?"

Michael looked at her for a moment as the morning light sieved its way through the heaviness of the hotel curtains. "You're a good guy, Michael. You'll make some lucky girl very happy some day."

Michael cast his eyes downward. "That's a nice thing to say."

"I mean it," she said reaching for the doorknob.

Their get-together was over at sunrise. No longer dark or under the influence, they both saw things clearly and rationally. They'd never see one another again. A goodbye handshake would have sufficed. She wasn't Angela. And he wasn't her husband. In no time, they'd both be a distant memory to one another. She'd be going back to her daughter to teach her not to make the same mistakes she had made in her own life. And Michael would be going to do the right thing in a war that never should have happened.

Waiting for his mother to show up in the lobby before their return flight to New York, Michael sat on one of the lounge chairs and flipped through the Sand's Hotel brochure. He thought about how memories can make you feel disoriented. Even the hotel was filled with recollections. The landmark was an oasis in the middle of the desert with a 500-room tower owned by aviation pioneer, Howard Hughes. He raised his chin to look out the window and saw the penthouse.

All this will only be a memory, someday. We're all an enigma, soon to be forgotten, including all the celebrities who performed here. He read their names: Louis Armstrong, Sammy Davis, Jr., Joey Bishop, Milton Berle, Dean Martin, Peggy Lee, Nat King Cole—*and this strange girl I just made love to. Discarded. What was her name? Melissa? Melissa, in a naughty town called Vegas.*

He wanted to blame his mother for his unfaithfulness to Angela. He wanted to blame his mother for everything that went wrong in his life.

Once back on Long Island, Michael went to the Massapequa Service Station on the corner of Merrick Road, across the street from the soda fountain where he used to hang out as a kid. He pictured himself, ten years old, spinning all the stools lined up at the counter as the clerk made his egg cream with milk, chocolate syrup, and seltzer.

He wished he was still the same free kid and wondered who that little person really was, as he lay across Mr. Doobie's worn out seats and squeezed his hand between the leather, feeling for any personal belongings that may have fallen there. He picked up something between his two fingers. A girl's hair-clip. *Angela's?* He stuck the hairclip in his back pocket, pulled out the 8-track from the player, collected more trash, old paper cups and whatnot, picked up his tried and true Road Atlas and threw it on top of the pile of garbage. Then he slapped a For Sale sign across Mr. Doobie's windshield and walked away without looking back.

Michael had passed his army physical with red, white and blue colors and had soon grown to hate what people always called his "gentle side." He worked on developing another side—an angry one—to get ready for the army. He obsessed with bulking up and joined Vic Tanny's Gym across from Bar Harbor Shopping Center where he pumped iron with a vengeance. One day he worked his upper body and the next day his lower body. He did the bench press for his chest, the military press for his shoulders, crunches for his abdominals, squats for his quadriceps, leg curls for his hamstrings, barbell curls for his biceps, push-downs for his triceps, and standing-calve-raises for strengthening his calves. In between his conditioning, he ate healthy, high protein meals.

One night after Michael left the gym, he felt helpless and overpowered; he headed toward the bay on Alhambra Road to a dive called Arthur's Bar. The place was known as a hangout for a variety of outcasts—perfect for the way he felt. He slipped in through the exit door and got into a conversation with the bartender about boot camp as he downed one Southern Comfort after another. "If it's good enough for Joplin, it's good nough for me," he slurred, oblivious to his surroundings.

A girl with teased hair stared at him with the slightest grin. She made a remark. "He's probably getting shipped off to Saigon or—"

Michael walked over to her, sloppy drunk. He leaned up against her shoulder, ignoring her huge Harley-clad boyfriend. "Ya know. Ya know, I can never figure out why—why, now what I was saying? Oh yeah, why-y-y they call it "shipped" out, when you don't actua-leee take a *ship* anywhere."

"Hey, get off my girl!" the guy almost twice his size yelled.

"I beg your p-pardon," Michael stuttered. "Your girl with the hairdo over here, implied I'm going to Viet—and I am most def-in-itely *not* going to Viet-viet NAM!"

"Apologize to my girl, now, you moron!"

"Huh? Yeah. Oh yeah. I'm sor-sorrreee—sor-r-r y you have such *bi-i-ig* hair," he said touching her head with one extended finger. He saw in doubles—two of the tattooed giant and two of the girl with the over-teased coiffure. The wood-paneled room seemed to close in on him, and the unpainted poles that held the structure together seemed to sway...the ceiling tiles circled over Michael's head like bees at a hive. The king bee was buzzing by now and came straight for him.

Michael felt his feet rise off the floor and his body being thrown onto the pool table. A rough crowd, unimpressed with bar fights, was obviously annoyed he ruined their game and quickly shoved him out the crooked side exit door like a sack of rubbish.

Eventually, he came to and stumbled home, holding his jaw. Confused, his feet moved forward, but he didn't think he was getting anywhere. Most of the houses looked the same. He stood outside the one with a tall chimney for a minute and watched a feminine figure in the window consoling a crying baby. Then there was quiet, and everything went dark. Either she turned off the light, or he passed out, he wasn't sure.

By the time he reached his mother's house, he was feeling sick. He paused at the old oak tree by the driveway and leaned against the solid trunk as he saw ghosts of himself and Angela—the first time Angela had gone to his mother's house. Michael had told her his mother was away for the weekend and Angela had told him afterward that she had the feeling he never wanted them to meet.

"I can't believe we're doing this," he had said, turning the key in the front door, stepping into the spacious foyer with Angela close behind. Michael and Angela had dared one another, earlier, to an egg-eating contest after seeing the movie,

Cool Hand Luke. "You can't get much cooler than Paul Newman in a prison flick," he said.

"Especially when he ate those *fifty* hard-boiled eggs." Angela laughed, while placing the brown paper bags onto the kitchen counter. "Bet's on, Mikey, I can eat more eggs than you." She unloaded the five cartons of eggs they picked up at the Dairy Barn drive-thru on the way home from the theater. Michael placed a large, dented, silver pot of water on the stovetop to boil.

"We'll just have to see about that," he said. "It may be your last dare. No joke. Or should I say no yolk?"

"Ha. Ha."

He left her to slide the eggs into the water one at a time with a slotted-spoon, while he went into the living room to put a record on the player. She seemed curious about his mother, calling out questions to Michael from a distance. "*When* did you say your mom moved to the states?"

"I told you already," he said, looking through his record albums. "My mother came to this country right after the war ended, in 1945.

"Are you in the mood for Gimme Shelter or Whiter Shade of Pale?"

"Hold on, I'm almost done with the eggs."

"Well, hurry up and get your butt in here and see our art collection."

She followed his voice into the other room. "Now, that's a line, if I ever heard one."

"Okay. You're right," he said, lifting her chin closer to his. Mid-kiss, they were suddenly interrupted by a loud thud—the elusive Mrs. Beckman. She dropped upon them as unexpectedly as a hot wire off a telephone pole. Angela smoothed back her hair to look presentable and smiled coyly.

"Hi, Mom," Michael said, ignoring the kink in his neck. She

stuck her face out to her son, ignoring his company, and he gave her a peck on the fine lines of her cheek.

"I see you weren't expecting me, Michael," Sylvie said, throwing her Burberry coat over the back of her chair, showing off her green and navy wool skirt, a Jaeger original. The two females stood across from one another in opposition, next to the mix of chrome and antique furniture that filled the stark white living room.

"Mom, this is Angela." Michael said.

Angela eyeballed his mother's glossy manicure and then extended her own hand with stubby fingernails to Sylvie who simply ignored her gesture and turned away, preoccupied. Michael was the only one who could read her unreadable eyes as they sized up the girl in one quick glance.

Angela hid one of her scraped moccasins behind her calf. She hadn't a clue that Sylvie was the one threatened by *her* presence, and the fact that she might take her only son away from her.

"Michael, Michael, always entertaining." She shook her head. "Who was that last girl you brought here? Rebecca? She was a pretty one with that short Twiggy haircut," she said looking at Angela's long ponytail but still not her face.

"Who's Rebecca?" Angela looked at Michael, biting her fingernails on the same hand rejected by his mother upon introductions.

The back of Michael's neck instantly broke out into a rash. He gave his mother a hand signal, a warning—"enough" behind Angela's back. "Uhh, Mom, you told me you'd be returning in the morning, didn't you?"

"Sorry to disappoint you." She frowned. "I left Vegas early…"

"No problem, I just wasn't expecting to see you, that's all."

"Oh, wow, Michael." Angela's attention was abruptly drawn to the wall. "You weren't kidding about an art collection. Tell me what I'm looking at, exactly. I want to know about what is on those walls."

The room got quiet. Michael looked at his mother and then at Angela.

"I left Vegas when an earlier flight became available. Besides, the casinos weren't at all generous this time."

"Vegas? Wow. I can't imagine *my* mother in a place like *Las Vegas*. My mother wouldn't know how to maneuver a one-arm bandit...unless it comes in the shape of a ladle or a spatula." Her attempt at humor didn't work. Maybe Sylvie took the remark as condescending.

Sylvie spoke only to Michael. "So, it's just as well I left a day early. I broke even. I went with Stella Passman this time. Remember Stella? Her husband bought her that cream-colored Mercedes last year. Thinks he's a big shot. A big chain smoker. That's what he is."

"Mom?"

His mother grabbed her pocketbook. "Where's my—"

"Mom? I'm glad you two finally get to meet."

Sylvie was removed. "Where's my lucky rabbit's foot?" she said, feeling at the bottom of her unscuffed Italian handbag.

"Mom? Let's start over. This is Angela."

"I'm sorry, where are my manners? Angela what, dear?"

"Martino," she answered.

Disapproval danced in his mother's eyes. This time Angela didn't extend her hand and his girlfriend's expression reminded Michael of a kid in grammar school who got the word wrong during a spelling bee. He started to perspire as he watched his mother leave the room in her usual hurry-scurry and cartoonish fashion when avoiding something. Michael followed his mother into the kitchen with a serious expression, and Angela could hear every other word.

"Ma, what are you doing? You were rude to Angela."

"What the hell are *all* these eggs for . . . who?"

"Angela, mom. You know, the girl in the other room I just introduced you to."

"She's real cute, but a *goy*, Michael?"

Angela's heart rattled in her chest as if it became loose. *But, what? I can hardly hear them now. What did she mean? Mrs. Beckman said something about Goya. Why is she talking about Goya beans?*

She heard Michael coming back and quickly sat in a garish arm chair. "Is everything all right?"

"No," he said. He grabbed her hand and pulled her up to her feet. "Let's go. Nothing is all right."

Outside, he opened Mr. Doobie's passenger door for her. After she got inside the van, he came around to the driver's side and slammed the car door behind him. "Don't you know?" He pounded the steering wheel. "You're not good enough for me. Because you're *not* Jewish."

"Oh." Angela sat in silence for a moment before she started her nervous hiccupping. "I have a confession to make."

Michael looked at her.

"At first, my mom didn't exactly want *me* dating a Jewish boy, either. Now, she seems okay with—"

"No. No, it goes much deeper than that. It's my mom's background . . . the Holocaust. But, you know something? I'm tired of patching the wounds of my mother's past."

"Her past?" Angela hesitated.

"She makes it harder on herself because she sleeps with a lot of secrets and mistrusts everyone. She believes that at any moment someone will hurt us, so she is over-protective, to say the least."

"Michael, you're her son. She really *loves* you."

"Yeah. She loves her mink stole, too. So what."

"Michael, you and your mother share the same blood.

"Yeah, Jewish blood. Jewish blood carries a lot of torment."

This hadn't *really* occurred to Angela that the Holocaust wasn't just something that happened long ago.

"Oh shit," Michael said.

"What?" Angela hiccupped again and looked at him.

"The eggs. My mother's gonna have a whopper of a breakfast tomorrow."

After one solid week of dark and drizzly weather, Sylvie resorted to cleaning out her closets. She'd bring her garments to a second-hand shop on the North Shore where they'd pay good money and make her trip worthwhile. She could use the money to buy *new* things. The last time she was there, she only brought one bag of her fine suits and dresses, and they had given her nearly three hundred dollars. Happy with herself that she packed four full bags by the middle of the afternoon, she decided to take a break before the long drive and put her feet up.

She turned on the living room light under the print of Rembrandt's "Saskia" and sipped a cup of hot tea, calculating in her head that this time she'd ask for one thousand dollars for the four bags. They'd probably make a counter-offer of seven-hundred. She already knew she'd accept because she had no choice. Again, she looked at Saskia. *To think my father had the real one*, she tsked.

Angela came to mind again . . . the night they had met. She had watched the girl fuss over the art, like her childhood friends used to do when they came to her house. Angela tilted her head at four small oils of men with frilly collars, then moved on and became fixated with Saskia's portrait. "Huh, look at that," she said, fixated on Saskia's distinct features. "How the light shows on only one cheek."

Sylvie knew the girl wondered where the light comes from. From a lamp burning nearby or from within the subject? She could sense Angela taking in the smell of the old art work. The smell of its *value, that is.*

Over the past two decades, Sylvie had sold much of the antiques that were salvaged, but she went through money quickly to satisfy her gambling debts and her shopping sprees. A far cry from the days of butlers and chauffeurs; still, somehow, she managed to spoil herself with the amounts allotted her and her siblings in escrow from her father's will.

Angela had wandered over to the age-darkened paintings above the formal settee and stepped closer to look at the ornate frame, reaching her fingers upward to touch the chipped paint, when she noticed Sylvie's scowl. The girl withdrew her hand, as if caught by a museum curator.

Michael watched his mother watching his girlfriend. "She wants to study art someday," he explained. Sylvie gave him a look, as if to say, "What, finger-painting?"

Angela continued to examine the darkness and the canvas that showed through in some spots. She had never seen art like this, so European, except for once at a museum in the city on a school trip.

"Did you see these?" Michael had pointed to blue and white miniatures on a glass shelf, "It's the last thing my mother's father had sent over from Holland."

"You're Dutch?"

"*Ja,*" he said.

Angela smiled cautiously. Michael was aware she was intimidated by Sylvie.

"It's delft. Some of Opa's favorites," he said.

"Is your father in America, too, Mrs. Beckman?" Angela inquired.

Sylvie tensed up, mumbling something about remembering

where the rabbit foot might be. She was thinking of herself as a young girl who once loved baroque art, especially Rembrandt's work, so full of emotion and drama. She had been enthralled by the master whose life was filled with strife and tragedy, and then bankruptcy. At the time, she wasn't sure what being bankrupt meant, but she wanted to equate the importance to her own life. After all, the Rosenbergs lost many of their possessions, too.

She loved all of Rembrandt's work, but one of Sylvie's favorite paintings was called a "Jewish Bride," with the subject being a Jewish father standing beside his daughter on her wedding day, after having placed a necklace upon the girl's neck. Sylvie used to think that someday she would see that same look in her own father's eyes when she'd wed. *Of course, Father would insist the necklace be solid gold, to prove his devotion to her, wouldn't he?*

FIFTEEN

SMYRNA, TENNESSEE
1969–1970

When Angela was old enough to drive, she sometimes borrowed her dad's car, opened all four windows and drove to the airport to watch the jets take off. On the way to JFK, she'd pull the taut rubber band free and, let her long hair whip across her face the whole way, as if she were flying. She loved driving fast.

Then, from the air terminal, she'd stand for hours peering out from the enormous plate glass window on the highest floor, regarding the flight of each of the giant silver birds, as they turned into sugar grain size.

Now, *she* was going off into the wild blue yonder... a brave "fly girl" who looked more like a frightened, baby bird. Although the terminal at Kennedy was quiet at that early hour, people in uniform walked quickly to where they had to go. Angela was feeling partly lost, until she met the two other girls she'd been corresponding with over the past few weeks, both from the New York Metro area. The three of them had scheduled the same flight to Tennessee.

One girl wore a black polyester pants suit, her hair in a bun at the nape of her neck, with matching black pumps and handbag. She remained quiet and sat stiffly as they waited for their flight. The other girl with the wild blonde locks and low cut dress, nervously dug into her purse, either spraying herself with *Chantilly Lace* or *Aquanet*, both of which made Angela's nose twitch. Angela had to pinch her nostrils to stop herself from a fit of sneezing. And from a fit of laughing at the girl's animation.

Angela was curious how they assessed her—was she trying too hard to look mod in her new geometric mini-dress that flaunted her legs? She had always wanted to make a dramatic statement that she wasn't prudish like her mother, but she also didn't want to come off looking like—well, the girl sitting next to her.

The yappy, jumpy one, looked as if she'd just stepped out of an *Archie* comic book and kept touching her designer carry-on as if it held plutonium. "Hmmm, would ya look at them!" The girl pointed, as entire crews from Braniff and Eastern Airlines passed with luggage in tow. "They sure look sharp, don't they?"

When they arrived for training in a hick town called Smyrna, not far from Nashville, they were met with oppressive heat and an airline representative who escorted them to an abandoned Air Force base that accommodated almost one hundred girls in training from all over the world. Soon, they'd all be assigned roommates. Angela set her suitcases down on the curb and looked at the line of small brick buildings in the middle of nowhere.

The rep chattered as she opened the door to their free rental. "The housing is old, but it's spacious. We refurbished it last year, you know, and we provide all the furniture."

"Waterbeds? Oh, this is so cool," Angela heard one of the other girls say. "And it's king size."

"Yes, there's one in all the bedrooms," the agent boasted. "The girls always seem to love how they bounce."

Angela blushed.

Her two roommates were Susie Pearson from Sausalito, California, and Eileen White from Fredericksburg, Virginia. Like Angela, they had never been out of the states they were born in. All the girls were busy over the weekend setting up their modest living quarters while they waited for training to begin. Most days Angela only had time to think of Michael in short spurts, while she ate her three meals or while in the shower. Every night, she would collapse onto her water bed, until the last ripple settled her into sleep.

Stew School was a trip in itself. The first Capitol Airlines meeting started early on Monday morning. It was too early for Angela to concentrate on the welcoming speech, but she was awake enough to study the panel of airline recruiters, mostly ex-stewardesses, seated at the table in the front of the room.

Would you look at that? They never lost those Stew smiles.

"And, please welcome the Director of Stewardesses, Miss Donna Doyle."

Whoops, except for that one.

Miss Doyle stepped up to the podium with a stern look on her face.

No way was she ever a stewardess.

"Ladies, on behalf of Capitol Airlines, its management and board of directors, I'm thrilled to welcome you to Stew School."

Eileen drew a picture of a face with an exaggerated frown and tore it out of her note pad, placing the caricature on Angela's knee under the table. Angela smacked her leg, and tried to hold back a laugh in the quiet room.

"Girls, you are about to embark on a glorious, and yes, glamorous career as hostesses of the sky. As told to you during your preliminary interviews, this entails a lot of hard work. And I do mean *hard*. It is not *all* glamour. In this demanding field of travel it takes much aptitude—"

Angela whispered to Eileen. "She means *altitude*, doesn't she?"

"After screening hundreds of girls over the past six months, we have complete confidence in the select few we have chosen, which of course includes all of *you*. I'm quite certain that you will prove to be an asset to this company and in a short time after training, you will be ready for graduation and a promising future. Oh, and of course, you will have *earned* your wings."

Applause.

On the first day of class, eighty-six bubbly girls had shown up to be enlightened that in order to pass the FAA test, they'd be required to know *every* centimeter of *every* aircraft the company flies, know things like how much fuel each particular plane carries, etc. They were deluged with charts and books and tedious hours of study. Then they applied their knowledge to locating the equipment in a timely fashion on mock planes, where they were challenged to respond appropriately to every kind of emergency that could possibly arise.

Angela gradually realized the seriousness of the lessons, but she wasn't frightened off. She had to wonder, though, how long her flying career would last once she satisfied her hunger of seeing the world. She could see herself going back someday to the boring community college where she'd already accumulated credits when she was unsure about her future, seeing herself ready to go for her degree.

The airlines classes were scheduled daily, from 8:15 a.m. to 6 p.m., and got more complicated each day with a plethora of information to learn in two short months. Angela smiled, recalling the surfing terminology that Katie tried to memorize on the way to the beach.

Angela's roommate, Eileen, griped about all the rules and regulations as she read aloud. Some girls gathered around her as she scanned the chapters of the thick manual.

"It's ridiculous how strict they are with everything. Have you seen all the paperwork? The passports and visa requirements?"

Eileen, who looked like she was constantly sucking in her stomach, continued to grumble. "Did you check out the weight and height requirements for all flight attendants? Oh my God, the print is so small. How do they expect us to *see* it?"

"Well," Susie chimed in over her shoulder, "NOT with our glasses on, I can tell you that much; according to section 11-1 -5. It states right here: 'Have good eyesight without contact lenses; vision can be no less than 20/40 in the better eye and 20/70 in the weaker eye.'"

"Are they serious? Oh, good, here it says, contact lenses are acceptable. Applicants must have worn contacts at least three months previous to employment."

"Here's a section on our responsibility to Chief Flight Attendant, to the Captain, to Field Reps. For example, cockpit courtesy limits your visit to the cockpit from 5 to 10 minutes."

"Who'd wanna stay in there any longer with those dirty old men?" one girl exclaimed.

"I would," added a girl wearing a low cut blouse.

"Ewww," Susie squealed.

"Then there's the time conversion table. We're supposed to have a complete understanding of Greenwich Meridian Time ("Z" or Zulu Time.) It goes on and on," Eileen whined.

The girls were giddy from the amount of information. When they got to the Aircraft Statistics section, which included

such things as the length and wing span, take- off weight, cruising speed, cabin pressure, etc., they all cracked up.

Eileen was so overloaded with facts that she broke out into
song to the tune of the "Bone's" riddle that kids sing to help
them remember human body parts:

*"Oh-h-h, the Aileron's connected to the Flying-Tab, and
the Flying Tab's connected to the Trim-Tab, the Trim Tab's
connected to the Spoil-er, the Spoiler's connected to the
Wing-Flap, the Wing Flap's connected to the Exhaust-Gate,
the—"*

Someone slapped a hand over her mouth.

Repeated lectures were given about the seriousness of instruction at the beginning of each class, and they were told over and
over that the main responsibility of the job had to do with life
and death. The students practiced procedures for evacuation
over land and water. Some girls were afraid of heights, others
afraid of the water. Some were scared of everything. Of course,
those who panicked were immediately expelled.

The day they practiced with life rafts, there were six girls
and a supervisor to each raft. It was obvious right away who
the leaders were. First they had to employ the inflatable chutes
at the exit doors, keeping up with the frantic pace.

"Let's go, girls. Move it! Move it!" the instructor yelled. "If
the girl before you hesitates, push her out the door of the plane."

The girls whispered stories to one another. "Did you hear about
what they did to one girl on her first flight? They put pepper in

her Demo 02 mask, and she had a sneezing fit throughout the whole demonstration in front of hundreds of people, while the senior stews laughed it up. Poor girl, she quit the next day."

Angela practiced her announcement:

"Good morning, Ladies and Gentlemen: On behalf of Captain McDermott and crew, I'd like to welcome you aboard Capitol Airlines Flight no. 217 to Frankfurt, Germany, with an intermediate stop in Iceland. Our flying time will be approximately 7 hours and 5 minutes. We will be cruising at an altitude of 34,000 feet. Please fasten your seat belts, position your seats in the upright position, and stow the table trays for takeoff—"

"Excuse me, Miss Martino," Miss Doyle interrupted, "We've run out of time today. Girls, don't forget to study! Tomorrow we will go over the Hydraulic and Pneumatic systems."

"I can't wait," Susie said as they exited. "Before this, I thought the hardest part would be the baby diapers and the barf bags."

"Yeah," Angela agreed, getting onto the Stew courtesy bus. "We have to wear too many hats for this job. But the worst hat for me is the nurse's. I get very queasy around blood and guts. What am I supposed to do if someone needs me to apply pressure to a gaping wound or is having an epileptic fit or a diabetic attack?"

"Oh crap," Eileen joined in. "I forget the difference. It is so darn confusing. Is the diabetic coma—lack of insulin—when they're drowsy, the face is flushed, the lips are red, and they have rapid breathing? And, um, insulin shock is—is what? Is what? Oh, no, I forget."

"Ashen color, clammy skin, kinda the way *you* look right now," Susie told Eileen who kept scaring herself and everyone around her on the duration of the ride.

"Oh, my God, and if someone has a heart attack or a baby on board, whadda we do with that whatchamajig?" Angela asked.

"You mean the placenta?" Susie said.

"Yeah, I don't care for the sound of that thing." Angela recoiled, as the bus pulled up to their complex. They laughed as they walked into the mailroom. Angela pulled out a form letter from her mailbox. "Hey guys, Capitol's getting *new* uniforms, and we'll be the first crew modeling them; that is, if we pass the FAA Test and graduate."

Eileen grabbed the paper out of her hand. "Did y'all see the rules?"

"You must adhere to the standard uniform rules, which consists of skirt, jacket and blouse, and must be cleaned and pressed at all times. The hemline is not to be shorter than three to four inches above the knee.

"In warm climates, the jacket may be removed at the discretion of the first flight attendant. When worn, the jacket must be kept buttoned.

"The hat may be removed in the airplane, only after the doors are secured and must be replaced prior to landing. No adornment of any kind, other than the authorized insignia, may be worn on the hat. Bobby pins may not be used to secure the hat. Hat may be worn off the face, but must be visible from the front.

"You should only wear neutral shades of pantyhose. Shoes are plain navy leather pumps and may be changed to cabin shoes out of view of passengers."

"And there's a lot more, here. I suppose you prefer I skip that part? Hey, where y'all going?" She quickly followed. "Hmm...whada 'bout girdles? Does it say anything about girdles?" she asked herself, sucking in her stomach even more.

Angela had to get ready for her *big* day. She'd shave her legs, polish her nails, put her hair in large rollers...on the inside, though, something felt irregular. As the shower water trickled between her eyelashes and ran down her shoulders, thoughts of her sister struggling underwater came back to her.

She reached for the knob and twisted it to the right. The sensation of the water stopping so abruptly, reminded her of the recurring dream she had the night before. The salt on her skin was washed away by fresh water. She dried off and sprinkled on some dusting powder, still not feeling clean. How many times had she dreamt about drowning?

The graduation was held outside the old air base on a sunny day with the girls seated in folding chairs lined up on the lawn. Angela's eyes gravitated upward at the clouds passing overhead. *Look, Anna, I'm going to have wings, too.* She wondered if Anna would also graduate soon...*past the clouds, maybe past the stars?*

All the girls looked spiffy in their new blue uniforms and little white gloves, eagerly waiting for their names to be called over the loudspeaker. *Funny how a uniform makes you feel like a different person.*

Something touched Angela's arm. She watched the insect gently flutter its red polka dot wings. *A ladybug.* Her eyes immediately teared-up thinking about one of the first days she had ever spent with Michael...he leaned in close, and picked a ladybug off a strand of her hair. They watched the teeny bug, together, as it flew *home.*

Once *she* flew off, would she ever fly home again to Michael? This seemed impossible, all because of Sylvie. His mother couldn't possibly know what Angela felt when she was with her son—how she knew him in another lifetime; how right he looked sitting behind the steering wheel in his Volkswagen camper; how he tugged on her sleeve for attention;

how his blonde stubbly whiskers felt against her smooth skin; how alive and warm his writing made her feel on the inside; and how he always smelled "summery."

"Angela Martino." A voice called.

The girl sitting next to her elbowed Angela. When she got up to get pinned, by good ol' Miss. Doyle, the ladybug remained on her arm. Angela touched the golden breast pin on her lapel and walked off the stage, imagining her mother's proud face. At her kindergarten graduation she had grabbed Angela and wrapped her arms around her. Whenever she did that, she'd tell her they were a human "sugar wafer," and that Angela was her sweet center. Angela sniffled back the nostalgia. She needed to prove she could go *alone*, begin her life of spontaneity...her dream, now reality, was climbing up inside her throat like nausea.

Angela checked-in at Operations before her first trip and then boarded the steps of the fleet's largest aircraft, the DC-8, which held 250 passengers. She did her pre-boarding duties, and also made sure the cabin looked tidy for the flight. The galleys were ready, and the meals were delivered and placed in the refrigerators, including four vegetarian and two Kosher meals.

She was reluctant to do the oxygen and life vest demonstration on her first flight out of Frankfurt in front of a rough-looking audience, which included dozens of toothless Czechoslovakian hockey players.

"Watch out for row 17, Greg the Groper," the tall stew, affectionately known as Pearl, coughed the warning into her hand, while squeezing by Angela in the aisle.

That warning had been a year ago, putting up with irate passengers, flying the metal birds with rigid wings, and trying to fill the deep hole chiseled right out of the middle of her chest. One flight Angela would not forget was from Frankfurt to Washington, D.C. with a turnaround to Brussels. Angela and another girl were in the back of the plane setting up bar to take individual orders, when one of the other stewardesses announced. "Hey Angela, I think you have a fan—23B. He asked for you."

"Asked for me? What do you mean? By name?" Angela's face turned red.

"No, I don't think so. Oh yeah, he called you 'Angel Face.'"

Angela's face turned from red to white as she slowly walked up the aisle to Row 23B.

There's only one person who calls me that. As she got closer and saw the back of his head in the middle seat, her knees buckled...the sandy brown, sun-streaked hair. What if she fainted right there in the aisle? She moved forward and faced him, looked right into his eyes, and stopped dead.

"Angela, what's the matter? You look like you've seen a ghost," her co-worker said, when Angela returned to the back galley.

"Almost did," Angela said.

"Who is he? Do you know him?"

"No. I don't know him." Her mouth quivered.

"Don't you just hate the flirty, drunken ones?"

"Hand me one of those bottles of gin and one tonic, will you?" Angela asked.

"Sure. Is the gin and tonic for him? Or is it for you?"

"I *wish* it was for me."

Angela's flying experience entailed riding in limos, staying at fancy hotels, dining carte blanche in the finest restaurants, and indulging in long layovers. One day she was in a cafe in Paris; another day a museum in Madrid; nightclubs and shows in Buenos Aires; surfing in Tahiti. She finally lived the fairy tale. It wasn't the overindulgence she had been looking for.

As unearthly as it felt every time the wheels disappeared into the mechanical bird's belly, and she was off on another adventure, she wasn't totally fulfilled. She always felt short *one* miracle.

SIXTEEN

FORT BRAGG, NORTH CAROLINA
1969–1970

Michael stared out the bus window and then closed his eyes as the Greyhound pulled away. He thought of the summer and how Angela looked on the beach with the marble-cake blue and white sky framing her profile. He pressed the palms of his hands into his eye sockets. *Let go of her, man,* he thought to himself.

At 22, he feared his life was over. Soon, he'd have to trade in his love beads for his dog tags. The image of her handing him the lavender writing paper came to him—his going away gift, the last thing he had packed, as if this would be his only connection to normalcy. He'd keep his promise, respect her wishes and wouldn't send her any letters. *Maybe I'll just write the letters, never* actually *mail them,* he thought in despair.

As the bus picked up speed, the white lines on the highway blurred into images of grand waterfalls spilling out of massive rocks—his last moment of peace before he fell asleep. He didn't wake up until the ten wheels rolled past a brick wall with bold lettering: WELCOME TO FORT BRAGG, N.C. U.S. ARMY.

After he reported to the Reception Center to begin his induction, Michael unpacked his bags, and began to panic. *How could I have thought lifting a few weights could prepare me for this place? Shit, I don't want to be this army guy. I'm such an idiot. I've ruined my own life.*

Oh no, that's just perfect—the kid with the baby skin's in the bunk next to mine. Tom McCready, from Amarillo, Texas. Talk about naive—soon after turning 18, Tom had enlisted to escape problems back home. Michael considered the kid his reason for being there. He supposed he could help someone else get through their life, even if he couldn't get through his own.

The squad's drill sergeant entered the barracks. "Hey, what's the matter with you *ladies*, can't you take the pressure?" he yelled out. "McCready, step forward. You call that standing at attention, woman? I'm gonna make a man out of you today if it kills me. Do you hear what I said? And we're all about killing here, you understand?"

"Sir, yes sir."

"Don't call me sir!"

McCready was so nervous he repeated louder, "Yes, sir."

The drill sergeant pulled at both his ears. "Can't you hear me, sissy boy?"

McCready grimaced and the drill instructor ordered him to run in place, until he told him to stop.

In no time, the inductees' heads were shaved, and they were immediately taken into a large auditorium where they were further yelled at and cursed at by their drill instructor. The fat barber smelled of BO. Michael was grateful the head-shaving lasted less than ten seconds.

Whenever the sergeants got bored, they made someone totally miserable by enforcing the infamous 'Drop and give me 50' for the slightest infraction. After a while, part of Michael disappeared, and he was only lugging his *body* around on demand. He was hardly motivated to eat the slop they called "meals" in the mess hall. He knew exactly what John Lennon meant when he said, "nothing is real."

After orientation and classification, Michael discovered he'd been made squad leader. *Who the hell is that?* he asked himself as he passed a full-length mirror in his army duds. *Ha! Funny, how a uniform changes you into a different person.*

The instructors drilled the men nonstop. The grunts did pushups in the rain and ran in heavy boots until their shins ached. They walked the horizontal ladder until new blisters formed on top of old blisters. The only consolation was that sometimes the physical stress helped to override the mental stress.

One night, he heard Tom crying in the bunk beside him. In the dark, Michael whispered, "Hey, what's up, buddy?" Tom was inconsolable. Michael finally had to bury his own head in the pillow. Still, he planned all night how he could comfort Tom the following day, make him open up. *Oh, yeah, right. Who am I kidding? Who delegated me as the "father" figure?*

He thought of his own dad who left when Michael was only six, one week after he started first grade. *Daddy, will you take me fishing tomorrow?*

Fishing? Mitchell had repeated, turning the pages of the newspaper, sitting on the fireside chair with his legs crossed. *Smelly-fish fishing?* He wrinkled his nose.

We'll see, he had always answered his son—to fishing, to learning how to ride his bike without training wheels, to throwing the ball, to just about everything. It was true that he never made promises he didn't keep. It was easy for him. He never promised Michael anything.

Michael would sometimes shut his mother out, as if the abandonment was her fault. She annoyed him with the coddling and overindulgence to the point he would have to walk

away. She'd give up, for a while, anyway. The look on her face
was blank and lonely. He'd watch his mother on those days,
how she'd absorb herself in soap operas or paperback books
with pictures of men and women hugging and kissing on the
cover.

Being an only child, he would play by himself outside in
the backyard. He'd gather leaves and rocks and sticks, anything
he could find under the earth. He'd squat with muddy knees
next to the biggest of trees, collecting an assortment of bugs,
then he'd set them up on parallel tracks in the dirt for a race
and he'd root for the caterpillar.

For years, Michael had tried to remember what his father
looked like, what his voice sounded like, but the memories
eluded him.

Michael marched his squad hard, also encouraging them to
take good care of each other. Sometimes they'd sit and have
a rap session or grab a smoke. He worked them strenuously,
until they were the best in the battalion. In a way, his pride had
sickened him.

One day they practiced bear hugs, and he taught them how
to break through when someone came up from behind. Sanko
had gotten too cocky, and Erickson managed to slip his arms
out of the hold and flip him hard onto the ground. Fists were
flying, but the sergeant wouldn't let Michael stop the fight. All
part of the discipline.

"A bloody lip and a black eye. Not too much damage,"
Michael told them, afterward.

Michael also had to discipline the pacifist within himself
at the rifle range. He repeated pumping holes from 500 yards
into a silhouette. *Hey, look at that. I didn't know I had it in me.*

They took apart M-14s, cleaned them and put them back

together again in the dark. They learned how to hit targets and how to use the bayonet and butt as weapons. Many hours were spent in the classroom and on the range and about disarming booby traps the Viet Cong were famous for. When Michael did "Advance & Fire Training," he was reminded of when he was a kid and used to play army games with his friends. He was always coerced into being the one who got killed.

They also had to learn about First Aid, gunshot and other wounds, they'd likely encounter and how to defend themselves from chemical attack. When Michael felt the tightness of the gas mask on his face, he thought of scuba diving. But there were no exotic fish in sight. After they had trudged through knee-deep mud, they ran the infiltration course laced with barbed wire and other obstacles. He suffered a few deep cuts on his chin.

He wiped the blood from his face. "Hey, I'm starting to look the part now, guys," he said.

"Yeah, it's about time, pretty boy," one of his comrades teased.

This was starting to feel like the *real thing* with live machine gun bullets firing overhead and deafening explosions inside of sandbagged pits. Tom looked dazed in the hole, covering his ears, and Michael had to shove him a bit until he obeyed orders.

Finally, graduation. In eight short weeks, they marched in perfect formation, changed from a bunch of wise guys into fighting warriors.

On Thanksgiving Day the warriors ate turkey. They had no idea if they should be grateful for where they may end up by Christmas.

* * *

Anthony Martino noticed the look of trepidation on his wife's face as she turned another page of *The Tribune*—their Sunday morning habit, the two of them sipping coffee and reading the paper side by side. He gingerly placed his folded eyeglasses on top of the section he had been reading, and commented, "Too many boys are dying over there—not the same as *our* war."

Jean went back to the newspaper. "The photos are so vivid. I can't look at this." Her voice cracked.

With such advancements in media coverage, the horrific image of war was in their faces—on their TV sets in the comfort of their living rooms.

"They're burning flags. We never did that," Anthony said.

"I'm worried about Angela," she finally said.

Her husband's "I've-heard-this-before" look froze her words, mid-sentence. Her worries remained inside her own head: *I hope Michael never has to go to Vietnam. I'll never mention this to Angela. She was upset enough when they had split up. Why should I upset her more, especially long-distance?*

Anthony looked at the sewing his wife was working on next to her on the couch. "What's this?" he asked.

"It's a blouse. For Angela. Do you think she'll like it?"

He nodded. "Everything you touch turns into something beautiful," he said, stroking her sewing hand.

After they had retired to the bedroom and her husband's snoring grew steady, Jean pulled her part of the blanket back. She made her way to her daughter's bedroom and looked at the old stuffed animals. She grabbed Angela's favorite—the gold horse, and rubbed the toy against her cheek, like Angela used to do. It had been a hand-me-down from Anna.

Jean had always admired Angela's tenacity—the way she cared for those horses at the stable. *Once that girl settled her mind on something, she put her whole self into it ... did I ever tell her that? How proud I am?*

"She's got an outstanding rapport with the animals," the stable hand told Jean Martino once when she came into the barn looking for her daughter. It seemed he could not stop raving: "The vet was delighted when he made his rounds and saw such remarkable improvement since his last visit. For a petite girl, she's gotta use all her muscle to bring up a shiny coat on the horses like that," he said, while refilling the water buckets. "Why, she turned Midnight's skin around in no time at all. Only weeks ago, there were lumps and bumps and wounds on the horses' surface. Angela managed to get rid of most of them using a soft, rubber curry brush. She massaged them until she removed all the dead skin. You've got yourself one determined daughter, there, Mrs. Martino."

Angela's mother smiled as she remembered his words.

"Yep. That girl's got the magic touch," he said. "The *magic* touch."

The first time she watched Angela at work in the barn, she was in awe, yet she was petrified for her safety until she saw what a natural her daughter was with the animals. Phantom stamped his feet like a spoiled child when she closed herself in the small quarters with him. She talked to the horse, unaffected by his size. "I can see you're going to give me a run for my money, aren't you, boy?" she said, as he reared his backside into the pen. After Angela's coaxing, he calmed down, and she started with his face. "I found out that most horses love to have their faces rubbed," she told her mother later that evening.

Jean was sure Angela must be putting her whole self into flying now. *I hope she gets this flying bug out of her system.* She lifted the stuffed toy closer to her cheek and buried her words deep into the horse's soft acrylic face. A deep ache surfaced. She reached for the light switch and softly closed Angela's bedroom door behind her and made her way back into her own bed without disturbing the steady rhythm of her husband's snore.

"My little girl. I wonder when she'll be coming home."

Michael's new squad was a mix of older guys, some looking shakier than others as they boarded the plane. Even after boot camp, Texas Tom, the youngest one in the squad, managed to stay at Michael's side like gum stuck on the bottom of his boot.

Guess it was meant to be, Michael thought.

None of the soldiers had much to say on the long trip to Okinawa. After their connecting flight, they stopped temporarily in Can Tho, south of Cambodia and Saigon and never knew where they'd be going next. They were always on the move.

Under normal circumstances, Michael would get melancholy during the holidays, but being in 'Nam—well, it didn't get tougher than that.

His mother's depression had always worsened during that time of year, too. They never celebrated Chanukah in the traditional sense. To Michael, the eight gift boxes were filled with nonsense. He went to his friend's houses and watched how it was supposed to be done. He envied them having a mother and a father and siblings. The way they all participated, stringing the popcorn on the tree, hanging their stockings on the fireplace, and baking cookies. He vowed someday to have children to share such joy. It didn't matter which holiday they'd observe, as long as they were a real family.

Michael ran outside of his hootch at one point when he heard "White Christmas" coming out of loudspeakers from aircraft overhead. The hardest part to him was looking at the expression on kids' faces around the village. If only they could see what other kids had back home in the "world," singing Christmas songs, drinking eggnog, and eating homemade pie.

Instead, there were rumors of civilian massacres and burning of humble huts people called home. He was grateful his platoon hadn't dealt with any of that. The guys talked way too much about the hideous war crimes—the raping and murdering of young girls, blowing away mothers and children, even beheadings. They sounded like boy scouts sitting around a campfire exchanging ghost stories. The guys played a game, passing their hands slowly through the flame to see who could endure the most pain.

"Ahhh, damn, that hurts like hell," Texas Tom said, pulling his hand back from the fire with a sick cackling.

Michael had to walk away to sit on his own. He had given Tom more advice than his own father had ever given him, but he refused to be his round-the-clock babysitter. He pulled off his helmet and looked at Angela's photo that he kept hidden in the lining. She was coming out of the surf, her cheeks pink from sunburn, her hair messy and loose. The waves were rolling in behind her wide smile. He could hear her slight laugh. Then he tucked the photo back safely, keeping her forever happy.

For ten days, Michael's unit was stuck in the boonies. The tent was small, lit by a bulb hanging from a cord. He started to feel disoriented. One day someone got hold of a record player, and played the same song repeatedly—Eric Burdon and the Animals: *We Gotta Get Outta This Place*. They knew the lyrics by heart...where there was a *better* life waiting for them—far away from 'Nam.

Michael started chewing tobacco so he wouldn't be tempted by all the heavy drugs going around. He needed to stay alert. For the most part, they took turns playing security guard, making sure no Viet Cong got anywhere near their base. Checking the ID's of civilians going up and down the road became routine, yet he knew things could change at any second.

Time dragged on and luckily most of his unit got through

the rest of the year with only a couple of major injuries and a few heat casualties. They were choppered into a field thick with elephant grass and couldn't see where they were going when Bull's Eye, they called him, stepped in the wrong place at the wrong time.

His unit then started sweeping villages. Michael approached an old woman from the back. She was squatting over her basket of goods at the dark roots of a banyan tree. The image made Michael think of Angela, and how she loved drawing her subjects from behind. He was grateful she wasn't there to draw such a scene. The mama san once lived above a popular bar before the war. She turned all the way around to look at Michael while chewing on what appeared to be some kind of rotten leaves from a bowl she held up close to her skeletal face.

He flinched when he saw that the other side of her face was totally missing. Her eyes were blank. She wanted *no* part of his friendship. He wondered if she blamed an American for what had happened to her.

In another remote village, he met a friend for life...he was only ten and his name was Tsan. He worked and lived in a noodle shop with this curious old woman—ông ngoai—his grandmother. They were hunched over on straw mats, when Michael walked in.

Michael could only nod at the old woman who excessively repeated unintelligible words, and Tsan laughed at the miscommunication between the two and was able to speak some English to help interpret. He wondered where the rest of the family was, but he didn't ask the boy.

Every time Michael would come through the village and pass by the shop, he'd feel something tugging on his sleeve. Always the same boy was looking up at him. "Mikeel," he would say. "It is me, Tsan. Friend? Friend?" he would ask. Michael would give him a hug, assuring him they were friends, and give him leftovers whenever he could.

Incense burned in the air around them—something to do with the *soul* of the city. Baskets of jack fruit and alligator pears, bins of rice, dried fish, and cages of chickens were sparsely scattered among the markets. Michael feared he was getting too attached to Tsan. Whenever the American trucks rolled into town, he saw the young boy looking for him and calling his name, "Mikeel?"

All the kids' faces were harmless and pure as they ran over to the trucks, waving the omnipresent peace sign with small wiggly fingers. They'd give the salute and stretch their hands out for goodies, like sticks of Wrigley chewing gum.

Sometimes the air strikes began early and lasted all day. The mix of dirt in blood was horrendous. The smell was unbearable. There were North Vietnamese everywhere, and orders came in as consistently as clockwork, "Guns Up!" Feeding ammo into the guns on a daily basis forced Michael into a trance, void of feelings—his body's natural way of protecting itself. Many civilians were killed because the rice growers looked the same as the North Vietnamese... it was hard to tell who was who, especially when overcome with fear.

Whenever the supply chopper came with a mailbag, Michael imagined receiving letters from Angela, but those were letters he knew he would *never* see. Instead, he heard the teasing. "Beckman, another Care package from Mama." It was mostly sweets and other rare treats. Once he got special soaps and a New York Yankees hat from a friend.

Dr. Rothman tended to the guys who cut themselves up on the concertina wire and handed out more salt tablets, malaria pills and mosquito repellent. "I want to remind you boys to keep your sleeves rolled down."

"Yes, sir," Michael said, thinking that the bug bites were a minor problem compared to everything else.

The slightest things started to set him off, especially in the middle of the night when he heard every trifling sound and quickly felt for his M14. His head would fall back onto his pillow when he'd only see a rat scurrying by. Most maddening were the popping sounds and the smells. It always smelled like straw burning. Michael's only solace was staring at Angela's photograph.

Word came that Tsan's village would be forced to relocate to a refugee camp. He'd probably never see the boy again, never know what would become of him. Michael was glad he had given Tsan a Mickey Mantle T-shirt—he'd always think of him wearing it...but when he returned to the village in his jeep from his military reconnaissance, he found Tsan's village destroyed and smoldering. He didn't know if Tsan and the old woman survived, but it didn't seem hopeful. Michael doubled-over, and while holding on to the side of the jeep, he stumbled into the weeds, where he vomited out of view from the rest of the guys. He kept his pain to himself, and they drove away as if nothing happened.

Another day, while on a march, Michael spotted a land mine. Everyone assumed the prone position until the extent of the mining was determined. The trap was emplaced on a foot-path, affixed to a bush with a trip wire tied to a grenade pin. He never knew he could hold his breath that long. For a fleeting

moment he could feel Angela's breath, how she practiced holding her mouth closed under water.

At times Michael could look at the mountains beyond the
roadway and be aware that killing was just plain wrong. With
everyone growing more paranoid by the day, it was getting
tougher to keep that in mind. *Don't forget*, he would tell himself, *this is not right. None of this is right.* He shook his head, until
it stuck.

Days were long and the men felt charbroiled under a sun
that had no mercy. Nights were lonely, and the dark ate them
up, made them forget being human, all over again. He cupped
his head in his large hands, trying to remember good things
and what he used to like about himself. And not to let fear
make him into someone he hated.

Michael slogged through the red dirt path that would turn into
cement after the rain dried. Once they got back to their hootches,
they'd rest until 2300 hours when the temperature would drop
to around 90 degrees, and they'd move their convoy like a slinky
serpentine through narrow roadways. As they were taught, they
kept distance between each other to throw the enemy off as to
the *number* of men in their unit, in case they'd run into a trap.
The trap would be less effective if they were spread out.

What Michael had thought at first was friendly fire, turned
out to be enemy bullets, mortars, rockets and artillery. He
dived for cover in the dirt with the rest of his men, scattering
like mice running to their holes.

"Holy shit!" someone cried out. "Now I know why they say
there are no atheists in a foxhole. Jesus! Jesus Christ. Help us."

His comrade had a deadpan look as he sank deeper into the
ground. "War *is* hell," he said, joking nervously.

Days earlier Michael had found a small Bible under his bunk and started reading the Scriptures. He had opened the Old Testament for some comfort, stunned at the amount of violence in what he read. *All along, I had this misconception that the Good Book would be filled with love and spirituality...nothing makes sense anymore.*

After they had sandbagged their new digs, they tried to make it homey by hanging up a map of the United States, a dart board, and a poster of Raquel Welch. The hominess faded fast when he saw a scorpion at the end of his bunk. He frantically tore at his bedding searching until he gave up in exhaustion. He couldn't sleep, consoling himself that at least if Charlie should surprise them with an ambush, he'd be wide awake for the attack.

I'll show 'em. Maybe even kill one of them gooks, chop off his scorpion head. He didn't sound like himself. Maybe he dreamt the whole thing.

While on patrol one night, Jimmy, whom they called "Stick" as he was as thin as a piece of uncooked pasta, killed a young enemy solider with his jack-knife. The guys reminded Stick of their brainwashing: "Either kill or be killed." Stick beat himself up over what happened. He got physically sick and couldn't stop dry-heaving.

Michael was aware that he might not last much longer before going crazy. He was always waiting or watching. The blue Vietnamese buses inched their way up an adjacent road like fat snails; wicker baskets, frames of dilapidated old furniture and cardboard boxes dangled from the roof. Time had stopped for him. Late spring, when he had lost his calendar and stopped marking off the days, he noticed he was running low on the writing paper and low on words.

"Hey, we're out of the God damn tourniquets," the medic yelled.

Tom started breathing heavily. "It's getting really hairy. I know we're gonna be next. That's how they got Snyder. Snuck up on him and dropped a grenade in his trench."

"Settle down, Tommy boy. Snyder never knew what hit him. If you gotta go, that's the way to go. Fast."

"Yeah, but the screams...squealing like those God damn hogs back home," Tom said. He looked up at the helicopters. "At least the choppers give us a fuckin' breeze."

Michael unfurled his tight body in the upper bunk that night. He still saw the phantom helicopters medevacking boys out, replacing them like old furniture...the chopper blades were twirling the seven-foot tall grass in circles. As he tried falling asleep in the unbearable heat, he imagined the breeze coming from the blades. He had trouble thinking of anything except what he'd have to face in the morning. He was told they were going on a special assignment, a risky one. *As if it's been a piece of cake so far?*

He reached for the box of writing paper that Angela had given him almost one year ago. He wrote *one* last letter...he hoped if anything should happen to him, she would somehow get this final one, the most important one:

Dear Angela,

Well, the box of writing paper is now empty. Turns out I'm down to my last piece of paper, which I suppose is not a very promising sign, especially since tomorrow I'm assigned to go on a rescue mission.

I wonder about the day you went to buy this statio-nery—how your mind guided your hand to pick this par-ticular one to take home for me. What grabbed your brown

eyes first? Or was it the scent of lilac that floated under
your perfect little nose? I promised you and myself I would
never profess my love to you in letters sent from Vietnam.
Being this is near the end and in case I don't make it, I may
as well let you know that my feelings for you have never
changed. Of course I never expected you to wait for me, but
I think about you every single day and of our time together.
I tried my best to remain the same on the inside, saved
that part of me just for you. Writing these letters marked
with "angel" in your name has gotten me through all of
this, even though you never got to read them. I am grate-
ful that knowing you has saved my sanity. It never mat-
tered that they weren't sent by long distance mail. They
were special-delivered on a spiritual level.

If I'm still in sound mind and in one piece when I
get out of here, I will find you. Until then, I don't want to
weigh you down, and I don't want to ever hurt you again
the way I did our last night together.

Meantime, I hope you've been living your life free and
high as a bird. I will never forget how, together, we followed
the seagulls with our eyes all summer long on the beach.
All my love,
I Cross my heart,
and hope not to die.
Michael

He sealed the envelope. Then he scrupulously drew angel
wings around her name, placing the envelope on top of the pile
with the others.

SEVENTEEN

QUEENS, NEW YORK
1971

Sylvie reached into her mailbox. Ever since she moved from Massapequa to Queens, she was concerned that the mail wasn't being forwarded to her new address. The space in the apartment was limited, again her world shrinking, but at least she was closer to the airport for impromptu flights to Vegas. And further away from the memories of where Michael grew up.

More bills. Nothing but bills. She told herself she'd eventually pay them. She felt something way in the back of the tin receptacle. She lowered her head to see better and pulled out a small piece of paper folded in half—a hand-written note in red ink, stuck in the back of the metal compartment. She ripped the paper, pulling it out, but it was only another reminder that she was late with the rent.

Mr. Gerard, the landlord, was no longer being patient with her tardiness. How could she know her last junket to Vegas would have turned out so sour? She had already explained to Mr. Gerard that soon she'd be receiving her annual stipend from her father's trust fund—not enough to afford her the same lifestyle she'd grown accustomed to when she was young, but still it was a substantial amount for most people to live on. What was he worried about? He'd be getting his rent soon enough.

Sylvie stepped outside her lobby onto the street and crumpled up the paper into a tight ball and threw it high into the air watching it land in a green dumpster. *Oh, I wish he'd stop bothering me,* she thought, re-evaluating the dead-on shot she made. *But right now I need a boost to pick up my morale. It's been a while since I bought anything for myself.*

She stuffed the rest of her mail into her bag and continued walking down to the main thoroughfare, stopping at the window of a pricey boutique. Her eyes lit up at the mannequin modeling an empire waist maxi-dress, and she instinctively reached for the door handle. She stopped when she saw Michael's ghostly image blending in with the dress in the window's reflection. An optical illusion? She gasped and quickly turned around to stare at the young man standing behind her on the sidewalk.

"Oh!" His resemblance to Michael was uncanny.

He looked at her strangely. "Ma'am? Do I know you?"

"I thought you were someone else," she said. "Sorry."

He smiled, curiously and walked away, making her miss her son even more. She still felt Michael was somehow watching over her, persuading her to make the right decision, and she quickly let go of the door handle and backed away from the boutique.

She was reminded of her youth and how her mother hadn't paid much attention to her until she transformed herself from duckling to swan. "You're a Rosenberg, not a ragamuffin," she told her stubborn gamine daughter who soon enough became obsessed with window shopping. She sighed, remembering how her mother broke her like a horse. Gretta abhorred Sylvie's transformation, first the interest in art to win her father over, and then fashion to win her mother—a more difficult feat.

Later that day, Sylvie returned home with some basics, still thinking about that dress. "How boring," she said to the items she pulled from the brown paper bag: bread, milk, cereal, napkins, two bananas, and one lousy tomato. She held up the tomato. "Darn," she said, turning it in her hand. "It's rotten. I didn't see these bruises when I picked it out."

A tapping at the door caught her attention. With the tomato still in hand, Sylvie opened the door without looking through the peep hole. She shrieked at the force of the door flying inward.

Mr. Gerard stepped forcefully into her apartment and closed the door behind him.

"What do you want, Mr. Gerard?" The look on his face scared her.

"You know what I want."

"I told you. I'll have the rent money soon. I'm expecting the check any day now."

"Hmm...any day, huh? What about today? I thought *today* would be my lucky day. What do you say, Mrs. Beckman?" He stepped closer. He looked funny at Sylvie. "You sure do smell pretty, you know that? New perfume?"

Funny, she was just thinking how grotesque he smelled— a combination of booze and strong coffee. Sylvie struggled to find words. "As soon as I get paid, I'll—"

"I think you can make it up to me now, don't you, Mrs. Beckman? Maybe we can work things out, buy you more time," he said in a heavy voice.

He walked toward her, and she stepped backward until she was up against the wall. His face seemed large and disfigured. "Please, stop," she barely uttered. She turned her cheek to one side. "I said stop!"

Mr. Gerard moved closer. He pushed hard into her, rubbed his light beard along her cheek. She slid down the wall, crouching, like a child. She squeezed the tomato still in her hand. Its red juice seeped down her leg. Sylvie pushed him at his knees, staining the legs of his wide gabardine pants. He didn't budge. His power frightened her. She was reminded of being helpless years ago. In fact, she was reminded *every* night as she fought sleep, fought the dark.

"STOP!" She finally let out a scream. And then another and another and another. "I said STOP! STOP! STOP!" She held both hands over her ears, her eyes shut tight, her body convulsing.

"What the hell?" Mr. Gerard said. "Okay, okay, calm down. No need to holler. What's wrong with you, anyway? You some kinda nut?"

Sylvie carried on, sobbing.

"Hey, I'm sorry. Didn't think one harmless kiss would set you off like that. Just wanted to have some fun, that's all," he said trying to help her up.

"Don't touch me!" She remained on the floor, her face buried in the crook of her elbow. "Don't touch me! Don't you *ever* touch me!"

"You know, lady, the way you parade yourself around the street 'n all, I thought—"

She stood up, gave him a look to kill.

"Oh, never mind," he said, moving away.

"Leave! Get out!" she cried, pointing to the door.

"I'm going. I'm going." With his body half out the door, he leaned back in. "And I'm counting the days, Mrs. Beckman, until I receive your rent money. I'm gonna have to start charging interest."

Sylvie threw the gushy tomato at the closed white door and watched the yellow seeds slowly slide downward with red juice, onto the white linoleum.

She could hear Mr. Gerard's muffled voice, as she double-bolted the lock and put the chain into the latch. "One more week, I'll give that broad. Then, she's outta here!"

When she peeked out the peep hole of the door, she could only see her nosy neighbor in the hallway, calling for her cat.

That night, Sylvie nervously fumbled with the alarm clock. She couldn't remember the last time she had set a time, but she was afraid if she lay awake the entire night, she'd sleep through the morning and not beat the rush hour traffic on the way to Massapequa. She planned to track down her old boss, Mr. Hudson. He never did send her last paycheck. They hadn't gotten along very well the last couple of weeks of her employment at Mays, but still, he owed her the money, and she would be damned if she didn't collect.

What a predicament. I have to get the money from one creep in order to give it to another creep. This better be worth the trip, so I won't have to get close enough to smell the stinkin' breath on either of them again!

It will be strange going back to Massapequa though. Hmm, while I'm there, I may as well make a few stops at some of my old favorite places again.

* * *

"Can you please write down your *new* phone number on the check, Mrs. Beckman?" The cashier at White's department store held up several customers on line while she asked the woman for some information. One of the people waiting was Mrs. Martino who held a card of tortoise shell buttons and some scraps of material she intended to piece together for a blouse.

"Yes, certainly," the woman answered, tapping her lacquered fingernails on the counter and jangling her wrist full of gold bracelets. She grabbed the pen. "Where would you like me to write the number?"

"Right there, Mrs. Beckman," the cashier smiled.

"Remind me never to move again. I'm still not getting all my mail forwarded from Massapequa to Queens, and between the bank, the post office and, well, you don't need to hear all this."

"You don't have to tell me about moving," the clerk said, "I moved here to Massapequa over two years ago, and I still haven't unpacked everything yet." They both laughed.

Mrs. Martino perked up. Angela's vivid description—the flashy clothes, the mixture of phlegm and a heavy European accent. She stopped breathing for a second when she realized who the woman before her was, digging into the bottom of her *Gucci* bag for her car keys.

"Uh, Mrs. Beckman? Excuse me, Mrs. Beckman?" Mrs. Martino repeated. "You wouldn't be Michael Beckman's mother, would you?"

"Who are you?"

"Oh, I'm sorry. I'm Jean Martino, Angela's mother."

She could see beads of perspiration settling on Mrs. Beckman's nose, as she grabbed her keys and rustled her packages, as if she had somewhere else she had to be.

"Mrs. Beckman, please," Angela's mother said, losing her place in line. "Is Michael okay? We haven't heard from him in such a long time. Did he end up going to Boot camp? Where is he now?"

Mrs. Beckman's face and neck flushed with the lie. "Oh, didn't you hear? Things worked out well for him. Michael's living in California now with his 'fiancée,' Rebecca—Rebecca Cohen, an old college girlfriend. I'm sorry, but I do have to hurry back home. It's a long drive to Queens."

"Oh, fiancée? That's nice. Good for him," Mrs. Martino said, perplexed. Is she fabricating this whole story? Unless, Michael didn't pass the army physical and never went to training...anything is possible.

"We always liked Michael. Tell him we wish him all the best," Mrs. Martino said.

"I will," Sylvie answered, turning on her heels. "He was once fond of Angela, too."

Mrs. Martino started to go back to the end of the line, when she decided to give it another try, for her daughter's sake. She caught up with Sylvie and tapped her on the shoulder before she got to the exit.

"I know you're in a hurry, Mrs. Beckman, but would there be an address you can give me, so we can send Michael a birthday card or a Christmas card?"

"Pardon me, Mrs.—what did you say your name is? Marino?"

"No, no. It's Martino. With a 'T.'"

"Well, Mrs. Martino, Michael's *Jewish*, in case you're not aware, and he doesn't celebrate Christmas."

Mrs. Martino bit the inside of her cheek.

"Have a good holiday," Sylvie said, putting an end to their chat.

Mrs. Martino went back to the end of the line, which had doubled in length, and thought about what she'd tell her daughter. Her nostrils flared with emotion. Maybe she'd tell her nothing. She'd lived with this all by herself and spare her the pain. "Yep, that's what I'll tell her—nothing," she said to herself.

Sylvie ran from the exit door, her keys jingling in her hand. She hurried to her car, got in, started the engine and drove fast out of the parking lot, thinking she would burst. About half a mile down the road, she spotted an isolated area. She turned off the engine and sunk low in her car seat. *What did I do? What did I do? Mrs. Martino appeared to be a decent woman. No, but I can't let appearances fool me. I had to do what's best for my Michael. I had to lie for my son's sake. That girl will have to find someone else, someone more like her.*

Her thoughts went round and round until she leaned back on the headrest and looked outside the car window at the long arm of a tree branch that scraped her windshield in the breeze. "How do you like that? It's a Weeping Willow."

She laughed at what the tree symbolized. Then she reached inside the glove compartment and pulled out the Kleenex.

* * *

The military flights Angela was assigned to were the most exciting trips of her flying career, picking up boys at a base and dropping them off where they'd be shipped off to Vietnam or picking them up still wrapped in bloody bandages from Bangkok, Thailand, bringing them back home. There was an overt difference in their morale, as the ones going out looked like scared boys, and the ones coming back looked like men with deadened senses.

On one trip out of Andrews Air Force Base at 0:500 hours with her final destination in Okinawa, they arrived at the assignment base near Naha, to take some wounded GIs back to the states. She opened the front cabin door with her white cotton gloves to a glaring sun and boisterous commotion below on the tarmac. Her gloved hand shielded her eyes from the brightness, as she heard a cacophony of cheers, shouts and whistles from the soldiers. Her crew could not focus on where the sound came from in the blinding light. They could hear the eager voices yelling up to them.

"Hey, sky girls, when are you coming down?" one of the uniformed men called up from his cupped hands.

"I feel like one of the Beatles," she said to her co-worker. "Yeah, yeah, yeah."

The girls made their brave descent down the plane's stairway to a bunch of guys waiting upon them like vultures. Many of them hadn't seen females in a long time. Angela's crew stayed on a one-month layover between Okinawa and Tokyo, doing military runs. The guys got to know the girls and treated them like queens, fighting over who got to talk to them, and who got to eat with them in the mess hall.

One night Angela went on a double-date with another stewardess and two infantrymen; they sat barefoot on the floor in a Japanese restaurant. The four of them talked about the war. She thought of the many times her parents talked about the hardships of living through World War II and suddenly regretted not sharing in their conversation. She thought of all the generations rolled into one, all the heartache and misery during the depression. In all of mankind's progress—had human spirit changed very much?

Is the world insane? People are tortured and murdered, even by our fine, freedom-loving American democracy. But if we didn't get involved—what then? What if we turned our heads in the 40's, during the Holocaust? What about now, during Vietnam? What will happen by the year 2000? When is war right?

Angela was temporarily put on furlough. This was her big chance to experience the epitome of freedom that she talked about for so long. She was finally going solo. Everywhere she went, she carried her bible—a book called *Europe on $5 a Day*. She loved not knowing where she'd be from day to day, just as she had always dreamed.

One thing was certain—she never did feel freer. Free to do whatever she wanted to do, and to see anyone she wanted to see…she still kept Michael's words in her head, "Now's your chance, Angela, run free."

Day after day, she was the solo traveler. She finally had time to herself to think about her life. One day while she was eating a messy dish of Hungarian goulash for lunch near where she was staying, she spotted a young man sitting nearby, smiling at her.

Why is he staring at me? Am I slurping?

They continued the eye contact back and forth, until she rested her spoon in her bowl and shrugged her shoulders at him. He walked to her. He was tall and on the thin side.

"I beg your pardon, Miss, I'm usually not forward, this way," the young man said. "I am Martin. Do you wish I join you?"

"Umm, sure." She pointed to the chair opposite her, and knocked the soup spoon out of the bowl, splattering goulash on both of them. "Oops."

"Let me order you another bowl," he said with his Polish accent.

"Oh, no. Don't—"I mean, really. Unless you want me to buy you a new shirt."

He smiled.

"Please, sit." She found him attractive, and after exchanging a few stories about themselves, she felt comfortable with him. Then there was awkward silence. He cleared his throat and, invited her to the opera.

"An opera? I've never been to an opera. That would be fantastic."

"This is good then, no?" he said, rising from his seat, shifting his weight from one foot to the other, as if he just pinned a strike at the bowling alley.

"This is good," she said.

"It will be you and me and *Madame Butterfly*. We grab the quick for dinner, first, around 7 o'clock, the time?"

She realized that was a question.

"Okay. I will meet you back here at 7 o'clock, then."

She was surprised and excited when he showed up on a motor-cycle. "Oh, man. Are you serious?" she asked him, in her suede mini-skirt.

"I am sorry," he said, looking at her short skirt. "We trade for car?"

"No. This is absolutely perfect." She hopped on the back with her skirt riding up on her legs, rested her boots on the foot pedals and put her arms around his waist, thinking how life was such a ride. *One day I feel like a caged rabbit and the next, I feel as free as a bunny in the briar.*

"Where are you from?" she asked with the wind blowing her words wildly into the air.

"I am from Warsaw."

"I've never been there. I'm from New York. Ever hear of Long Island?"

"Hold on," he yelled, as they took a curve and merged with traffic around a circle that looked like a free-for-all. "Are you afraid?"

"No. This is insane!" She laughed out loud.

"Long Island, you said? You are surrounded by water there?"

"Yes," she answered dreamily. "Surrounded." *And sometimes, suffocated.*

The 50-piece orchestra played music that filled her heart with extra beats, making her feel a little melancholy. Her eyes welled, thinking about the old days.

Martin looked concerned. "I am sorry. Not the best seats, no?"

"Huh? Oh no. It's not that. It's, uhh, the music. My dad has this record album. It made me pretty homesick, that's all," she said, wondering how *homesick* translated. She looked around

the horseshoe shape of the opera house with five levels of balconies. There were different compartments separated by velvet
drapes for small parties.

"I've seen this in the movies dozens of times," Angela said
in a small voice.

People around them pulled out their pocket-sized binoc-
ulars and quieted down as the orchestra played and the curtains opened. The stage setting was oriental, with trees in the
background, a small house, a bridge, and a well. The first act
showed for one hour:

*Lieutenant Pinkerton of the U.S. Navy came to Japan and
wanted to rent the house for his honeymoon after taking "Butterfly"
for his temporary wife. She had to change her religion to do so, and
Pinkerton didn't know all that she sacrificed. She was going to have
his baby son, just as he left for the Navy again. The son was known
as "Trouble," later to be named "Joy," when the father would someday return. She waited three long years and one night heard news
of his ship coming in. She fixed up the house pretty with flowers
and sat by the window, waiting. He didn't return by dark, and she
still sat there with her son, as it turned morning. There was a long
silence of a woman who waited forever.*

*When Butterfly saw that he brought back a wife from America,
she was crushed. Her young son pitifully patted her head. She gave
the little boy to Pinkerton and later stabbed herself with a knife.
The curtains closed.*

Martin looked over at Angela, her eyes ready to overflow.

"The music?" he asked, not knowing she was wondering
about Michael and where he'd been since she last saw him at
The Beach Club parking lot.

"Yes, the music." She nodded.

Martin reached for Angela's hand and leaned in for a kiss.

She pulled away. "You know I'm leaving tomorrow."

Martin looked back at the stage, watching the actors take

their bows as he answered her. "Yes, I remember," he said, letting go of her hand.

Because Angela wanted to keep moving on, she knew she'd no longer see Martin; it didn't matter, he became another stone monument in Europe, nothing more. Also, she was still contending with her feelings about Michael, although she never admitted these emotions to anyone, not even herself.

She boarded the 8:15 a.m. train to Munich. The steam engine made short explosive sounds as it chugged through dark fir trees spread on snow-capped mountains, and the speckled buildings of aqua, pink, red, and green rushed by her.

Angela found a hotel around the corner from the railroad station, "Fremdenheim Rainer," for 14 marks, $3.36 a night. A woman with thinning hair showed her to her snug room in which she only spent two minutes before running out again. She didn't want to miss the 11 o'clock display at the public square. She grabbed her umbrella and walked in a light drizzle where no motor cars were permitted on the streets, and she scampered along with all the shoppers caught up in the ambiance.

There was a huge clock across from the town hall at the plaza, and promptly at 11 a.m., giant mechanical figures came out of the clock and danced. Tourists stopped in their tracks to watch, while some of the zany tourists imitated the dancers.

When she got back to the corner of the railway depot, she had almost forgotten which hotel she had checked into. Fatigued, the monuments, churches, hotels, and train stations had all melded into one. She heard an American voice and turned around to a spunky girl with short strawberry-blonde hair. "Excuse me, are you staying here, at this hostel?" the girl asked her, standing at the threshold.

Angela looked perplexed. "I think so," she chuckled. "All the buildings are starting to look alike." She read the name— The Fremdenheim.

"I was wondering if the rooms are nice," the girl added.

Angela then remembered that the room was clean and cozy, and the hotel proprietor, a charming, humble woman. "Yes, I'm staying here," Angela answered. "And it's fine."

The girl laughed. "I know how confusing traveling can be."

"I'm staying in the loft. It's the smallest room."

"Do you think she has a vacancy for three more Americans?" the girl asked.

Angela looked at two other girls sitting on their suitcases at the curb.

"Yes, I heard her say she has one spare room available on the 3rd floor." Angela pointed up to a window. "The bell doesn't work. So, knock hard."

"Thank you. I'm Rachel by the way. Hope to see you later."

"Me, too. I'm Angela."

"After you settle in, knock on our door," the girl said to Angela. "Maybe we can all hang out."

Hours later, Angela, Rachel, and her two friends, Mindy and Carolyn headed for the Mathaser Bier Stadt, the largest beer hall in the world. They were immediately overcome by the scene of unruly German men sitting at long tables with their stout-bodied beers. The waiters carried as many as 15 mugs at one time while the oompah band played loudly. Were these fun-loving Germans the same people she'd always heard about from the Holocaust?

EIGHTEEN

DACHAU, GERMANY
EARLY 1970S

The gravel spinning under the wheels made the tour bus shake violently as it made its turn. Angela looked up from her pamphlet the bus driver had handed out and rubbed the condensation off the window. There it was in the distance, behind the mist—Dachau. The first "murder school," just like the brochure described. She squinted to read the words below the entry gates: *"Arbeit Macht Frei*—work will set you free."

She refolded the pamphlet in fourths, along its creases, and buried it deep inside her backpack. She thought about her dream trip, now coming to an end. This was to be her last stop, the end of her long journey. She'd be going home....

Again, she looked out the bus window. She smiled at the fog in the distance, thinking how she accomplished what she had set out to do. She found her independence on the road, backpacking solo around Europe. How she had longed for the journey, longed for the luxury of absolute freedom. She concluded it *must* be "the end," because here she was, feeling a profound loneliness. For what, she asked herself?

Michael was probably no longer there, in New York. He'd enlisted in the Army. Angela had punched him repeatedly in his arm when he had told her... *Why, Michael?* She cried while

231

she hit him. *Why'd you do it? So you don't have to face your mother, about us?* She watched his eyes get swollen and heavy.

"You're right, Angela," he confessed. "Actually, it *is* a lot easier to join the army than battle my mother." He broke down in front of her. But Angela was so angry, she couldn't console him. How she wanted to hold him one last time. But she just couldn't.

*God, how I miss him, the way he used to squeeze me, the way he smelled like the beach, the way—*she stopped herself. Had she forgotten some of the other reasons she needed to escape on her odyssey? She had often told others they were different, she and her mom. Angela could not imagine her mother traveling spontaneously like she did. She wondered if she'd surrender after all to her overprotective upbringing.

At least she'd always have her travels to look back at—all the interesting people she met, and promised to keep in touch with after kissing both cheeks of strangers, letting go of hands that wouldn't pull away...she'd never forget picnicking on the grounds of Versailles; playing hide and seek with the feral kittens at the ruins of The Coliseum; having a stare-down with the Mona Lisa at The Louvre. What had these extravagant jaunts really proven?

Partying the night before with her new friends had finalized her odyssey. She was grateful, though, that she passed on that last stein of beer. By the time she returned to the youth hostel, she barely had enough energy to pack her bag and take a hot shower. Once in bed, she methodically propped herself up with an array of bed pillows. The glow of the nightlight fell over her shoulders onto the thick book held stiffly on her lap. She thumbed through the pages, a myriad of historical facts about World War II, preparing herself for the somber excursion she would go on the following morning.

As much as she had tried, she hadn't been able to identify with its magnitude and had fallen asleep with the rise and fall of Hitler spinning through her head like the giant spool atop her mother's black cast-iron sewing machine.

The quiet of the bus suddenly became loud. Had the jitney stopped? The rows ahead of her were empty. She hadn't been paying attention and was the last one left on the bus. Feeling slightly dizzy, she stood up from her seat in the rear, to exit. Stepping off the bus, the chill hit her face hard.

Catching up with the bus group, Angela overheard two English-speaking tourists, talking.

Americans?

One woman said to the other woman, "I don't know why we're going to torment ourselves, going to this place of horror. Whatever happened here happened a long time ago."

"Let's make sure we leave by noon. I saw this adorable little place where we can go for lunch," the other responded.

Angela ignored their mindlessness.

At first, nothing seemed real. Angela looked around her, taking in the panoramic hell, setting her left foot before her right, trudging along behind the others. This was one of many concentration camps, with a punishment system that surpassed any others in history, run by the SS—Schutzstaffein.

Angela looked up. What color sky was Michael looking at that very moment? The clouds joined together, like closing doors, darkening a room. She envisioned her sister's wings folding at the sight of such gloom. She looked down at her feet, hoping that when she had dressed, half-asleep in the morning, she picked matching shoes. *Yes, both black. What a mundane thought.* She realized everything in her everyday life was trite by comparison.

The group of tourists marched together in one huddle, past the fences surrounding the camp, past the long side of the bunker houses. As they proceeded under the entrance gates, this caused her heart to beat faster.

How many other hearts under yellow stars worn on the left side of the chest thumped in this place? She tightened her grip on the railing along the museum wall below the hundreds of black and white photographs. With each step the Nazis' mistreatment of the Jews intensified.

Then the guide hit the light switch off and she stood with strangers in the blackness as the projector flickered above their heads. They watched propaganda films, including the distorted perspective of Leni Riefenstahl and the amateur footage of Hitler marching in the streets after one of his frenzied speeches with military police at his side. His followers saluted and waved banners at der Fuhrer. At first, they only threw stones at the Jews.

One little Jewish girl on the big screen, around five or six-years old, was wearing a torn coat and had a shaved head. Her eyes looked directly at the camera. She and her mother were holding hands, not knowing that in a matter of moments they would be pulled apart and separated forever. Peculiar, Angela thought, how the mother had the face of a child, and the child the face of an old woman. She suddenly was overcome with missing her own mother... the many times she had cradled her like a sugar wafer, the many times she taught her about human kindness. She thought of the Halloween when her mother gave in and made her the cowgirl outfit, even though she knew her mother wanted her to be a princess.

Mom, can you hear me?

Her hand stroked the page as she read about the children of the Holocaust. They could serve no productive purpose. They were known as "useless eaters."

Wow! What a terrible thing to call a child.

Angela exited the screening room, feeling repulsed and

queasy, and tried to gather the strength to continue, but she did not regret that she learned what had happened there. If those people had to endure the atrocity, the least she could do was witness their hell. She wiped her face with her sleeve. *What did happen here? What kind of hatred? Enough to perpetuate more hatred?*

Angela could understand Sylvie's bitterness. She thought about Sylvie, how the woman rejected her as the *gentile* girlfriend of her son. Still, she couldn't understand why Sylvie didn't realize that Angela and Michael were more *alike* than different.

She sat down on a bench with her book, emotionally exhausted. Her reflex was to feel for the special gold star given to her by the one Jew she had gotten to know, gotten to love. She turned the pages to more photos of starving, frightened children dressed in rags and bandages, taken from their parents, wandering aimlessly.

Angela had a mental picture of her mother standing there with her needle and thread in her lap, so ready to help mend, to make do.

There was no such thing as kindness for the Jewish children during the war, and no reason to keep them alive. Most were killed immediately. One million children died at the death camps. Nazis believed the Jewish children represented the minds of the future Jewish race.

In other camps, Jewish stars were sewn onto babies' blankets. Newborns had prisoner numbers tattooed on the pudgy part of their thighs, above their dimpled knees. Angela thought how her own mother would tell her how she used to kiss the dimples on her knees when she was a baby. "Look, she would say, pointing at the old baby photo albums. "How I loved those fat little legs of yours."

And Angela would come back with, "Oh, Mo-o-m!"

For many Jewish infants, minutes after birth, came their

death. Full buckets of water were placed next to the delivery tables, ready for the infants' drowning. Jews, young and old, were shot in the back of the neck and piled on top of one another in mass graves. The not quite dead lay on top of their loved ones, buried alive, gasping for air and clawing their way through flesh and earth. Eventually, mass murder by shooting was much easier and less time-consuming for the Superior Race. Soon, they began large-scale gassing.

Angela walked through the barracks where the people had slept in bunks three decks high. She shuddered at what seemed strange to her. *The wood is so old yet it looks brand new.* Prisoners had been forbidden to make one mark or stain in the shelter without severe retribution. One spot stood out. She craned her neck to see and noticed small scratch marks under one high window, as if someone had been scraping there with their fingernails.

Further into the exhibit, she got to see the *actual* drawings the children had made. They weren't typical drawings of children with a bright sun in a blue sky, but they were profoundly disturbing renderings. Most of the pictures were done in plain black lead. One showed a boy crawling to the top of a mountain—perhaps to escape? His arms were exceptionally long, and his feet were blue, the only color. Maybe the artist had frostbite on that winter day.

Another drawing showed black and white butterflies with red swastikas on their wings, blood dripping to the ground, watering flowers that were Jewish stars atop tall stems.

What was it about art that always brought out the strongest emotions in Angela? She choked on her own tears. She held back some vomit in the back of her throat. In her dizziness, she looked for another bench to sit on, to digest the experience, feeling the need to tell everyone, once she got home.

Home? How she longed to be home again. She couldn't get

home fast enough. Surely, someone would be able to explain *how* such a thing could happen. *Damn. Where are my tissues?* The ache grew inside her. She wondered about the ache in her mother's heart for Anna's one little life. *Does she still smell her sweet child's young skin? How long did Mom have to wait for the hurting to pass? Did it ever really pass?*

She ran outside to catch her breath, into the large square, where the Jews were lined up twice a day to be examined by the guards at roll call. If someone was missing, the rest of them had to stand in the same spot the entire day until that person was found. Some had good excuses—some were found dead in their bunks. Others were found lying next to the electric fence.

With each step, Angela grew more upset. She was unaware that she entered an area *prohibited* to tourists and unaware it had started to rain. Drops battered the pavement like loud bullets. Afraid and cold, she quickened her pace, ripping her blouse on barbed wire. She turned to behold looming watchtowers. Sobbing, she couldn't see very well, couldn't hear.

A large stocky man with a demanding German accent called to her. "Fraulein? Fraulein?" The guard held the book she had left behind on the bench in his hand. "Fraulein, your book!"

Angela ran faster, sensing tormented souls at her side. She'd guide them to a way out, but it was too late. In her mind she heard the sound of machine gun fire: Tat a tat tat....

Ten months earlier...

Tat a tat tat...the sound and burning sensation hit instantaneously, accompanied by hideous screams and flashes of blazing light in the dark sky. Michael lay in the bottom of the trench while a thick fog hung suspended over the rice paddies.

He saw Tom get blown apart and heard the cracking sound of bone breaking, like Mom breaking apart chicken legs at the kitchen sink. Michael was numb. He somehow managed to reach out one last time to close his young friend's eyes—"Texas Tom" from Amarillo—gone.

Michael raised his head to the heavens and prayed. Questioning religion didn't matter. He *knew* someone was listening as he listened to the strangled cries coming from mangled bodies. He glanced around for his buddies among the men wet with blood.

He couldn't see his own body. He couldn't see that *he* was one of them. There was no pain. In the pandemonium of chopper blades whipping overhead, he felt himself being wrapped up in plastic. *A body bag?* He was being jostled, carried off, air-lifted. He kept hearing his name being called. *Michael? Michael? You okay, buddy?*

Angela ran down a long, winding road until she was out of breath. There was no traffic, and there were no people on the streets. Shadows were changing on the pavement, growing larger with the wind in the trees. Edvard Munch's painting came to mind. Mouth wide open. A silent scream. Eyes painted shut. Ears covered with both hands.

How easy, she only had to purchase a ticket to a museum to find out that the earth spins differently on its axis for different people. She'd always known the Holocaust was real...but not like this. How obscene it felt to walk through their hell as a tourist.

Michael was no longer in that same hell, but he had moved on to another one. He hadn't a clue how much time had passed. He had no idea how many weeks, months, he'd remain bedridden in the Thailand hospital he had been flown to by emergency helicopter. A comrade had stayed with him in the rotor-whipped grass until they were lifted into the air.

The open wounds on his body and bloody cuts on his face had healed enough so the ritual of being fed became less painful. The smells of astringents and piss had subsided but could never be completely scrubbed off. The bigger obstacle wasn't his loss of appetite; it was his loss of giving a damn.

Every few hours a nurse poked Michael to test his sensations. He wasn't ready to hear the reports. Dr. Wells, the orthopedic surgeon, gave a somewhat hopeful prognosis, but the painkillers rendered Michael unsure of what he heard . . . was the doctor sounding optimistic merely to bring him back to reality?

"Don't hold me to anything right now, Mrs. Beckman," the doctor pleaded with Michael's half-crazed mother on the phone. "I can't predict the future. It's tough to know Michael's condition early on. Spinal cord injury is serious business because there are varying degrees of severity. We'll just have to wait and see."

"Doctor, please tell me, if you had a crystal ball, what do you *think* you would see?"

His silence scared her.

Michael endured an arduous recuperation period, but he slowly regained his physical strength. It was his mental state that was complicated, and he found it difficult to pick up where he had left off—being that free spirit he once was.

The summer of '71, Michael finally returned to his beach house
from the recovery hospital he was eventually sent to in Germany, Sylvie waited for his state of mind to improve, but she
didn't think there was much change. Knowing better, she
didn't give him a hard time when he refused to move into her
Queen's apartment with her, but she was relieved when they
offered him back his editorial position at his local newspaper.
They allowed him to work from home, and he was grateful.
Whenever he found spare time, he'd dedicate it to writing his
first nonfiction book about his tour in Vietnam. But it was the
second book, the truth growing *inside* him about being swallowed up alive in Vietnam, about being with Tsan, that he was
passionate about . . . he was unable to start with the first word
at the moment—the weight was too heavy on his heart. *Someday*, he thought. *The words will heal me, someday.*

Sylvie tried her hardest to lift his spirits and drove out east to
visit her son every weekend, promising herself she'd try not to
smother him or else he'd discourage her from coming at all.
If it were up to her, of course, she'd move in with him, take
care of him, and keep him company. For the first time, she
even tried making sacrifices, passing by racks of clothing and
shelves of new shoes—in case he needed her help, financially.
But he never asked.

One weekend came when Michael told her not to make
the trip out east, because his old high school friend, Dave,
would be visiting him, and they had a lot of catching up to do.
She wasn't sure he was telling the truth. Maybe he wanted to
be alone. Maybe he was slipping lower into his hole.

Instead, Sylvie went into Manhattan, where she ended up
in a New York art museum, and by chance, found herself looking into the eyes of Rembrandt himself—a dark self-portrait.

Even in the shadows, his eyes were telling...*what* were they telling her?

What was it about the art that filled Sylvie's head with so many questions? She turned in circles in front of Rembrandt, trying to understand her family's struggle. What did her grandfather find in himself through the masterpiece which he acquired almost by accident and which became his passion? How much of his soul did Papa have to sell? How much of herself was really saved?

The painting made her look back and try to understand her own preconception and how she might end up alienating herself from her son. Sylvie looked for the answers through the art. Maybe now it was time to make sacrifices of her own—to help her son and finally liberate him so he could recover.

She *must* find Angela. She would finally show her the letters Michael had written her—letters never sent. Sylvie rushed up the stairs to the spare bedroom where she had kept all the boxes she still hadn't unpacked since her move from Massapequa to Queens.

What if Angela is still traveling? I can't go to her house. What if her mother answers the door? She surely wouldn't subject her daughter to more heartache. I'll have to call first, have Angela come to me, beg the girl, if I have to....

Sylvie threw stacks of boxes to one side, finally reaching the box she had in mind—the one with Michael's personal belongings the Army had sent her—the one with the letters proving his devotion to Angela. Sylvie slowly pulled the letters from the box neatly held together in the lavender ribbon.

I must call her, but—Oh no, what is Angela's last name? Sylvie smacked herself in the head, racking her memory. Suddenly, she pictured the dowdy neighbor standing at her front door. "Martino! That's it!" She flipped through the pages of the phone book, unable to concentrate on alphabetic order.

"Unlisted!" She slammed the book down, her eyes darting around the room like pinballs. She rummaged through more of Michael's boxes, through scraps of paper, hoping to find any numbers Michael may have jotted down somewhere. She faltered, choked on her breathless expectations, when she came across Michael's scribbling on the back of an old issue of the newspaper he used to write for. She saw the word "angel," the nickname her son had given her, and a number next to it: PY-8-56—Sylvie couldn't make out the last two numbers. "I will not give up until I reach her . . . how many *angels* can there be?" she said, dialing.

NINETEEN

MASSAPEQUA, NEW YORK
1971

On the flight home, Angela ruminated over living back in New York. She was anxious to start college soon and to see her sidekick, Katie, again. She and Katie used to talk for hours at the beach about going places, about romance, about their future. Now they were no longer the same two goofballs and Angela was on her way home from accomplishing what she had set out to do, asking herself if her dreams really had come true. She had no idea what life would bring next. She'd have to create new dreams. Both her parents loved to create, too, but they had always limited themselves.

She thought of her dad and how bigger than life he had seemed to her when she was small and he held her up above the crashing waves. When she was a little girl she used to think it was okay that her father never went to mass, because it was only a sin when mothers didn't go to church. One Sunday—she recalled it was Katie's thirteenth birthday—her mother had gone to mass without her because Angela had a cold, and she went to look for her father. She found him in the shed by his workbench. He appeared to be this miniature man below the high-pitched ceiling. Of course, she had always known he stood five-feet-five in his bare feet, and his size was squeezable to her.

"Hey, Dad, what are you doing?" Angela asked, plainly seeing that he was fixing the lawnmower.

"Hand me that Phillips, hon," he said, pointing to the screwdriver. "Mom left for church?"

She nodded and smacked the tool into his palm, as if he were a surgeon. "Huh? Yeah, church." It hadn't occurred to her that her father had spent much of his time there in the shed. She glanced at the metal shelves holding the unique birdhouses he made by hand. They made eye contact and smiled at each other among the neatly crowded rows of tools.

"What's up, Angie-girl?" her father asked as if he knew that she didn't just come to watch him tinker with the Toro.

She perched herself on one of her old bike seats. "I was wondering why, um, why—"

"Hmmm," he started, lifting his eyebrows. "Don't tell me. You're wondering why I don't go to church. Am I right?"

"You've always been my personal mind reader." She grinned.

"So, do you want to get into, what you kids call a heavy rap session, or do you just want a quick answer?"

"Somewhere in between would be good."

"I can't say I remember the exact moment I decided to stop going to church. I was probably around your age. One day I thought, God is way too big to fit inside *one* religion. Religion's one of our most cherished freedoms if that's what you choose. It's what people *do* within the organization that's wrong."

"I know what you mean. This may sound dumb, but I feel God's presence around me in *other* places, like when I'm sitting on a rock in the middle of a field, watching something simple...a white moth landing on a flower." She chewed on the inside of her lip. "And sometimes, if I see a monarch butterfly, I feel God's *right* there." Angela touched the middle of her father's chest to show him the exact spot.

Her father leaned over to kiss her forehead. "That doesn't sound dumb at all."

He's still a giant, she thought, almost letting the door slap the back of her heels as she exited his tool haven, which she finally figured out, was *his* church.

There, in the distance, beyond the plane's silver wings and in between swirly cirrus clouds, Was The Panoramic Skyline Of Manhattan. If Anna was watching from one of the clouds, she would have seen her younger sister running her fingers over the wallet size photo taken when Anna was only five. How she wished she had one photo of them *together*.

Anna had been taller than Angela at that age. Blonde and graceful. They were *different*. Although Angela never met her, she missed her sister as if they had always known each other.

When Angela learned of Anna's existence, she was actually slightly jealous of her dead sister. Once, after Angela's bath, her mother came into her room to help her dry her hair with the blow-dryer. When she pulled off the towel that was wrapped around Angela's head, Angela perceived a look on her mother's face—as if she had forgotten—as if she were disappointed it wasn't Anna's face, instead.

Now she realized this was her guilt—guilt of her own survival.

She kept Michael's picture right next to her sister's. What a coincidence—each of them being an only child. Was he lonely, too? Why had she not been able to talk about Anna with him?

Angela thought of the many places she had been over the past couple of years. *Nothing is what it seems, is it? I went so far trying not to be anything like my mother, but I never really had to go searching to find out I want to be just like her.*

She squeezed her eyes tight and pictured her mother

standing in her sewing room with thread hanging from her arms, like tinsel. She focused on her mother's sewing room, as if seeing the cramped space for the first time in her mind. She realized she admired her mother more than anyone. *How she takes lifeless scraps of material and turns them into something so beautiful. Oh man, here I am getting all sentimental, and I'm not even home yet.*

Angela smiled, remembering when her mother tried teaching her how to sew, and realized that it wasn't about the tacky rooster potholders at all. It was about the *two* of them.

She wiped her eyes dry as the wheels touched down. She walked out into the busy New York air terminal. Angela was *almost* home.

Angela had taken on one college course too many, and had been looking forward to a day off. She planned on staying in bed longer on this Friday morning, but the unexpected call from Mrs. Beckman had abruptly changed everything.

Sylvie summoned Angela, demanded, really, that she immediately come to her apartment in Queens. Angela hesitated at the urgency in her voice. "But, Mrs. Beckman," she begged, "How is he? How is Michael?"

The woman did not answer her. Was it her hearing this time? What was she hiding? Angela had to find the answers to some of the questions she'd been carrying around for so long about this mysterious woman—Michael's blood. Yes, Angela was determined. Mrs. Beckman would finally be sharing her secrets!

Angela found her missing moccasin under a pile of books on the floor and moved quickly, although everything felt slow motion. On the drive, she practiced how she'd get tough with the woman, but then she worried about the repercussions if she came on too strong. If Michael could never reach her all these years, how could she? *Oh my God, after all this time, I still don't know what to do. I'll have to bite my tongue a little longer.*

Angela and Michael? Together? Grinding her back teeth on a piece of hard candy, Sylvie knew better this time. She had no choice. She tilted her head to one side after she placed the handset back on its cradle, staring in silence at the black phone, as if something had just died. Her touch lingered over its smooth surface. Michael and Angela actually *did* seem good together—like milk and honey—before the milk curdled, and the honey hardened.

Sylvie admitted to herself that she had become obsessed with separating the two and had *promised* herself to keep them apart, no matter what. Finally, surrendering, she swallowed two tranquilizers which she knew would make her lightheaded but would take the edge off.

Here she was, sitting at her vanity table, waiting for this girl to arrive while examining her premature wrinkles in the lighted mirror. When had she begun to look much older than her age? The four walls tightened around her. She thought of the huge house she had once lived in when she had youthful skin. It wasn't the lines in her face that horrified her, it was the bitterness magnified in her reflection. She threw a ball of cotton in the wastebasket that she used to remove her makeup worn from the night before. She had fallen asleep in the arm chair, the television set still on, keeping her company.

There was a time when Sylvie was a young girl growing up in Holland, when she would have thought Michael and Angela's differences were *romantic*—that love between a Jew and a gentile could work. A time when she held on to stories with cheerful endings, where anything could happen—like the famous story about the little Dutch boy who plugged up the water trickling from the dike with one finger, until the good people from town arrived the following day to help.

It wasn't until Sylvie was a teen, when she learned stories of her own—that good people could turn into monsters called Nazis. They had invaded her Dutch wonderland—disturbing the pleasant sound of wooden shoes clomping past fields of pink and red and yellow tulips shadowed by the playful turn of the windmills, replacing them with the sounds of goose-stepping boots.

She thought about her bottle of sleeping pills in her nightstand drawer. How many would it take? Another cotton ball added to the top of the pile, her eyes reddened, she was finally ready to apply a new face for Angela.

Angela remembered the smell of *Chanel* when she entered Sylvie's house. The well-coiffed Mrs. Beckman did not apologize for her rudeness on the phone; she kept her gaze downward as she directed her into the living room to take a seat.

Angela cocked her head at Michael's mother, perched on her wing chair like a mature woman on a throne, but she took another glance at Sylvie's turned-in feet—something that had always impressed upon Angela—the mere child in the woman.

"Mrs. Beckman, why have you called me here? Where's Michael?" Before she could demand an answer, the look on Sylvie's face indicated who would be doing all the talking. Again, Angela had to force herself to wait for Sylvie to speak despite her desire to learn about Michael.

"Sit," Sylvie said, sleepy-eyed. The tranquilizers had started to kick in. She pointed to a chair she had pulled up next to her own. "Please. We will have tea soon. Tea. It is good for—for something, they say. The soul?"

"No, thank you. I don't want tea. Please, don't bother with that."

"You know, once I was young and in love." Sylvie's words came slow. "With a boy who wasn't Jewish." Sylvie was lost in thought as she spoke of her and Samuel sitting by the lily pond the day they had sneaked out the back door of the gallery and shared kisses.

"Samuel and I, we would hide in the broom closet at my father's art gallery and talk for hours. I have a feeling my father knew where we were the entire time, but he trusted my good judgment. My father and I were very close. That's why it was so hard to lose him." She closed her eyes. "May he rest in peace.

"When I learned of Papa's fate, I felt his spirit slipping away, mist between my fingers. He had lost too much, and could never get back what he once had. His art was *who* he was. His business is what he sucked into his lungs, and when it was taken away, he—." Sylvie stopped and stared blankly.

Angela touched Sylvie's arm. "Mrs. Beckman?"

"In his closet, next to his good business suits and shoes—" Sylvie stopped again. "They found the chair kicked over on its side, beneath his limp body."

Angela's eyes grew larger. When she heard the word "liquidated," she pictured the dried paint turning into liquid again, dripping from the framed masterpieces...all the colors running together.

"The rest of us—at the camp, were celebrating the end of the war when my father must have been contemplating his end. We were all packing our bags to leave. The others would be going back to Holland to take care of loose ends before joining my father, but I was determined to see him sooner. I chose, however, not to fly, so I had to wait for the next boat that would depart for New York. I had a fear of flying...maybe because I thought my luck of surviving had finally run out.

"I didn't let him know I'd be coming. I wanted to surprise him once I got there. I wanted to tell him I'd help him get back his art. So many times I imagined the expression on his face when he'd open the door and see me standing there—his daughter, the heroine.

"Do you know what I miss most, Angela?" Sylvie asked in an uneven tone. "I mostly miss the feel of Papa's hand when it touched my cheek." Sylvie gently stroked the side of her own cheek. Up and down.

"I went to the city and I finally found my father's business partner on 57th and Madison...a man by the name of Schaeffer. He told me about Papa's death. He told me about my father's state of mind as he tried desperately to reclaim the masterpieces and would only locate one at a time, then have to go through hell to prove ownership. 'Not an easy task,' he said. 'And after all he'd been through with the war...the obstacles were just too much for him. Your father was not a quitter, but he gave up. He confided in me how troubled he was, more each day, about his failure to negotiate enough deals to save Helene's side of the family, too.'

Sylvie brushed her hair falling over her eyes."I remember feeling great relief when Mr. Schaeffer said he didn't believe Papa knew anything about my being assaulted." Sylvie didn't look at Angela's face as she revealed this.

"My family must have kept their word, not to add more heartache to a man already in such despair. Besides, they knew the baby would simply disappear."

"The baby?" Angela asked in a whisper.

Sylvie thought of her mother's relatives that had perished—65 in total. There were almost 150,000 Jews living in Holland, prewar, and less than 20,000 left by the end of World War II, and a fact that Holland lost a greater proportion of Jews in the war than any other European nation.

"Although Mr. Schaeffer was in poor physical health, he took me under his wing. After staying a short time in the city, when I was running out of money for hotels, he welcomed me to stay with his family at his bay-front home in Massapequa until I'd find a place of my own. That's when I fell in love with the area and eventually purchased my house with my father's first stipend. I collected the furniture from his apartment, including some of the antiques that he had sent over to him from Holland."

Sylvie realized how uncanny it was that it was the girl's presence that gave her enough nerve to fetch the old journal. She got up and walked to the tall cabinet, where she retrieved a small brass key and unlocked the door that held the leather book. She set the journal on her lap, but she did not open it. The room quietly waited for the older woman to speak again.

Angela worked hard to sit still and listen. She tried to interpret the look in the woman's watery gray eyes. At first, Sylvie didn't read the cursive that had once been inscribed by her calligraphy pen. Without opening the book, Sylvie recited from memory about her family, the art collection, Samuel . . . .

"Papa and Uncle Nathan had gone on to Basel, where they finalized the big deals. And on the day we were forced to flee, he personally spoke on the phone to German officials at the Spanish border in order to be sure we would safely pass. Only then was the Rembrandt handed over to save our lives. To think it was because of art—why art?" Sylvie said. "Why did the Germans fancy it so? I go over it in my head, and to this day, I don't know. What is it that they desired? Was it the genius and remarkable skill the artist possesses? To understand how he created atmosphere with the use of light and shadow? To know the artists' innermost feelings? Was that what the Germans craved, the proficiency to show humanity even as they led the Jews to their deaths?"

Angela nodded as Sylvie spoke, as if anxious to hear more, anxious to finally hear about her son, too. "I'm sorry such evil existed in your lifetime, but—"

"I know you enjoy art, Angela. To think that an artist born in 1606 had indirectly saved our lives...his full name was Rembrandt Harmenszoon van Rijn—The Netherland's greatest artist. Papa often talked about Rembrandt, a man whose own life was tragic.

"Our freedom had been granted in exchange for a tangible thing—another Rembrandt from Father's private collection—allowing 25 of us to board the Marque de Comillas," Sylvie said, sounding drugged, her words starting to drag...The heavily tethered ropes finally released the boat, and we pulled away from the dock in Barcelona, heading for the West Indies...I don't recall how long the journey took, but I know it seemed forever for me to feel settled in our barracks once we arrived at the internment camp in Jamaica. The camp was called Gibraltar, made up of about 400 buildings, divided into 20 blocks, each with smaller laundry and toilet buildings. Each building had six rooms, 15 by 20, with beds that were long and hard on our backs."

Sylvie's eyes got further away with memory. "How I missed my smooth soft sheets and lace covers," she said "and those embellished curtains that clutched the dormers in my bedroom like kidskin gloves.

"Even though we were 'protected Jews' I was like a prisoner, trying to peer from the barred windows too high for me to see. Like a ballerina, I was always on my tiptoes. There were many English administration employees and a few hundred soldiers at the camp. The military police were positioned in guard towers with search lights. We were free, yet fenced in. This is where we were told to wait. And *wait*."

Angela heard the intensity of the word *wait*.

Mrs. Beckman went on. "Every night, I'd lie down on my bed by the warm light of a candle while everyone else was sleeping, and I'd think that it wasn't enough that I was alive. Inside, I was half dead. I'd been stripped of my identity. I didn't know who I was anymore. I learned at a young age that *nothing* is free, especially freedom."

Angela wiped her face dry and leaned in closer. Sylvie noticed her expression.

"Life is strange, Angela, isn't it?"

Sylvie thumbed the pages. "As you can see, there are some pages missing from my journal. But not from my mind. I will *never* forget. How can I? I can still hear the dreadful news about Papa, as if for the first time."

"I'm so sorry, Mrs. Beckman," Angela whispered.

"I questioned what kind of a man my father was to have abandoned us. Why wasn't our survival enough? Why wasn't his family enough? Why did he have to keep the business going at all costs?"

Angela shrugged her shoulders.

"And my Oma. When she was taken away...poor Oma. We never recovered her body from Westerbork."

"That's so sad," Angela said.

"War does crazy things to people, Angela. My family had survived the Nazis, but we ended up estranged from one another, as if we're all still waiting for Papa to return in order for things to go on as before. We live separate lives. I chose to stay in America—maybe because that's where Papa had ended up. I was his pet, you know." Sylvie smiled faintly. She seemed to be looking at her father at that exact moment.

Sylvie fought back the effects of the tranquilizers and a

yawn, and then opened the journal with trembling hands to a page marked with a playing card from an old deck. She held the Ace of Hearts close to her face and smelled a slight odor of the mansion in Holland where she and her brother and sisters would run up and down the three flights of stairs.

She strained to open her eyes wider and read from her heart:

It seems I've been at this camp forever now. I am now sixteen. Mama seems more depressed than ever. She must miss Papa, like I do. It's difficult for me to write about all that has happened, specifically about some of our relatives, who reached a different fate than us. Uncle Nathan calls us from Switzerland whenever he has the opportunity, to tell us bleak news about what has been going on in our own country—atrocious things—the fate of some of my young girlfriends I knew from the Jewish school, who were forced into sterilization rooms. What they did to Margaret was unspeakable.

Time spent in the internment camp has forced me to grow up awfully fast. The days of fancy attire and meticulously looking through rows of party dresses in my oversized wardrobe are long gone.

Thinking back to the day we left on the train, Mama had to tear some of my favorite things right out of my hands. I had managed to hide what was most special to me—the Star of David, seconds before we were 'on the run.' I fetched my necklace from its hiding place and vowed to give it to the child I'd have someday—my first Jewish son.

The head guard, here, Dennis Kenny, is probably in his 30's, and he's very nice to me. He comes and talks to me quite often. He's more soft-spoken than the other

*guards. I don't know, there's something about him…oh,
how I miss my Papa.*

*Once we settled, things aren't so bad. Sometimes we'll
barbecue outside, and we even get to travel into Kingston
with the same guards who look over us. I notice the dash-
ing Officer Kenny especially watches over me. He let me
know that I am not "invisible" after all.*

*He always compliments me on my hair or my blouse
or skirt. Finally, someone notices me. I'm elated to be alive
again!*

Sylvie shifted in the chair, stretching her body, before she
read again.

Angela also shifted in her chair as if afraid of what was to
come.

*I haven't written in my journal for a long, long time. I
couldn't bear to write about what's happened. The man
with the soft voice turned on me—like some of my friends
turned on me, like Samuel, like the German people, and
like my own father.*

*Officer Kenny with all his decorations and fancy insig-
nia plastered on his uniform, repulses me, now…like one
giant swastika. And to think, he's not even a German. He's
no longer stationed here in Jamaica. I don't know where he
went—hopefully, straight to hell.*

Sylvie had a wild expression. After a long inhale, she continued, garbling her words:

*One night, he found me alone in the room, trying on my
new skirt, the one my Aunt Chelley from London had sent
me for my birthday. What can I say? He was strong, I was*

weak. I fixed my eyes on the reflection from the ceiling light—flashes of my six-pointed-necklace bounced off the light fixture like fluorescent moonbeams—like fluttering colors of a hummingbird's wings.

I saw the officer was also wearing a chain. From it, hung a crucifix. And as he jerked his body on top of mine, the cross abrasively scraped at my face. My own small star, a chunk of precious metal, was the only thing that hadn't betrayed me, the only thing I could focus on as he had his way with me, violated me....

Angela looked horrified. She patted the star on her chain without revealing it. The point felt extra-sharp on her forefinger.

Sylvie touched Angela's knee with her shaky hand. "I must tell you more."

That man's face was distorted, his eyes wicked. His hands, alien, as they pressed heavily on top of my extra layers of fancy slips. He wore a grin the entire time. From that day on, life has been ugly. I lost almost all feeling. I wasn't sure what to feel anymore. God forgive me, but I sometimes think the girls from Amsterdam forced into the sterilization rooms met a better fate.

I told Mama that I was in trouble.

"Would you like your tea now?" Sylvie asked without waiting for an answer and rose.

Angela thought she'd lose her mind at this point. "Oh no, that's all right."

"I will get you tea." Sylvie shuffled out of the room, repeating. "Time for tea."

"All right, thank you, Mrs. Beckman."

Angela watched Sylvie walk away, wobbly on her feet,

but she continued to sit stiffly on her chair. She tried not to look at the paintings she remembered seeing on the wall that night when she and Sylvie had first met and not look at the college photo on the shelf, where Michael's eyes were emphasized under a spotlight. Something felt stuck inside her chest, and she was afraid to take another breath. Had she finally surpassed the point that would cut off her air supply?

TWENTY

QUEENS, NEW YORK
1971–1972

As she waited alone in the kitchen for the water to boil, Sylvie went back in time to when she had moved the blue blanket away from the baby's scrunched-up face and looked at the little stranger. To her, the baby looked like a little old man, already weary from life.

Sylvie had been relieved that the baby was all right, though she immediately tried to detach herself from him. She was wheeled down the hall after the delivery, shaken up from the experience. She wished she could stop *feeling* anything at all. Afraid of the past, afraid of the future, she closed her eyes to make her world go away.

The nurses will find my mother in the waiting room and tell her how brave I was through the ordeal. She'll help me raise the baby, nurture the child....

Sylvie had fallen asleep mumbling those words. In her heart, she knew it wouldn't be that way. Mother wouldn't have the patience to wait and see if it was a boy or a girl, and the nurse would only find a slight hint of her perfume in the waiting room.

For years, Sylvie had to hear how lucky she was to have survived the war. She was told repeatedly, it is because of a famous work of art. But she would always question why *her* Jewish star was the lucky one. What about all her Jewish friends who didn't have important art dealers for fathers? Couldn't they have shared a Vermeer? Traded a Jan Steen or a Ruysdael for one of their lives? Many nights she'd wake up in a sweat and see murder camps before her as the train doors opened. She'd hear the German voices, so curt and demanding: "Mach Schnell."

Sylvie had finally released all the screams she had kept inside with her last push. She had no choice but to let the baby boy enter the hurtful world. Having lived such a privileged life, maybe she deserved all the pain and the anger, but she didn't wish the child any harm. She made up her mind—there would be no connection between the two of them. He would *not* be the son she'd choose to wear the Star of David.

The memory gripped Sylvie fiercely. She covered her eyes with the back of one hand, and stirred teaspoons of sugar into the two Royal Albert cups.

Angela waited, still too leery to move. Sylvie re-entered the living room, the cups and saucers jiggling on the tray and pushed the tray at Angela who stood to help Sylvie. She never asked Angela how she liked her tea prepared. "Take a sip, sweetheart. Funny how tea always makes you feel better."

Angela tasted the overly-sweetened tea, pursing her lips.

They both sat down again and Sylvie continued as if she had never stopped. She held her hand over the journal's leather binding and looked at Angela. "A few days after the birth, my sister Gretta came to me while I was holding him, after I whispered his name. She pulled the baby from my arms, and I didn't fight her. She said she found a woman who'd raise the boy. I just let her take him. I hated that *she* was the one taking him from me.

"I knew it was Mother's orders. Gretta always obeyed Mother's orders, but I hated Gretta for it. I didn't fight her," Sylvie repeated. "Because I couldn't make sense of life . . . ."

Angela shook her head once again.

"At that moment, as I felt his warmth leave my body, I questioned what I was feeling inside. Wondered if the baby knew . . . it was the last time I ever touched the child. I looked in disbelief at the little blue cap that he wore on his head."

Sylvie tasted the sour guilt in her mouth and wanted to spit.

"So, you see, I have many unpleasant memories and regrets. I am no saint. It is *you*—you are the only angel in my son's life. You must be the one to tell Michael—tell Michael he has a brother, even if it means he'll never forgive me for keeping the truth from him."

Angela stood, with her hand on her temple, as if in deep thought. "Mrs. Beckman, I don't think you need to be forgiven by Michael. You have to forgive yourself. Don't you see? In the end—we're *all* the same—only human. And I'm now only starting to realize how hard it must be to be a woman, to be a *mother*."

Sylvie didn't waste any more time before telling her about Michael in Vietnam. Angela groped with her fingers, feeling behind her for her seat, before she'd collapse. *Michael had been wounded in Vietnam . . . but he's alive!*

"How could you have done this to us?" Angela's face was distorted, trying to hold back the tears. "Mrs. Beckman, you have no idea how much I love your son! I never really let go. I held his hand the whole time we were apart." Angela tapped her chest. "Right—right in here," she said. "I've thought about him every single day since I left and wondered why he—where he—"

She cried openly until Sylvie took the girl's wet face in her hands, cupping both cheeks. Sylvie looked beyond the hazel hue in Angela's eyes and saw an honesty she had never known in anyone before.

"Angela, I am so sorry."

Such irony, her acceptance of a non-Jew would be the very thing to give *hope* to her son. Sylvie moved closer beside Angela. "I know now of your feelings for my Michael. I believe they are sincere." She handed the girl the stack of lavender letters with her name on the front of each one and waited for Angela to ask why she had never received them.

Angela didn't speak.

"You and Michael aren't the different ones. It is me. I am different. I couldn't see *inside* the two of you—the part that is identical. Your love managed to survive through words. Words." Sylvie's face dropped, as she spoke.

Angela didn't like the serious look on Sylvie's face.

"I can't wait another minute! Tell me, is Michael all right? Where is he?"

Sylvie bowed her head. "I will tell you more, and then I want you to go see him..."

Angela headed for the door. Then she quickly turned around and went to Sylvie who still sat there with a curious look. Angela unclasped her necklace and placed the chain holding the star around the woman's neck.

"This belongs to you, Mrs. Beckman," she said and, then bolted out the door.

Sylvie fell asleep with the journal on her lap and when she awoke, she went to the antique secretary in the foyer to return the journal to its place; something slipped out from the book to the floor—the photograph of a baby's face. She got on her knees to look closer. It was the hospital photo that the nurse had taken. She hadn't seen the photo since the war ended in 1945.

Sylvie remained on her knees for a long time, holding the picture of the baby. She touched the boy's cheek with her fingers. "I thought I'd never see your face again," she cried. Still holding the two-inch portrait, she whispered a short prayer to God that she made up, one that maybe God would listen to for the child's sake.

The baby, he's a man now, but he'll always be a baby to me.

"Thank you God for..." she heard herself, and stopped. She hadn't realized she and God were on speaking terms again.

After midnight, Sylvie entered her bedroom and looked around as if trying to redress what was wrong with the room. She threw off her shoes and walked barefoot through the shag carpet. With calculated grace, she opened the double-hung window, thinking how for a change she'd like to hear the birds singing in the morning.

Then she placed the small photograph on the pillow next to hers, where her Prince Charming's head would never rest and stared at the infant's face, remembering the name she had secretly given him. Her eyelids got heavy. She sang a lullaby to her baby that her mother had sung to her. Sylvie never forgot the words.

When Angela last drove on the beach road in Southampton, she was looking for the house with the red roof, the one he'd rented while going to college. Now she was Michael's age, when they had met.

Her heart was beating as fast as the telephone poles which seemed to skip by her windows like matchsticks. It was hard to know which house was his because many were repainted, some houses had been built up into two-story homes; others had been washed away by storms.

"He *owns* the house now," his mother proudly had told her. Angela pointed her snub-nosed car toward the side of the road, where she paused at the modest white house with the red roof, freshly painted green shutters and empty flower boxes.

She hesitated in the driveway. Mr. Doobie was missing. She knocked on the rosy blush of the front door. First she tapped lightly, and then harder. No one answered. She peeked through the window. She didn't see him.

Her insides were fighting to escape a tight box. She walked cautiously around to the back of the house along the slate path until she got to the long decking that led over the sand toward the water. Everything that was ever *true* inside her, swelled as she saw Michael from behind, in an olive green flak jacket...there he was, just sitting there, validating they had *never* really been separated. His hair looked messy in the wind...how she always loved touching its softness—*like the feathers of a baby bird.*

He appeared to be meditating. She came up behind him, just as her mind had done many times in its imaginary canvas and put her hand on his shoulder. She came around him and stood at his side, as if they'd seen each other the day before. He choked up, pulling on her sleeve playfully, the way he used to do, directing her to sit on his lap. She gently placed her dainty body on top of his, cupping his face with her hands. She looked into his blue eyes, searching for answers. She had a lot of questions. But she didn't ask him anything for a long time...they didn't need to speak. They hugged, kissing each other's salty tears. She closed her eyes to the empty canvas in her mind, waiting for the two of them to be sketched in, giving it life.

Angela got up and pushed his wheelchair back toward the little beach house. When she paused to look at the sky it was purely blue, no clouds, not even the beach angel, not a shadow in sight.

Almost one year to the day after Michael and Angela reunited, Sylvie received a large package in the mail. She didn't recognize the scratchy handwriting spread across the front; she speculated by the shakiness that it was written by an elderly person.

Her eyes widened when she realized the return address looked familiar—yes, this is where Papa had lived when he moved to Manhattan during the end of the war, up until his suicide.

Sylvie felt sickened, and took a seat. Nervously, she opened the package with the tip of her thumb nail. She reached inside and pulled out a pile of loose yellowing papers, only the top sheet, fresh baby-blue stationery. Sylvie trembled as she read the note:

Dear Miss Rosenberg,
I hope this letter finds you well. I found these old papers dating back to the 1930s in a shoe box behind a dormer in our storage room. I believe it belonged to your father who rented this loft before my wife and I.
I'm sorry it has taken me so long to discover your father's things, as you may have been seeking them over

the years. I've only recently come across the box and mailed its contents to you immediately. Unfortunately, the envelope came back to me, marked "return to sender."

I assume you had moved, but because these documents look important, I am determined to track you down, and give you back part of your past, an obviously important part of history.

The best of luck to you, and God Bless.

Mr. Arthur Goodman

Sylvie read Mr. Goodman's letter twice, the second time aloud. She stroked at her throat, touching the Star of David that Angela had returned and examined the other musty papers. One in particular captured her attention, a letter from her mother to her father. She was reminded how flighty her mother's script was, compared to Papa's prosaic style. The letter was sent to where her father had stayed in Switzerland on his business trips during the early occupation of The Netherlands by the Germans.

Sylvie closed her eyes, visualized her mother's face, her figure. Her beauty was captivating, much like the art so desired by the Germans.

She stopped. Immediately, the words of endearment struck Sylvie as odd. Never before had she heard either of her parents act or speak with such tenderness. She never thought much about their feelings for one another. Papa was busy with his work and Mama with her social life, and then her *mysterious* outings.

Sylvie rechecked the names. Yes, it was written by her mother, meant for her father. The salutation:

My Dear Josef, my love…and the closing, your loving wife, Helene.

She read the content of the letter:

You were so perturbed this time when you left for Basel, and I didn't get the chance to explain…I had to do what I had to do, my darling, I had no choice with those men. You were away so long on this final trip, arranging visas for our escape. The Germans knew when you were away on business because you required special permission to travel. I was warned not to mention their abusive visits.

But after what happened to mother, taking her to Westerbork, I dared not refuse the Gestapo. I was never one hundred per cent certain that the art alone was all we needed for protection. What if something went wrong? Even though you were negotiating our safe exit from this country, I never believed we would survive in the end. How could I trust promises from such beasts?

Please understand me, my darling husband. I had to make sure beyond a shadow of a doubt that our children would survive at the hands of the Nazis.

My heart belongs to you. I hope you can forgive me.

Your loving wife, Helene

Sylvie dropped the letter on her lap and sat in shock. It wasn't only the art that had kept the Rosenbergs alive. Mother had also been forced to make a few deals herself, doing "favors" for those despicable men.

Sylvie's hands shook after figuring out the innuendos. "Oh Mama, I'm sorry I doubted you even for one minute…you kept your promise, after all, you kept us all safe." She thought of the one exception—Little Rose. She could still hear her mother breaking the news to them that their baby sister died from an illness. Was it pneumonia?

Then there was the tumultuous getaway.

She folded the letter back into thirds and opened another envelope, postmarked only weeks after the war's end. This one was from Gretta…Sylvie clutched her chest as she read the words her sister had written to their father.

Dear Papa,

I hope you are well. May I start off by saying that the family misses you greatly. I cannot imagine what it is like living in New York. Ever since the war ended, we've been trying to get everything here in order, as I'm sure you are doing, too, before we could come join you in America.

As you know, Mama has been suffering from deep depression, but I'm afraid it's only gotten worse since we returned to Holland. I don't know how to tell you this, other than just come out with it: The doctor caring for her at The Sinai Mental Health Institution of Amsterdam, said she's suffered a nervenzusammenbruch—a nervous breakdown. He brought me to see her, but I could not believe how she has deteriorated.

Oh, Papa, you wouldn't recognize your beautiful Helene anymore. She's so overcome with grief that she refuses to eat. She's nothing but skin and bones. She repeats things over and over again. Her guilt has consumed her about all the things she was forced to do during the war—mostly her ultimate sacrifice with Baby Rose in the root cellar.

The Nazis were conducting stringent raids throughout Dieren that day. Mother told us to go along with whatever

*she said, pretending to play a game for Ruthie's benefit, so
she wouldn't be scared. Well, you know how that turned
out... we knew the soldiers would be back, but fortunately,
you returned with our visas and we were able to flee in the
middle of the night to go on that horrid train ride.*

*When Mama stops crying long enough, she asks for
you. Most days, she's comatose. I'm afraid we are going to
lose her. Our only hope is if she could see you and you can
forgive her. I implore you to come.*

*Maybe if she improves, we will move her to London for
a while, before we come to America. It is much too painful
to stay here in Holland any longer.*

*Aunt Chelley is living on the outskirts of London now,
where it is not bombed out and she has offered her help in
caring for Ruthie, so Wilhelm and I can go back to school
and also work. I hope Mother will be well enough to join us.*

*Your loving daughter,
Gretta*

Sylvie choked on the welled-up emotion stuck in her throat.
She went back in her mind. How could she not have known
that the infant Mother was holding was no longer breathing....

Sylvie rubbed her eyes. She saw them again that day, going
down to the root cellar through the small doorway. Mother was
holding Rose in the pink blanket, gripping her tightly against
her body. After the house once again grew silent, it was safe to
go back upstairs. Mother was still caressing the blanket. Was it
lifeless in her arms at that point?

Then something else occurred to her...maybe it was not
Father's child. "Is that why he had abandoned us? Is that why—
?" Sylvie put both hands over her ears, and rocked back and
forth, shaking the image of a Nazi baby out of her mind.

She now understood her mother's reaction to the baby she had to leave behind in the Jamaican hospital. She let herself sink down to the floor, and rested her head on a stack of glamour magazines, waiting for her pulse to slow down. Or to stop entirely.

When Sylvie regained some strength, she sorted through more papers—a stack of documents—she stopped dead at one invoice in particular—the Rembrandt her father had traded for their lives.

"Proof!" she screamed. She wiped her brow, feeling crazed and professed to the empty room. "This is it, all the proof I need! One day, I will get our paintings back. I will right this wrong for the Rosenberg heirs—my future grandchildren. Restitution for my half-Jewish, half-gentile grandchildren."

Nathan & Benjamin Katz
DIEREN, HOLLAND, CIRCA 1936

Firma D. Katz Art Gallery
DIEREN, HOLLAND, CIRCA 1936

Firma D. Katz Art Gallery
DIEREN, HOLLAND, CIRCA 1936

Nathan Katz (second from right) and to his left his brother Benjamin Katz.
THE OTHERS ARE UNKNOWN. PHOTO ARCHIVE KATZ

Firma D. Katz Art Gallery
Dieren, Holland, circa 1936

Hitler gives painting to Goering

Marques de Comillas

Gibraltar Evacuee Camp in Jamaica during the World War II evacuation circa 1942-1945

*Vogue Katz-Berg (daughter of Benjamin Katz, aka Sylvie Rosenberg in novel,
Rembrandt's Shadow) with two of her children, 6-year-old Alma and infant son,
Murray at the Gibraltar Internment camp.*

Benjamin & his wife Marianne - 1946

FERDINAND BOL (1616-1680), MAN WITH A HIGH CAP

"Man With High Cap" by Ferdinand Bol was restituted by the Netherlands to the heirs of Nathan and Benjamin Katz. Art dealership Katz sold the work to Hans Posse at the end of November 1941 under duress from Nazi occupation.

"HOW REMBRANDT
SAVED MY FAMILY'S LIFE"

The pressure mounted daily as the family endured beatings and vandalism. Warned by the resistance, they moved from town to town in order to avoid the Germans. David recalls hiding in open graves and riding around with a Rembrandt in the trunk of the car. "My grandfather and his brother continued securing paintings for the Germans in order to keep their family safe."

"How could they refuse? In 1943, my grandfather's mother was sent to Westerbork, which was a holding camp for those awaiting shipment to Auschwitz. When Nathan was informed of his mother's arrest he wrote to military attaché, Major General Von Tricht, *I just received the news that my mother, an 85 year-old-lady, who has just suffered a cranial fracture, was taken to the camp in Westerbork. Don't you think this is deplorable?* She was later released when a trade was made for a Rubens meant for Hitler's April birthday."

With special permission to go to Switzerland, Nathan was able to trade the Rembrandt painting the Nazis had their eye on, for the 25 visas which saved 25 lives. Even though some of Nathan and Benjamin's immediate families had escaped, the 65 family members, who did not make it out alive, haunt the survivors to this day.

After the grandmother was released, a postcard dated 5

December, 1943, recently discovered, was sent to Nathan Katz in Switzerland, and recalls the anguish they felt and concern for those not as fortunate.

"Grandma is well again but she talks about the children who were left behind there all day long. Uncle, can't you do something for them, if you can't please write us. Then, we'll at least know something. Now we can only hope you can do something. It is terrible for Grandma and Ben. Grandma says she is dying of sorrow and worries about it all day long. Things are so difficult here. Annie and husband and child are there, too, now, and so are the Nijstadts. The only "something" that could be done was to continue to provide the Nazi monsters with the art they craved so desperately ... the lives of children for oil paint and canvases. Where is the choice?"

Even as I learned new details about their escape, I was perhaps even more surprised to find out what exactly happened after the war.

The Second World War obviously took a tremendous toll on so many. With the initial invasion, in the summer of 1940, it has been reported that over 700 Jews committed suicide unable to face the horror they knew awaited them. But my grandfather and uncle endured in order to save the lives of their families and so many others.

After the war, Nathan suffered an untimely death, leaping to his suicide, September 27, 1949. Benjamin, though, had to endure something beyond imagining: a zealous investigation by the Dutch government in which he was accused of economic collaboration. Those paintings that saved his family? How could he make such a deal with the Nazis? It was a ridiculous accusation, one that was never proven.

But the experience left him so shaken and weak that they were eventually unable to continue questioning him. Almost to this day, the Dutch government maintains that the Katz' brothers were acting freely and without duress.

The Katz heirs are seeking restitution for nearly 200 paintings, but were disappointed only to get back one - Ferdinand Bols, which shows the Dutch have now acknowledged that the dealings with the Germans were not all done freely and without duress. Their refusal to acknowledge the obvious is somewhat baffling, and may stem from their own guilt over the Dutch treatment of Jews. Meanwhile, an unwillingness to return paintings which line the walls of their museums to their rightful owners is somewhat appalling.

The Katz family is asking the Dutch government to return the paintings that my family lost under insurmountable difficulties. So far, they have only returned one painting, but we are pleased that they acknowledge the fact that dealing with the Germans was not voluntary in this instance and it must be concluded that many other paintings were secured under similar circumstances.

I am determined to understand what my grandfather endured in those dark days. I only remember a sweet old man who enjoyed sharing little coin tricks with his grandchildren.

These brave men, Benjamin and Nathan, were brilliant art connoisseurs but they were so much more. They had generous souls and great determination.

After the war, Nathan was given Medal of Appreciation for Support of Refugees from Queen Wilhelmina. They stared into the faces of true evil, but they endured so that my children and others could survive. Including me.

—BRUCE BERG

THE TIMELINE

1938–1939: Hitler targeted his choice of art collections.

May 10, 1940: Germany invades the Netherlands.

June 29, 1940: Katz provides Dr. Hans Posse with quotation for 25 paintings.

July 19, 1940: Katz confirms sale of 17 paintings to Dr. Posse for Linz for NLG 358,000.

August 2, 1940: Katz's sell 500 paintings to Alois Miedl for NLG 1,822,500 which they received (Benjamin:" ... would not even have considered selling such a large batch of paintings in a single transaction... we had little option...")

Sept. 27 1940: Goering visits Katz house; it is sealed off; Nathan feeling ill.

Oct. 1940: Katz instructed by Wilhelm Wickel to "immediately notify Posse by telegram if he found anything "special".

End of 1940: Nathan Katz goes to Switzerland on behalf of Dr. Possee with Visa arranged by Wickel to negotiate for Lanz paintings.

Feb. 17, 1941: Katz firm goes into liquidation on orders of Wirtschaftsprufstelle.

May–Aug 1941: Nathan Katz reported his findings about the Swiss art market to Posse, including photos of paintings that were of possible interest.

Dec. 1941: Across Europe, Nazis begin running deportation trains....

Jan.–Feb.–Mar. 1942: With help from Schmidt, Dr. Posse helps with arrangements for Nathan Katz and immediate family leaves for Switzerland; David Katz describes trip as 'frightening.' Benjamin Katz stayed behind to continue to work for Dr. Posse under duress.

281

June of 1942: ¼ of family assets go to looting bank.

Sept. 1942: Benjamin Katz promises to trade REMBRANDT painting to Dr. Posse "if he and is family could leave country safely." Exchange takes place. Arrangements are made for Benjamin Katz & 25 others to emigrate to Spain accompanied by high-level German officials in charge of "deportation of Jews from Amsterdam"; "escort" was probably meant as a guarantee and intended to ensure that the family did indeed reach their destination...otherwise the Rembrandt painting would not be released.

Oct. 18, 1943: A meeting of high-level SS Intelligence Unit officials & others concerning the fate of the Katz family members remaining in the Netherlands.

End of 1943: Katz family members "arrested on orders of the SD & taken to Westerbork."

1944: "While he was in Switzerland, Nathan Katz had attempted to get his family freed by making works of art available to Sonderauftrag Linz."

1944–45: Katz family members deported from Westerbork & 65 die in camps or in transit.

POST-WAR: "The majority of these (claimed) works were returned to the Netherlands from Germany after WWII following which the State of the Netherlands incorporated them in their national art collection."

1946: Dutch government awards Nathan Katz Medal of Appreciation for support of refugees.

EXCERPT FROM THE SEQUEL
"RESTITUTION"

The stealing started unintentionally.

Sylvie simply had to have that darling champagne-colored crepe de Chine blouse she saw in Lord & Taylor's storefront window. Once inside the iconic shop, she spotted only one blouse left in their newest French line. She could sacrifice *some* of the luxuries she had been accustomed to when she was a child in Holland, not all of them. Since her sisters living in England had stopped sending her designer clothes, she felt she was going through haute couture cold turkey. Sylvie promised she'd reimburse them. Maybe after her next stipend from her father's estate; but still no new pieces for her wardrobe arrived.

Yes, it has my name all over it, she thought, feeling the fabric of the blouse. She reached into her bag for her eyeglasses to read the size on the tag, when another woman grabbed the blouse and held it up, to admire.

Sylvie couldn't close her gaping mouth until she noticed the woman had a rather *large* neck, which reminded her of a tree trunk. She fingered her diamond "S" necklace that hung around her own neck. "That blouse runs small, you know," Sylvie lied.

"Excuse me?" The woman stared at her.

"The blouse. I have the same one. And it runs small. Especially trying to get it on and off over, you know, over your neck." Again, Sylvie moved her fingers over her own slim throat, to show her.

"Well, I'll just have to take it home and see, now, won't I?" The woman walked away in the direction of the nearest register.

"Aagh, all the nerve!" Sylvie called after her in her guttural tone. Nearly 40 years living in America, she couldn't rid herself of her Dutch accent. Aroused by such indignity, she threw her empty hands up in the air and shouted at the woman now out of earshot. "I'm a Rosenberg, I'll have you know—an aristocrat back in my country."

Why is it others always take what belongs to me? Sylvie had to do something to squelch her temper. She had no more chocolate truffles left in her purse, a usual quick fix to fill the emptiness inside. She was anxious and desperate as she flipped through the one-of-a-kind skirts, dresses and slacks hanging on the rack, now minus the blouse, *her* blouse.

"Hmm. This one's not from the French line, but it's not *too* bad," she tried to convince herself, holding it up to the light, looking for its sheen. She picked through the other blouses until she decided on a peach-colored one. Methodically, she rubbed the plastic string tag back and forth over the teeth of her car key until the tag separated from the blouse and fell to the floor. She made sure no one was around before she slipped the garment into her shopping bag and casually headed for the exit.

Was there someone behind her? For a minute, she panicked about where she had left the car. Like a mischievous child, she ran through the parking lot with her exaggerated pigeon-toed gait. Then she remembered the giant rabbit's foot she had recently stuck on top of the antennae. She giggled at her ingenuity as she squeezed her thin figure between the rows of cars, making her way to the gold Caddy glowing in the sunlight as did her thick gold hair. She turned the key in the ignition, the same key she used to commit her first crime and pulled out of the busy shopping center.

"So what, I took one lousy blouse. It's not even satin. Besides, they should be thanking me. I'm the only one who sets a trend for fashion around here."

Lost in thought, she still had desire for something sweet. At the last minute, she made a sharp turn off the highway, without signaling, into the parking lot of Simon's Bakery. She pulled into a vacant space, oblivious to other drivers honking their horns.

Rewarding herself for her first misdemeanor, she blurted "Mocha. Yes, I'm in the mood for mocha." She felt in command. Lately, sudden impulses came over her and she had to submit to them or she thought she'd go crazy. The urge to steal was new and the most exciting of all her compulsions. It wasn't that she even needed the blouse. She had a dozen new blouses hanging in her closet, most with the tags still on them.

Between visits to her son's beach house, Sylvie became covetous of Michael and Angela's bond. She wondered if when a child came along, they'd have any time left for her. She feared she would be pushed out of the picture. *Although, it would be fun to take the kid out for ice cream cones and buy him or her lots of toys and fancy new outfits....*

As she approached the pastry counter, she wrapped her arms around herself, as if she needed a hug at that very moment.

"You're cutting the line. You have to take a ticket, like everyone else. Ma'am?"

"Oh, all right, already!" Sylvie waved her purse at them, always *sensitive* about her hearing issues. "I can *hear*, you know!"

"Mommy, why is that lady yelling?" A little girl asked her mother.

"I think she *really* needs a cookie!" the mother answered.

"I want a cookie, too!"

"Don't cry honey," Sylvie patted the child's cheek. "I'm going to get you the biggest cookie in the bakery—as big as your head."

She continued her crying, digging her face into her mother's side.

Sylvie bent down and whispered, "When I was your age, my mother told me that every time I wanted a bite of my cookie, I had to take a sip of my milk. I didn't like milk, and I made it bubble out of my nose."

"I like chocolate milk. But, I still want a cookie."

Sylvie poked the customer currently being served on the shoulder. "If you don't mind, perhaps you can wait for your babka, so the little darling over there can get her cookie."

The woman stopped eyeing the fresh breads. "I beg your pardon?"

"Oh, here we go again," the Polish clerk moaned, recognizing Sylvie from previous visits.

"That child over there." Sylvie pointed. "You see the one crying? It's because she wants a cookie. She wants it *now*. Would you mind, terribly, if she—"

"Of course. Go ahead of me."

The child's mother was speechless while Sylvie stepped up to the counter ahead of five other customers. "I would like a black and white for the little girl, please."

The clerk grabbed a cookie and Sylvie held up her hand. "Not that one. The one in front of it looks an *ounce* bigger, wouldn't you say?"

The girl nodded her head.

"Oh. And while you're at it," she tapped her fingernails on the glass, "Give me a piece of that mocha cake and I'll be on my way." Sylvie licked the mocha off each finger, while walking out of the bakery and, looked back at the little girl taking bites out of her cookie. First she bit the vanilla side, then the chocolate.

That's what I like to do—help people. I'm good at it. Sylvie got into her car, and pulled out into heavy traffic, a cacophony of car horns in her wake.

After only five minutes in her small apartment, Sylvie paced. She was *always* pacing. She didn't know where she belonged— she was always running from *something*. She certainly didn't belong out east in the countryside where her son lived and where locals dressed in denim and overalls and wouldn't know a Gucci from a horse's feed sack. Sylvie thought of her son, now labeled a "war veteran." She cringed thinking of the scars on his back, the limping and his depending on a cane.

She grabbed her light Burberry raincoat and headed out the door for a walk in the early evening chill. Immediately, she saw two women coming toward her.

"Damn!" She pulled her silk scarf down over her eyes. Too late. Mrs. Silverman and her daughter, Rachel, started waving. Sylvie had run into them only the week before in the exact same spot outside her apartment building. *From now on I'll use the other exit.*

"Mrs. Rosenberg?"

Mrs. Silverman was pushing the stroller with her daughter's dozing toddler and was obviously in the mood for small talk. Rachel was almost nine months pregnant now.

She needs another one like a hole in the head.

"How are you today, Mrs. Rosenberg?" Rachel asked in a nasal voice. "Nice fall weather, isn't it? I simply love autumn."

Sylvie stared at the toddler. The child wore a ring of chocolate milk pasted over his mouth. *Like Hitler's mustache.* Sylvie tasted vomit in the back of her throat.

ACKNOWLEDGMENTS

I had always thought of Rembrandt as my favorite artist ... and then along came Mary Vettel, author and book doctor who shaped my book like a sculptor with clay, chiseling my words, slicing them, shaping them, building them, and guiding them into form until they were softened and smoothed out. I am grateful: to my family who believed in me over the arduous years of filling empty pages, especially to my mother-in-law, Vogue Katz Berg, who lived the story, and to my own mother, Jean Marino, who lived to "create" and make something beautiful out of scraps...and to my father, Anthony Marino, who lived to "invent." Thanks for passing down those genes, which my children, Janelle and Jeffrey have inherited...and to Mike Gomez—my 2nd son and hero, and friend, Sean Gibbons, who helped me find my way. I am forever grateful to Ryan Scheife for his patience, to Corinda Carfora for shining her light on me, and for Anthony Ziccardi and Post Hill Press for bringing me to the end of my journey.

To my golden retrievers Jade, Jewel, and Jude, who sat by my side through it all, keeping me company in this isolated world of writing. And to my selfless sister, Judith Anne, who was my first reader and to my blood sister from childhood, Kathy Ives Lamberta—a character in my book, who knows me like no one else. I so appreciate my helpful editor friend Eileen Obser, who always seemed to be on the same page as me. Also, thankful to Rita Kushner, and for the last beat of the drum by Dr. James Kennedy. I cannot forget Debbie and Lon

Dolber, who gave me the *perfect* title. Thanks to Dan Rattiner, who gave me my *first* writing job—who knew?

Appreciation for those who sparked me to learn how to write through a Master's Program at Stony Brook University where I absorbed bits and pieces from my authored professors, including the late Frank McCourt, and also a special thank you to my friends, JoAnn Phoenix, and Kathleen Powers-Vermaelen, and those like family, Judy Paulsen and Eileen Costanzo for their *extra* support; and to those I met quite by chance, who shared their advice, including mentor Julia Noonan; and literary agent, Jill Marr who never let me give up by *not* sending me a rejection letter. I'm especially thankful for the generous seeds Fern Michael's planted along my path.

Here at The End, I have no words that can describe my gratitude for my husband, Bruce—my soul's mate...who wanted my dreams to come true as much as I did, and who believes we lived another life together before this one. I hope we share many more lifetimes where there will be more stories to create on blank sheets of paper.

3190105979414